NO FUCKS GIVEN

PART ONE: OUTGOING

RUNNING WILD

RUNNING WILD PRESS

NOBODY FN IMPORTANT

CONTENTS

CREEPING DEATH

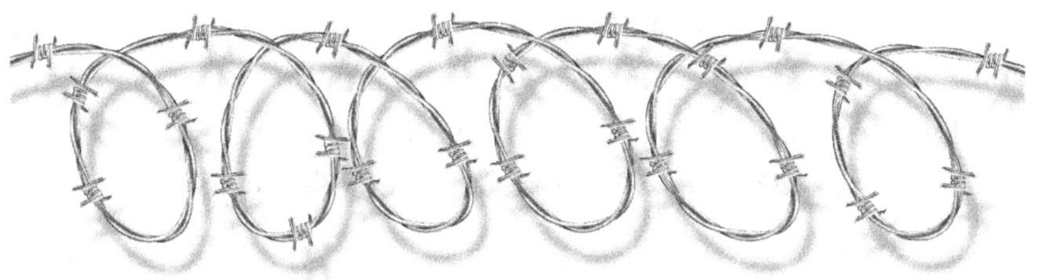

A **HOOK HANGS DOWN FROM** the ceiling of our jail cell where we sleep inside Abu Ghraib Prison, located just outside Baghdad, Iraq, far from the safety of the Green Zone. The U.S. Army's new forward operating base is right smack in the middle of the most dangerous place in the world called the Sunni Triangle.

Saddam's guards used the hook to hang prisoners from as examples to deter other inmates from disobedient behavior. And sometimes, according to local rumors, his son Uday Hussein would use the prison as a sadistic playground to take pleasure in torturing soccer players who lost international matches. The human guinea pigs were beaten, whipped, and hooked up to primitive electric-shock machines until the pain became so intense, it knocked them unconscious.

And for some other unlucky bastards, they were tossed into the prison's septic tank and forced to swim in a pool full of piss and shit; with the taste of liquid horror flowing into their nostrils and down into their throats with the same devastating force as the great Mesopotamian flood, drowning out any hope for humanity.

Multiple torture chambers were discovered inside the prison soon after we invaded Iraq last year in March of 2003. One room still had the hot plate that prisoners were forced to stand on while having to make the gut-wrenching decision of allowing their bare feet to burn or pull the handle that released the floor, dropped the plate, and tightened the noose around their neck until death did they part.

The corpses of nearly 1,000 Iraqis have been found buried throughout the compound, giving the prison a paranormal chill that gives my 21-year-old brain an uneasy feeling every time I walk through its frigid hallways. Dripping rainwater sounds like a heart beating as it pumps the blood of the dead through the cracks in the concrete ceiling and splashes down onto the floor into a pool of nothingness. And sometimes late at night, there is a ghostly wind swirling through the prison that sounds as if it's trying to whisper secrets to me in some ancient Babylonian language that this private first-class soldier can't quite translate with his basic high school diploma. But it doesn't take a fancy PhD degree to make an educated guess as to what it might say if it could speak English to those of us still living on Earth.

I bet if the cold-concrete walls could talk they could tell tales that would make Steven King stories sound like nursery rhymes.

There is something about the history of the hook's brutality that reels me in as if I am a largemouth bass being caught in a small Florida lake. I often find myself treading water in an aquarium size fish tank of despair as I lay on my cot, looking up at the hook, focusing on its paint peeling like an Eastern Diamondback Rattlesnake shedding its old skin. That's when the wondering, and the pondering of the probability of a mortar round blasting through the roof and ripping me out of my own skin begins to take hold.

The thought sends an electric shock through my chest as if I am the one hooked up to Uday's homemade torture contraption. And knowing it's only a matter of time before life drops that hot plate from beneath my feet, I can feel the noose getting tighter around my throat as the days go by. Living here does that to a person. It gives you the not so funny feeling that it will soon be your turn to eat shit and die in this septic tank of a prison.

It's torture to think about the reality of death at such a young age. I should be out partying with my friends in bars all around Tampa for my 21st birthday, clinking our shot glasses together as we toasted with cheers to good times and bad decisions. Instead, I am out here getting shot at in some dried-up desert hell hole on the edge of the world that's far more sobering than living in one of those dry counties back home in the bible belt. Cheers to making it out of here alive assholes.

CIA reports have stated thousands of prisoners we call EPWs (Enemy Prisoners of War) are coordinating their riots with Iraqi insurgents on the outside to overthrow the base and free everyone inside. There are even reports that the enemy has built wooden ladders to scale the compound's reinforced concrete walls. The terrorists have been unable to penetrate it with modern technology such as rocket propelled grenades and car bombs, which is bad enough to deal with, but now we have to worry about something as primitive as a fucking ladder breaching our gated community and leading to our modern military's downfall.

Every time an attack is about to kick off, thousands of prisoners begin rioting and roaring in Arabic with the same intensity of a soccer stadium full of drunk fans during the World Cup after the home team scores a goal. And it's not long after that when the enemy's offense unleashes a mortar bombardment that comes thundering down on our position, with the Grim Reaper always just an arm's length away... waiting to pull us across the wire and into his realm at any moment.

Mortar rounds are different than small arms fire, especially the 120mm variety. Even the anticipation of one hitting will put the fucking fear of God in you. The saying is true, there are no atheists when your position is under attack. Especially when you see the rocket-propelled grenade's red glare or feel the rattle beneath your feet as those air-burst mortars go bursting in the air. You start praying to whoever out there will listen; God, Allah, Buddha, Zeus, Apollo, Mother Teresa, Santa Claus, the Easter Bunny; it doesn't matter who your flavor of the week is, you just pray like hell someone out there in the afterlife will hear your all-points bulletin over your brain's secret electromagnetic radio wave and bless you with another day on this giant rock that is floating in a big empty space.

It wasn't until experiencing this phenomenon in person that I fully understood why they called it shellshock during WW1. Mortars shock you to your fucking core... mind, body, and soul. It causes young men to have the eyes of 80-year-olds. I try not to let it get to me, so I always stand next to the blast craters like a tourist and take a photo of the aftermath while throwing up a "W" with my fingers to signify this is WAR. It's my way of making light of a heavy situation.

The attacks are so frequent though, that I haven't seen anyone under the rank of major in the three or so months since we've been here. And the U.S.O. concert tours always detour around these haunted grounds. Hell, George Bush and a convoy of fighter jets flew right over us and into the Green Zone without so much as a wave.

We are ghosts to the outside world. But I don't blame them. This place is far worse than any horror movie I've ever seen. *A Nightmare on Elm Street? Friday the 13th?* Hell, even *The Exorcist.* They are all child's play compared to Abu Ghraib Prison.

"Combat operations" may have ended on the TV screens back in the states when George Bush declared "MISSION ACCOMPLISHED" after landing on an aircraft carrier in a Navy S-3B Viking anti-submarine plane. But out here in the world of the deployed, whose boots are actually on the ground, the war still rages on.

Every week the enemy continues to attack us with rocket-propelled grenades, mortars, car bombs, roadside bombs and suicide vests.

Boom... boom... boom.

They keep pounding our position with everything they have.

Boom, boom, boom.

They dropped so many bombs they should start calling themselves Ashton Kutcher's and Jennifer Lopez's acting careers. The thought of sitting through movies such as *Dude, Where's My Car?* and *Jersey Girl* can be just as painfully terrifying as sitting through a rocket attack. Yeah, they get lucky with a hit every now and then, but so does the enemy. But on the whole, they mostly fall flat, out in a field where no one ever sees them land.

Boom!

Dude, where are my fucks to give?

Hey, don't get sensitive on me now. You read the goddamn title of this book. I'm sorry you seem to have me confused with someone who gives a fuck. Words mean absolutely nothing to soldiers. And we certainly don't get offended by them so you shouldn't either. In fact, we say the most fucked up things to each other to prepare us mentally for seeing images way more horrible than words could ever describe. That's why when someone tries to hurt our feelings with a weak ass vocabulary, we're all like sticks and stones and fully automatic machine guns motherfuckers.

Now if you can't handle that sort of R rated language that stands for spittn' real shit then maybe you should put this book down and go listen to some dumb down for mass consumption bullshit like The Backstreet Boys or Taylor Swift or Justin Bieber or go read some flowery ass poetry or go get a fucking facial because this ain't no god damn fairy tale trip down the yellow brick road. My job as a Mark 19 gunner is to light up the night sky by dropping bombs from this fully automatic grenade launcher at a rapid-fire pace, not blow smoke up the reader's ass. Now put on a Kevlar helmet and strap on some body armor assholes, the firework show is just getting warmed up.

You see, actions mean everything to soldiers, not words. People talk all this shit about how big and bad they are but when the bullets start flying, they shrink down into a shell of themselves. That's why we only care about who has our back when we run out the door during an attack, not who's running their mouth the loudest while posturing during peacetime. Which is hard for civilians to understand because it's the opposite in the civilian world. Star quarterbacks sexually assault women, and no one says a word as long as they say they are sorry the victim feels that way. But let someone say some stupid shit and then all the torches and pitchforks come marching into town.

But for us you see, after seeing death, facing death, and living in this hellhole for so long, it forces you to reevaluate things. And you learn real quick that words, celebrities, reality TV stars, and actors whose job is to be as fake as possible mean absolutely nothing. But for some reason the more fake people are, the more our society loves them. Why do we idolize these morons who don't give two shits about us, who flaunt their wealth and privilege in our face as we scrape by in order to put scraps on the table? What makes these dickheads so important anyways? With their photoshopped photos, fake tits, fake lips, fake asses and fake personalities all wrapped up into one giant fake TV show called Keeping up with the Kardashians; a clan of carnivorous cunts clinging to the coattails of Kim, whose only claim to fame is taking a D-list rapper's dick in her mouth. Now that's an A-list, Pulitzer Prize winning paragraph right there that all my former English teachers who gave me a F would be proud of.

Fuck 'em all, I say. Out here in the reality of war, the only people that matter to us, are us. And the only thing we care about is helping each other survive this nightmare. Not honor, not glory, not medals, not awards and certainly not for the hollow "thank you for your service" sentiments that allow civilians to wipe their hands clean of it all so they can say they did their part for the war effort and go about their lives guilt free; the money's on the table, thanks for the service.

None of that bullshit matters to us–for us, it's simple–just simply to survive. And dark humor is the only way to survive without completely losing our shit.

So welcome to our reality show. Which is far from the "let's live like there's no tomorrow" and "you only live once" parties going on all around college campuses in America. To us, death isn't some abstract painting to be hung on a hook and drunkenly cheers to from behind a wall of safety by some rich white sorority slut and her sweater-vest-wearing boyfriend who prances around through life in a pair of boat shoes while never actually stepping foot on a fucking boat. The song "Bombs Over Baghdad" and those YOLO slogans have a literal meaning for us. Out here in the sandbox, death and brutality are four-dimensional. And it's real as fuck. Indulging in this reality–facing this reality–is the only way to survive.

It gets inside you.

It becomes you.

You become it.

You see, there's something animalistic about war that's in the very fabric of our DNA. There is a barbaric beast inside every one of us. Ask any mother what they would do if someone were to threaten their child. The momma bear is alive and well inside them. But for the 99 percent, the beast has been locked away in a cage of rules and laws. Humans are, by their very nature, a tribal war like species such as the Native Americans and Vikings. But somewhere along the way, Homo sapiens started building safe spaces like the ancient city of Babylon and Jerusalem in order to wall themselves off from dangerous animals such as lions and tigers. Then somewhere along the way some slithery snakes began attempting to "civilize" these residents within their gated community by turning these wild animals into domesticated pigs and sheep and a cheap obedient workforce by brainwashing them with religions and governments and big-screen TVs.

But every so often, they release a few back out. And what happens to soldiers is similar to what happens to a domesticated pig after being let out into the wild. Within two weeks, its hair will grow long and dark, and its docile nature will turn aggressive. I witnessed this phenomenon firsthand.

WELCOME TO THE JUNGLE

IT'S JUST AFTER SUNRISE. I am lying on my cot inside our converted jail cell at Abu Ghraib Prison that the US Army has turned into barracks for us to live in. The stench of sweaty feet and sweaty balls and sweaty armpits of four Army roommates fills the 12x12 foot cell with the pleasant aroma of a high school gym locker room. My eyes are not quite in focus yet when I glance over at a supply soldier, whose name and likeness will remain redacted because of the classified nature of his actions, which includes the fact he has a striking resemblance to pencil sketches of a midnight groper of female soldiers' tits all across military bases in Iraq and Kuwait, standing in front of his cot with his pants down around his ankles while rubbing cocoa butter on his balls, his routine ritual he's been doing all deployment.

My battle buddy, Specialist Vega, an Argentine college boy who joined the Army an hour before 9-11 happened and who is now a self-proclaimed conscientious objector, looks up from some bullshit book about Buddhism.

"What the fuck are you doing?" Vega shouts in horror.

"What?" the supply soldier replies. "Huh, huh. It feels good. You should try it, huh, huh, huh."

Vega throws a piece of paper at me.

"Ruger, do you see this shit?"

"Don't ask, don't tell," I reply, shaking my head while trying to focus on anything but a grown-ass man rubbing cocoa butter on his balls.

Thankfully, the immoral thought is interrupted by the clanking sound of the blue jail cell door opening. My Puerto Rican team leader, Sergeant Rodriquez, storms in wearing his full-battle rattle gear.

"Ruger, get your gear on," he says in a serious tone. "We are going on a mission."

He looks over at the supply guy. "Dude, what are you doing? That shit is nasty. Pull your pants up."

"What?" he replies. "Huh, huh, huh."

I sit up in my cot and ask, "Where are we going?"

Rodriquez replies, "We have to go to the hard site (where they keep all the Iraqi prisoners that have attacked coalition forces) and help transport an EPW (enemy prisoner of war) to BIAP (Baghdad International Airport.) Get your stuff on and meet me downstairs in the motor pool in 10 minutes. And bring your Gore-Tex jacket. It's freezing out."

As Rodriquez walks out of the room, Vega looks over at me.

"Holy shit, Ruger. Isn't BIAP down Ambush Alley where Specialist Ramirez was killed?"

"Yep," I reply, throwing my green woodland camouflaged body armor over my desert-colored uniform jacket and strapping the Velcro shut. "I'll take my chances out there. It seems a lot safer than being stuck in this jail cell with Specialist Cocoa Butter over there. You two love birds have fun."

"Huh, huh," he mumbles, still rubbing his balls. "Looks like it's just me and you, Vega. Huh, huh."

I reach under my cot and pull out a water bottle full of vodka and take a swig, just enough to take the edge off. I toss it back under and pull a can of Skoal Cherry tobacco out of my back pocket and put a pinch in the left side of my lip. After grabbing my M16 and Kevlar helmet, I make my way down to the motor pool.

The sky is overcast, making everything look as if the landscape is being televised on a black and white television screen. An icy breeze blows into the top of my Gore-Tex jacket and down the back of my neck. Rodriquez honks the horn from the driver seat of the deuce-and-a-half. I hop in the passenger side and we pull out of the motor pool and make our way to the hard site. Usually, the lower ranking person drives, and the senior person takes on the role of truck commander. But Sergeant Rodriquez is a bit of a control freak who always likes to steer his ship in the right direction as evident by his perfectly bloused boots and pressed uniform. And I am the crazy one with the itchy trigger finger because... well, chicks love the trigger finger. The unique setup works for both parties involved.

As we arrive at the hard site, we realize the truck is too wide to fit through the gate. Rodriquez cranks the transmission into reverse and backs up to the opening in the chain-linked fence.

"Fuck it," he says, shaking his head. "Let them bring the motherfucker to us."

About 10 minutes go by when an escort of MPs comes into view. A large Black soldier from a different unit rolls our human cargo out in a wheelchair, laughing and slapping the back of the enemy prisoner of war's head in some sort of twisted remake of the movie *Driving Miss Daisy*. They nicknamed the prisoner "Trigger" because after a member of the IP (Iraqi Police) smuggled a 9mm pistol into the prison, he used it to shoot the Black MP in the chest. Luckily, he was wearing his body armor, and it stopped the bullet from making him another statistic scrolling across the bottom of the TV screen on every news channel back home in America.

Thirteen soldiers were killed in Iraq today. In other news, Rush Limbaugh reveals he's an Oxycontin addict and Courtney Love claims drug charges against her are "retarded."

Trigger is wearing nothing but a pair of black shorts and a brown sandbag pulled down over his head. He jerks back and forth in the wheelchair to the point of almost knocking it over. Most of the MPs laugh and smile as the Black soldier continues to slap Trigger's head.

"I'll see you when you get back, motherfucker," the MP says with a grin. "Motherfucka gonna shoot me then cry like a little bitch when I slap him around. You better enjoy those nice nurses cause when you come back, your ass is mine."

The MPs' smiles flip upside down faster than the safety switch on a M-16 when they realize they will have to carry Trigger to us because the road in between is nothing but rocks and sand, and not suitable for the proper operation of a wheelchair.

"Get up!" a Staff Sergeant yells, his white cheeks turning as red as the stripes on the American Flag. "Get the fuck up and start fucking walking!"

"Mista, I can't," the prisoner cries out, pointing down at his bullet-ridden legs.

"Fuck this," the MP shouts as he and a Hispanic Staff Sergeant each violently grab an arm and drag his fat ass down the rocky road, his bare feet bouncing up and down off the ripples in the gravel covered ground, which instantly invokes memories of a fishing cork bobbing up and down through the ripples of the ocean's surface and the ensuing violent struggle of a fish being reeled into the boat.

"REEEE... REEE... REEEEE," Trigger screams out in pain, still jerking back and forth as if he is trying to jump out of his reptilian textured skin. But no one hears a word of it. He shit his bed, now he has to lie in it.

The MPs dump his helpless body in the back of our truck like a giant tuna being poached from the sea. I peer through the side of the deuce as they climb in the back and place Trigger upright on the troop carrier seat. His battered body is covered with black and blue bruises the size of fists and combat boots. Several stitches covering bullet holes line the inside of his calves. Underneath his left armpit is a shotgun pattern the size of a basketball where he was shot several times at point-blank range with non-lethal rubber shotgun pellets, leaving a permanent impression of tiny white circles on his dark tan body.

After some deliberation from the convoy commander, it is decided in some infinite West Point wisdom, that a mechanic, that being me, will ride in the back of the truck and guard the EPW while the pissed off MP rides in the deuce's cab with Sergeant Rodriquez. I reluctantly climb up in the bed of the truck and sit on the opposite side of Trigger. I almost throw up because of the stench. The battered bastard smells like a pig that's been rolling around in his own piss and shit. Getting a good whiff of it is as nauseating as swallowing a mouthful of chewing tobacco. I spit mine out before that happens.

I stare over at Trigger as if he shot my own brother. That's how it feels. It feels the same as when people mourn the death of celebrities they've never met, the way everyone mourned the day the music died in the 90s, when Kurt Cobain put that shotgun against his head, pulled the trigger and then he was dead. We feel connected to these people, as if they were family, because if it could happen to them, it could happen to us. That thought hits home a little harder. That's how cops feel when something happens to any cop. That's how firefighters feel when something happens to any firefighter. And that's how it feels to soldiers every time something happens to any soldier. We all feel as if we are one.

Fuck Trigger. He got what he deserved. If the roles were reversed, he would have done worse things to one of us. He probably would have strung up our mutilated body from a bridge like they did in Somalia and watched as the blood dripped all over the road as it was being broadcasted on CNN.

This is no place to be getting all sentimental with the emotions. It will eat you alive if you do. It's a kill or be killed world. It's Darwin's theory put into practice. It's all about survival. And if you haven't gotten the memo yet, getting home to our families in one piece is all that fucking matters.

The truck shakes violently as Sergeant Rodriquez fires up the engine. I point the barrel of my M-16 at the prisoner, tapping my finger on the rifle's trigger guard as we bounce our way through the muddy road toward the front gate. Trigger cries out every time we hit a bump in the road. And there are a lot of them in this fucked up war zone. He squeals like the wild boar my brother wounded while we were archery hunting in the swamps of Florida when we were teenagers.

"Reee... Reee... Mista... Ple-e-e-e-e-se... Reeeee... Reeeee... Mista... Ple-e-e-e-e-se... e... e... e."

I'd like to put him out of his misery just like I did that hog, popping one right into his fucking throat, but the Geneva Convention won't let me. I hold fire, hoping he makes a move that makes shooting him legal. His cries grow louder with every bump, but I feel no sympathy for him, I feel nothing at all.

Ever since sitting through Specialist Ramirez's memorial service, I've become... uncomfortably numb. It felt like the ball bearings from that roadside bomb had torn through my chest when his fellow soldiers started talking about him and his family, how he had the option to stay in the states after going home on emergency leave because of his ailing father, but chose to come back to be with his fellow soldiers. That pain burns inside with an intensity

I haven't felt since those planes slammed into the World Trade Center and melted them into nothingness.

It all has become too much. The pain, the sadness, all starting to consume me whole as if I'm a mouse caught in an eastern diamondback rattlesnake's meal plan, slowly drifting headfirst down into that cold-blooded heart of darkness. I had to cut off all other emotions. I had to–for survival reasons–replace it with an edgy attitude of not giving a fuck, which I wear like body armor in order to keep those emotional bullets from making me another 22-a-day statistic that no one wants to talk about on CNN or Fox News.

I try my best to keep the emotions locked away, but the anger is always knocking on my M-16's chamber door. It's hard not to want to hurt the people that made me feel this pain. Revenge does that to a person. It makes the line in the sand… blurry.

As we arrive at the base's exit checkpoint, the gate guard holds up his hand in a fist to signal for us to stop. We have to wait for clearance to leave the base. A few minutes later we get the go ahead to proceed. The convoy of gun trucks pulls through the opening in the wall and turns left out onto the hardball called MSR Tampa. I pull my black neck gaiter up over my nose and grip my M-16 tight. The truck's muffler and wind are blowing so loud, they drown out Trigger's screams as we barrel down the highway. My attention turns away from the prisoner and out toward the desert terrain, looking for any improvised explosive devices that might be set to turn us all into my X-rated roommate's endless supply of cocoa butter.

Everything is a possible threat out here; Coke bottles, dead dogs, tires, and dirt that looks fresher than the dried-out sand scattered along the side of the road. This war is different from the movies. Hunter S. Thompson said it best in the book, *Hey Rube*, "[there will be] no front lines and no identifiable enemy." You don't know who to trust out here because the enemy doesn't wear military uniforms which allows them to blend into the civilian population with a sort of camouflage that would make the producers of stealth jet technology look on with envy.

We are fighting ghosts that would rather plant a bomb on the side of the road than fight us head-on. CIA reports state that most of the enemy are trained in Iran and armed by the Russians. The Jihadists then crossed over the border to wage a Jihad War against America, which is really just code talk for another proxy war. I guess the Russians are still a little bitter that we armed the Afghans during their occupation in the '80s. Which was a Soviet lesson the US had learned in Vietnam when the commies armed the Viet Cong.

Now, I am all about tits-for-tats, but this constant tit-for-tat between the world's two superpowers that has been going on since the end of WW2 has become about as enjoyable as falling on a rack full of bungee sticks. But that is what this war is shaping up to be, another Vietnam. But instead of using bungee sticks, the insurgents are using shape charges–a cylinder the size of a soda can that shoots molten copper like a laser beam through the toughest of armor. Rumor has it these have even penetrated an Abrams tank.

But I don't have to worry about it penetrating our vehicle's armor because it doesn't have any. There's not even a cargo tarp to protect me from skin cancer.

As our truck continues to cruise down the road, I continue to scan my lane with rattlesnake eyes, looking over the cab of the truck at the forest of palm trees and lush vegetation appearing as we get closer to Baghdad, searching for any sign of movement or for some terrorist rat on a cell phone that might trigger one of those road side bombs.

As we approach an overpass, I notice some Iraqis standing on top while looking out over the highway. I duck down below the cab of the truck to avoid any wire that might be strung across the bridge with the intention of relocating a gunner's head to the middle of the highway because he/she/it decided to sit a little too high above the vehicle.

"Roadkill Cafe–you kill it, we grill it."

It's like David vs Goliath all over again, with the insurgents using primitive weapons to take down a giant and all its modern technology. They learned that lesson from the Viet Cong. Off with their heads!

The truck swerves violently as we pass under another bridge, trying to avoid any souvenirs in the shape of hand grenades that the bystanders might try to drop down into our gift bags.

After about a 20-minute drive, we make it to Ambush Alley, the same road where numerous coalition lives have been lost. As we turn left, the prisoner begins to dangle halfway out the troop carrier while flopping up and down like a freshly caught catfish on the side of a saltwater flats boat. But I do nothing to reel him back in. I am letting this one off the hook because I am not touching that bottom feeding motherfucker. Especially without a surgical mask or gloves or pliers. He probably has Tuberculosis or AIDS or who knows what else.

The truck suddenly swerves over to the side of the road and stops. The convoy commander jumps out of the Humvee behind us.

"What the fuck are you doing, Private?" he yells, marching toward me with a purpose.

"The prisoner is about to fall out of the God-damn truck."

I don't answer back. I just give him a blank stare.

What the fuck does he want from me? I think to myself. If he doesn't like the job I'm doing, then he should ride his bitch ass back here. Fucking pussies don't have the balls to do it. They're riding in their safe new little up-armored Humvees with the heater on.

Well, all of the gun trucks are new except the last one in the convoy that was given to our unit after it rolled over into the Euphrates River and sank to the bottom faster than Virginia Woolf with a pocket full of rocks, killing all four soldiers on board. Shit. I could have used a euphemism here to soften the Euphrates water landing for the reader, but I am not here to coddle you assholes. This isn't some self-help book. This isn't some hippy dippy Kum Bah Yah bullshit. This is real shit. This is war.

We now return to your regularly scheduled programing.

What the fuck does he want from me? This ain't my fucking job. I am not a MP. I am not trained for this shit. Not like anything could have prepared me for this shit show anyways. No amount of training can replicate the emotion of experiencing such sheer death and brutality and bullshit in person.

Nothing can prepare you to become an emotionless ghost.

But Fuck, man.

I used to care so deeply about people, and the world. Now it all just hurts like that Johnny Cash cover of the Nine-Inch Nails song. The American profiteers can have it all, this whole Middle East empire of dirt. I've let the world down; I've let myself down; I just want to stop the hurt. It's all a *Downward Spiral.*

What have I become, Johnny Cash? What have I become?

In our quest to destroy the terrorists, I fear we've become terrorists ourselves, destroying everything that stands in our way of freedom, including everything we once stood for.

When did it all go so wrong? How the fuck did I end up in this fucked up war to begin with? This wasn't what I signed up for. Iraq isn't why I joined the Army; 9-11 was, Afghanistan was. To fight the terrorists was. This is not what I am about. This is not what I believe in. I know deep down in the murky waters of my soul; this isn't who I am.

Goddamn.

Now I know how all those largemouth bass I caught in Florida as a kid felt. One minute you're swimming freely through the muddy waters of life, then something shiny catches your attention like a bright book in a dimly lit library. And when you reach out to grab it, BAM! you are transported into a completely different world–hook, line and sinker. And the only thing you know for certain anymore is that wherever you are now, is not a good place to be. It's cold as a cooler full of ice, you're surrounded by dead and dying bodies, and the world feels as if it's closing the lid on your existence...

I pull my neck gaiter down, light up a Camel Light cigarette and stare off into the village. Then this Hispanic Staff Sergeant comes around from the front of the deuce with a field jacket.

"We have to cover the prisoner up before we take him into BIAP," he says, wrapping the jacket around the Enemy Prisoner of War. "We'll get in trouble if we don't."

The convoy commander adds, "And keep him from leaning out of the truck, Private!"

I say nothing back.

I just stare off into a field of nothingness.

After the MPs get done covering their tracks, we proceed uneventfully down Ambush Alley and make it to the 28th Command Support Hospital (pronounced 28th Cash) inside Baghdad International Airport. The pissed-off white MP riding with Sergeant Rodriquez gets out of the deuce and proceeds to scream at Trigger again, demanding the bag of battered bones jump down from the truck. Sergeant Rodriquez races around the back side panel of the vehicle.

"No! This isn't right," he yells at the white Staff Sergeant.

The higher-ranking MP steps back and goes silent, stunned from the outburst of my usually reserved team leader. Rodriquez and the Hispanic MP lower the tail gate and help Trigger down. I just stare off at the cute blonde Army nurse rolling out a wheelchair, thinking to myself how soothing it would be to have her rub some cocoa butter on my balls.

She cracks a knowing smile at us, well-aware of the immoral thoughts rolling through my mind, then wheels the prisoner into the building. I hop down, put the tailgate back up, jump in the passenger side of the deuce, and we head back to base. I put my headphones on and try to drown out what we just witnessed with Metallica's *Ride the Lightning* CD, but the loud muffler sitting right outside the passenger side window of the Deuce sounds like Trigger screaming every time Sergeant Rodriquez hits the gas pedal. "Reee. Reeeeeeeeee."

We ride back to base in our desert combat uniforms inside of our desert-colored truck. We pass by desert-colored villages inhabited by desert-colored people. Rodriquez and I don't say a word. We don't have to say anything to understand what each other is thinking. We both know it was a fucked-up situation. But what can you do? Our rank isn't high enough to matter. It's a fight we cannot win. Now it's easy for armchair soldiers and civilians back home in the states who sit in an air-conditioned house inside the relative safety of a gated community to play Monday morning quarterback about the morality of war, about what is right and wrong, but after being out here in the desert for so long, everything starts to look the fucking same.

SMELLS LIKE TEEN SPIRIT

SPECIALIST VEGA AND I are huddled around our cots watching *The Sopranos* television series on a mini-DVD player. It's turned into our after-work ritual after turning wrenches all day. It helps transport our youthful minds out of this terrible reality we've gotten ourselves into. It helps to take my mind off all the fucked-up shit I've witnessed recently.

But as usual, the rest-and-relaxation is interrupted by the clanking sound of the prison cell door opening.

Our warden of a squad leader, Staff Sergeant Jackson, comes marching in with a serious look on his face.

"Let's go, Ruger," he says in a stern tone. "The First Sergeant has agreed to talk to you."

I grab my DCU top (Desert Combat Uniform), and we make our way over to the First Sergeant's wing of the prison. Jackson taps on the blue jail cell bars.

"You in there, Top?" he hollers with a frightened voice.

"Come in," the First Sergeant yells back.

Jackson opens the door, and we file in. The Cuban First Sergeant is sitting in a folding chair, dressed in black physical training shorts and a brown T-Shirt. He leans back with his arms stretched across the back of his head with an unlit cigar in his mouth like he's some sort of gangster, like he's Tony Montana from the movie *Scarface*.

"What can I do for you, PRIVATE?" he says with an annoyed tone stressing "PRIVATE" to let me know he knows exactly what he can do for me–or what he isn't going to do for me.

"Well, First Sergeant, I wanted to find out why I am not being promoted?"

"Well, PRIVATE, do you remember the day you thought you were badder than the First Sergeant back at Talil Airbase?" he replies, raising his eyebrows. "That's the reason why. And it's not going to happen, so you might as well forget about it. And this is the last we are going to talk about it, ok? Now get out of my room."

I grit my teeth while thinking to myself how if we were back in my old neighborhood, me and my homeboys would make quick work of this guy. *Fuck him.*

"Did you not hear me the first time, PRIVATE?" he yells.

I don't answer back. I just give him a smirk and storm out, my chest bursting like an IED blast with anger and rage. Jackson tries to calm me down with his usual God *this* and God *that* and God *has a plan* bullshit. But I don't want to hear any of it.

"I want to speak to the Battalion Commander," I tell Jackson, pointing my finger at him. "I am done with the First Sergeant's shit. I am done with this unit. I am going over their fucking heads."

"Okay," Jackson says with his hands up in the air. "But remember, you reap what you sow. You do realize they're not going to back down on you for this?"

"They can't do anything," I quip back. "They have no paper trail. They never gave me an Article-15 or a counseling statement. As far as I am concerned it never happened. It's just an old ghost story because they can't prove it happened because there were no witnesses. It's fucking stupid anyways. It's all a bunch of petty bullshit. And I want it pushed up the chain of command, or I will walk over there myself."

"Ok," he says, shaking his head while letting out an uncomfortable chuckle.

What a load of horseshit this is. Here I am busting my ass for my country 16 hours a day 7 days a week, fixing vehicles that the MPs keep breaking because they drive their trucks like assholes with their foot pushing the gas pedal all the way to the floorboard because they know they won't have to foot the repair bill or set one foot in the maintenance tent to do the repairs themselves. And here I am going on missions as a Humvee gunner, manning guard towers every time our base gets attacked, risking my life when I don't even have to. I could easily sit in the rear with the beer and the gear. I could easily hide out in the motor pool and mail it in like our worthless female supply soldier whose only job now is to deliver the mail.

But that's not me. That's not how I roll. I don't do anything half-ass. I am doing everything I can for the greater good of this unit, for the greater good of this country, and what do I get for my hard work? A thank you? A pat on the back? A promotion?

Nope. All I get is a big fat *fuck you* because I am not some bitch ass pussy who can be intimidated easily by rank, because I am not some bitch ass motherfucker who brown noses these high ranking shitbags. And to add insult to injury they just promoted a soldier to Specialist after demoting her to Private First-Class back in Ft. Stewart, Georgia after she body slammed a female Master Sergeant and broke her sternum. But I guess that's what happens when you get to ride around with the First Sergeant every night "delivering food" to the soldiers in the guard towers. What a load of bullshit man. It's contagious. Here I am now, stuck in Iraq with nothing to entertain us.

This is fucking bullshit.

This is fucking bullshit.

This is fucking bullshit.

This is fucking bullshit.

Fuck all this bullshit.

—WARNING—

Most of this book was written under the influence of performance enhancing drugs (green and caffeine.) It was also written after nearly a decade of consuming large quantities of black label Jack Daniels, blue Vicodin 500s, yellow Xanax bars, powdered cocaine, and crystalized molly in an attempt to erase the memories of my time in Iraq. You see, it's not easy to remember things you don't want to remember. But this is my best attempt at the truth from my point of view of the world. However, it may not be the truth as remembered by those around me. That's the funny thing about memory. You can have five people witness the same car accident and each will have a completely different recollection of what happened because each individual sees the world differently. We filter what we see through a lens of subjectivity that is based on our brain's subconscious biases that have been molded by the environments we grow up in. Cops interviewing multiple people at the scene of this train wreck called life is like opening the doors of perception to the minds of mankind. Inside you will find multiple rooms that are vastly different, and the witnesses' view of what happened reflect this reality because they will all give differing statements.

That's why some may say what is inside this book is pure fiction while others may say it is the absolute truth. But I say it doesn't fucking matter. All fiction is nonfiction and all nonfiction is fiction anyways.

All fiction is based on an element of truth. At its core it's based on the reality that the author has experienced in his/her/its lifetime and then filtered into an alternate setting. Hunter S. Thompson once wrote, "The best fiction is far more true than any kind of journalism. And the best journalists have always known this."

And nonfiction is fiction because it's not the absolute truth. It's the truth that the author and his/her/its interviewees want the world to see. There are nonfiction book publishers and newspaper companies publishing all sorts of shit such as a politician's direct quote even though they know it is a damn lie and then passing it off as the truth on the front page of reality. It's the classic, "Hey look, he said she said, it must be true."

Hell, journalists go out and interview people all the time, but are they getting the truth? *No!* They are getting the perception that the person they are interviewing wants the world to see. No one wants to be published in a negative light. That's why people are willing to harness the power of the newspaper in order to point out their perfections, but how many of these folks would still be willing to flaunt their flaws for that same 15 minutes of fame?

So, who can say what is real and what is not? Hell, we can't even agree on whether the dress is blue or gold or whether the shoe is gray or pink or whatever the latest stupid eye color test craze is on social media that is designed to get people all riled up because no one person sees this world exactly the same. Especially those who are just plain colorblind and those who are completely blinded by their own bullshit like an ostrich with its head in the ground, not wanting to face the facts going on around them. Sports fans are notorious for this shit. Their team is always the best even when they finish in last place. And their quarterback is the most moral upstanding citizen on Earth even when they are assaulting Uber drivers and young coeds in barroom bathrooms. But let the opposing team's QB do it and they put down the D-Fence and break out the picket fence.

This is why I consider myself genre neutral. I don't identify as fiction, nonfiction, or poetry. Like Bruce Lee, I don't believe in submitting to one style. Freedom of expression should never be chained and bound to some preconceived notion before the audience has a chance to experience the work without prejudice.

Besides, genres were created by control freaks with OCD who need to place everything into perfectly organized sections. Well, I think and write outside the TV box, so I refuse to be confined to some square with a label on it. I am not some can of dog food. I am not some bottle of hand lotion. I am not a can of instant coffee or instant mashed potatoes. And I sure as shit ain't no cheap ass mass produced Chinese made product ready-made for infomercials; on display in a town near you. I am a real motherfucker. I do my own thing. So hopefully book stores will accept me as is and not force me into some narrow-minded shit hole over in the dark corner of the building next to the self-help section–or worse, the poetry section.

Now that we got that out of the way, I would like to take this moment in time to say thank you to all the men and women who gave their lives so we can enjoy this thing called freedom of speech. I'd rather drink a beer in Hell with you guys than have a mocha latte macchiato whatever at the latest hip cool coffee cafe with all these crybabies left here on Earth. You fuckers are the real heroes and will always be more important to me than some overpaid athletes or mindless reality TV stars. *Cheers assholes!*

And I also would like to take this moment in time to thank the chicken shit motherfuckers who walk dogs for a living and work part time as theater critics and who have never risked their lives for something greater than themselves, for rejecting my story of doing just that because "It isn't suitable" for their fancy magazine full of flowery bullshit. Sorry I don't dress like a lumberjack and drive a Prius and write flimsy ass fairy tales and drink overpriced craft beers like it's a glass of wine. Swish, swish swallow it like the good whores you are motherfuckers.

Now I am going to be honest with you though. There are things in this book our soft ass society is going to find offensive. But I don't give a damn. Twenty-two veterans a day commit suicide, and our society doesn't give a flying fuck about their feelings so why should I give two shits about theirs? I don't. And I won't. They want to drive around in their BMWs with bumper stickers that say "support the troops so my kids don't have to fight and die in pointless wars" while talking about how my words offend them, well, I would like to talk about how their silence offends me.

So, in the words of my late great flannel shirt wearing, Budweiser drinking, Salem cigarette smoking, red meat-eating grandfather who lived to be 86 years old, "fuck 'em. To hell with all of 'em."

I'm done playing nice. I'm done trying to fit in. If the wine and cheese crowd standing at the gates of the publishing industry want to wear their Gucci glasses and boat shoes and thumb their noses at people like me, then fine… they are gonna need the proper footwear cause I'm fixing to start rocking the fucking boat.

Get it? Got it? Great balls of Fireball Whiskey.

And now that we are all on the same page, literally and figuratively, it's time to sit down, shut the fuck up, strap in and hold the hell on because this rollercoaster is about is to take the fuck off.

Please keep your arms and feet inside the coaster at all times.

And enjoy… your ride…

BORN IN THE U.S.A.

THE LSD TOUCHED MY tongue before the first bell even rang to start my freshman year of high school. I was riding in the truck bed of my surfer-looking friend Patrick's black two-door Ford Ranger, cutting up a ten strip of acid for my grunge rocker buddies as the 17-year-old circled around and around the castle-like school in Tampa, Florida as if we were riding horses on a carousel.

And round and round we'd go, where that story was gonna stop, nobody fucking cared because we were having too much of a blast just enjoying the ride to give two shits about how it was all gonna end.

Patrick and my redneck brother were hollering out the truck's windows at people they knew walking along the sidewalk in a zombie-like haze at 7:30 in the morning. Songs such as Nirvana's "Smell Like Teen Spirit," Sublime's "Smoke Two Joints," Warren G's "Regulate," Snoop Dogg's "Gin and Juice," Guns and Roses' "Paradise City" and Ratt's "Round and Round," blared through the speakers from someone's mixed cassette tape. Yeah, that seems like an odd combination of songs, but that's just how we rolled, that's how white boys roll when you grow up in the hood. Rolling spliffs and writing riffs. You know what I am saying, bro?

Pat and my brother were best friends, and the two buddies knew everybody because they were seniors and notorious party animals; the infamous class of 1996. Their hoots and hollers were met with smiles, sideway peace signs, and the occasional friendly middle finger that was accompanied by a devilish grin.

As the mobile party vehicle passed our friend Bryan's house, who lived right across the street from the aging brick school, Pat honked the horn, and the beat-up old truck slowed to a rolling creep. The grungy, long brown-haired junior who made all the girls smile, came running out with his worn brown book bag bouncing off his blue flannel shirt and jumped in the back of the truck next to me.

"Want a hit?" I asked with a grin.

"Hells yeah," the 16-year-old junior replied, holding out his hand.

He popped the tiny square piece of paper in his mouth, then pulled out a joint from a pack of Camel Light cigarettes and lit it up.

"You want to hit this?" he muffled, trying to hold the smoke in and laugh at the same time.

"Fuck yeah," I said, grabbing the Zigzag rolling paper that was wrapped around and around the weed tighter than a square's asshole from the oval office walking through the projects in the middle of the night, and pulled a strong drag.

Pucker up assholes, the show has just begun.

Smoke from the freshly lit joint drowned out the exhaust fumes, stale beer and cigarette butts that were stinking up the place as they lay scattered around in the back of the truck like dead soldiers on a Civil War battlefield.

Pat leaned out the driver's side window.

"Hold on to your nuts boys, we fixin' to get crazy," the bloodshot-eyed teenager yelled, flicking his Clove cigarette out into the street and revving the engine's 112 horsepower so high it shook the truck like dice in a gambler's hand hanging over the edge of a craps table.

After getting the RPMs up to the red line, he released the clutch, and the tires screeched off down the road in a cloud of white smoke, sending all the empty beer cans clinking back toward the tailgate.

Welcome to fast times at Hillsborough High.

The first day of the semester was always a waste of fucking time because it was mostly hours of listening to introductions and expectations from the teachers. Not much involvement on the students' end. It only seemed logical to prevent such a great day from going the way of Old Yeller by getting bored-to-death by a shotgun blast of useless information. But my carefully crafted day of doing drugs was rudely interrupted by a teacher who had other plans.

By the time my second period English class rolled around, the acid was on its way to reaching peak performance. I was staring down at the dark blue carpet, which was twirling around and around like a tornado from *The Wizard of Oz*, when Mrs. Beasley called on me to read from a book she had placed on all our desks. The ambush caught me off guard, and I got all sorts of sideways. Luckily this gothic girl sitting one seat over helped me get on the right page.

But I soon realized my mind was off in another section of the library. I attempted to translate Edgar Allan Poe's "The Tell-Tale Heart" from written words to vocal sounds, but I couldn't because the letters were literally getting lost in translation as they began flying off the paper and into the air. Frantically, I tried to catch them and put them back on the blank page, but when my eyeballs peaked up, they noticed the whole class was staring at me in horror. My heart began to pound so hard I was convinced the school resource officers could hear it beating from their office two buildings away.

To make matters worse, the teacher kept eyeballing me with her vulture eye. And it sent my nerves into a pit of pendulums that were hanging on by a thread. So, I put my head down and said I didn't feel good. She seemed to have bought it, probably chalking it up to a 14-year-old just being a teenager. Besides, who the hell would suspect I was whacked out of my mind on hallucinogens at 10 in the morning?

I was eventually saved by the bell, thankfully. And as if I was the singer Meatloaf, I ran out of there like a bat out of hell. But no matter how fast I ran, nothing could save me from fourth-period German class. Third-period history I handled. It was cool because Bryan was in the class with me. And because I've always enjoyed learning about The Native American Wars, slavery, The Women's Rights Movement, the Civil Rights Movement, the Anti-War Movement, the Workers' Rights Movement, the Civil War and how the Founding Fathers used the penny press to unite the colonial settlers to overthrow tyranny. There was just something fascinating about the oppressed rising up against the rich and powerful in the face of overwhelming odds. History always had a way of moving me to want to do something that was that powerful and meaningful for some reason.

But *Die Deutsch Sprechen?* Shit, I couldn't understand it half the time when I was sober, let alone when I was peaking on some high-quality acid. I could see the letters visually coming from the teacher's mouth, but none of them formed a single legible word; though the tone in her scratchy, cigarette damaged voice was crystal clear. I could feel the displeasure coming directly from her eyes because I couldn't stop talking to these cute metal-head chicks with long black hair; Laurie and Colleen. And because of my inability to comprehend what the hell the old hag was saying, in German or English. She gave me the squint-eyed death look. And you didn't need a translator to understand it either. It was worth a thousand angry curse words. And I bet she had an arsenal of brutal ones stored up in her mind's armory. I got the feeling she had seen and done things that most blonde-haired, blue-eyed Germans would rather not discuss when the sun is out and the booze is tucked away.

The laser beam of negative energy radiated down on my position with such a Luftwaffe-like intensity that it caused me to lose complete concentration of my ship's sail. A U-Boat torpedo of paranoia hit me right in the frontal lobe. I kept thinking the secret police were going to jump out of some hidden room behind the bookshelf and haul me off to a concentration camp. Sorry, Ann, I am just being frank. Once there, they would re-educate me by cutting off my long black hair and beating obedience into my thick skull. But I was too hard-headed for that, so I took a bathroom break and never went back.

Instead, I went to hang with my brother, Patrick, and all the seniors who were chilling in the center courtyard for their lunch break. It's where the infamous "H" is, a giant red concrete letter in the ground that is surrounded by one chain and four poles. Normally, freshmen are forced to kiss it by the outgoing athletes, but I was spared the humiliation since my 17-year-old brother knew all of them from his all-star football and baseball days - before he got burned out and screwed over by the varsity coach who was still bitter about the fact that my sibling, who was the starting pitcher for the JV squad at the time, defeated the coach's A team that had been propped up as the chosen ones to go undefeated and win it all that year, ruining any chance for his precious perfect season.

Hillsborough High was one of those athlete-driven schools. Built in 1928, the three-story brick building in the inner city is home to the poorest kids in Tampa; mostly poor blacks from the surrounding projects. Athletics is their ticket out of poverty. And the school did whatever they could to ensure their star players got out. So, they were given special treatment.

They were allowed to bring food and drinks into class.

They were allowed to sit in the back and sleep.

Shit, they could ace a test without knowing a single answer.

We lesser beings were written up for minor infractions and sent to see the assistant principal, who my parents were on a first name basis with, I might add. The rigged system gave the privileged athletes a sense of entitlement that radiated throughout the school like a bad case of jock itch, and it left a bad taste in anyone's mouth who wasn't in the cool kids' club, which was about 85 percent of the students. The male athletes wore their team jackets around campus as if they were bouncers at one of the many world-famous strip clubs that Tampa is known for, roughing up anyone who got out of line. And the cheerleaders followed them around like rock star groupies; sucking them off before the sweat dried on their jockstraps after the big game under the Friday night lights.

The terrier mascot and the red and black colors were fitting for the school. It was dark and mean. Bullying was rampant. Kids brought guns to school, and there were occasional riots. It felt like being in prison sometimes. We poor fucks were treated like dogs compared to the other schools in North Tampa, such as Gaither, where the rich white kids in Lutz went to school.

Our main rival's colors were a bright shade of white and blue. The yuppie fucks drove to class in brand new Mercedes Benzes and BMWs. They lived on lakes and in posh suburbs. The Gaither Cowboys (or the Gayfer Cowgirls as we called them) received more funding than us, which meant larger classrooms, smaller class sizes, and higher quality teaching equipment.

But more than anything, the privileged kids had hope.

They had a path to a good future laid out for them. All we had were outdated textbooks and a path that usually led to jail, the porn industry, or death.

Don't believe me?

Look up my old friend, porn star Avy Scott.

Hillsborough's finest alumnus.

Hell, Hillsborough High was so poor the wall in my history class on the third floor had several holes in it the size of a 12-pack of Busch beer. The only thing stopping someone from falling through it was a roll of yellow police tape wrapped around it. Any money the school did receive seemed to be used for homecoming rallies, football helmets, and baseball bats. The only nice building was the main entrance to the school. That's where they housed all of the trophies and jerseys of famous alumni such as Major League Baseball players Dwight Gooden and Gary Sheffield.

But athletics didn't mean shit to me, especially after taking a baseball to the left side of my face during a game that left a bad impression and a throbbing black and blue welt on my cheek. My redneck father, who worked at a paper factory plant called Weyerhaeuser, wanted me to play football and baseball when I was young, but I sucked at sports and hated everything about it.

"He wanted a pitcher, not a belly itcher, sitting in the locker, eating Betty Crocker."

Growing up, I wanted to be a musician in a rock-n-roll band. It was the '90s. Nirvana's "Smell Like Teen Spirit," The Smashing Pumpkins "Bullet with Butterfly wings," Pearl Jam's "Jeremy," Sublime's "What I got," Guns n Roses' "Welcome to the Jungle," Metallica's "For Whom The Bell Tolls," Bush's, "Glycerine," Alanis Morissette's, "You Ought to Know," Alice in Chains "Would," and The Cranberries' "Zombie" all ruled the airways. MTV was playing music videos instead of reality TV shows. Flannel shirts, blue jeans, long hair, and fuck-the-world attitudes were as normal to me as heroin is to a junky.

We didn't give a fuck about credit scores, batting averages, or 401k plans. We didn't give a fuck about fancy suits or fancy cars or fancy houses and we damn sure didn't give a fuck about slaving away our youth or slaving away the rest of our lives in some factory or cubicle while the corporate powers get to enjoy all of the time they have on Earth whenever and wherever they so damn well pleased because of the working class's hard work. We didn't give a fuck about any of that. We didn't care about anything except the music and holding on to our individuality in a growing corporate world that was increasingly trying to strip it away. That was the path to our promised land. That was the key to unlocking our happiness.

The only problem with my chosen career path, however, was that I played guitar about as well as a drunken hillbilly juiced up on bathtub gin and sang like a screeching rooster getting peppered by Kurt Cobain's shotgun at the crack of dawn. But even though I lacked the necessary skills to ever be inducted into the Rock-n-Roll Hall of Fame or accepted into any band in their right mind for that matter, it didn't stop me from partying like a rock star.

And party I did.

I took my first hit of LSD at the ripe old age of 13 while hanging out at a water park in Tampa called Adventure Island. My mother, who was a registered nurse at St. Joseph's Women's Hospital where I was born and where her mother retired from, also worked part-time at Busch Gardens as a RN and would drop my brother and me off at A.I. every day during the summer with the free passes she got from work.

There would be 20-30 of us misfit kids wearing blue jeans, black t-shirts from our favorite bands, and chain wallets that hung down to our knees. We would blast Bob Marley's "Jamming," Jimmy Hendrix's "Purple Haze," Cyprus Hill's "Hits from The Bong," Alice In Chains' "Junkhead," and Tom Petty's "Last Dance with Mary Jane" on someone's boombox or cassette player.

The volleyball courts, called the Pit and the Spike Zone, were where we would meet up and chill and get harassed by the security guards in their goofy green and white uniforms with gold badges. Apparently, we were scaring the wholesome family types that traveled from faraway places like Wisconsin and Nebraska to enjoy some good old fashion family fun in the sun only to arrive at what looked more like a Marilyn Manson concert than the fairytale beach commercial they were promised. We were bad for business, as the corporate types like to say. But hey, we were customers too, and there was no dress code listed on the ticket at the time. So, there was nothing they could do.

The Spike Zone was the scene of the crime for my introduction to hallucinogens. I met this rad blonde eighth-grader named Jen who lived in an upscale gated community in Carrollwood, which was on the opposite side of town from me. She had me wrapped around her finger like that Cranberries' song "Linger" had the whole country wrapped around in the 90s. There was something about her that reeled me in close, as if I was a line of cheap cocaine at the end of her rolled up hundred-dollar bill. She always reminded me of Cherry from my favorite movie/book, *The Outsiders*, taking a liking to me even though I was a poor metal head from the south side of Tampa. I was hooked from the day she came up to me with some white-on-white paper acid and said "here, eat this."

Hey now, if you had seen that sweet smile of hers sparkling in the Florida sun, then you wouldn't have said no either. I grabbed the dime-sized piece of paper and put it under my tongue like normal kids put a pulled tooth underneath their pillow at night. But instead of finding money under there, I found a key that opened the doors of perception.

About thirty minutes went by when the lines in the sand began slithering like snakes and coiling up around the palm trees that appeared to stand as tall as skyscrapers. Coins the size of baseballs rained down out of thin air. Turns out though, it was just the LSD fairy Jen and a couple of her prankster friends messing with me by tossing loose change at what they kept calling their "wishing well." Everyone would fuck with each other like that, making the echoing sounds fly fly fly, high high high while tossing paper airplanes through the air as we looked on from another dimension. We motley crew of kids were birds of a feather, and when it came to doing drugs, well, we all flocked together.

The best part of tripping at A.I. though was when we went up on the hill that overlooked the water park and stared up at the clouds floating around in that big blue sky. It was like we were on top of the world. Everything was at our fingertips. Anything was possible. The sky was our canvas, and we could paint whatever Picasso we wanted on it with our minds. My modern-day masterpiece had cloud-shaped tigers roaming across it and fish swimming by and wild horses running wild and giant blackbirds flying as free as every caged animal wishes they could be.

But Adventure Island wasn't the only place our LSD adventures ventured out to though. Sometimes we would walk down the road to Busch Gardens and hop on the roller coasters called the "Python," "Scorpion," "Kumba," and "Monto," dropping down into those vertical drops that lead into loops and all the twists and turns of a good book with the G-forces of a fighter jet.

Please keep all hands and feet inside your mind's coaster at all times. Thank you for visiting Busch Gardens and enjoy... your ride.

When we weren't traveling at high speeds through another dimension, we would stroll around the park to the pink flamingo exhibit with actual live birds in it–not just those stupid plastic ones you saw on the front lawns and on T-Shirts worn by dull-witted tourists all across Florida in the 80s and 90s. We'd stare off at the pink and white Flamingos as their feathers appeared to flock together into one giant Sesame Street Big Bird as the grass beneath their feet slithered into the water and turned into diamond-shaped eyes staring at us from deep within the abyss as a line of band members came marching by playing African music on drums and trumpets.

The fresh smell of churros, hot pretzels, popcorn and beer hops from the on-site brewery flowed around the theme park like the steam from the Serengeti Express train as it made its rounds around and around the Serengeti Plains full of zebras, antelope, rhinos, giraffes and elephants before dropping passengers off at different sections of the park called Congo, Nairobi, and Stanleyville.

But the theme parks were not our only source of amusement.

There was also the laser light show at the Museum of Science and Industry's IMAX Theater that we loved to trip balls at because the screen stretched from the floor to about halfway up the ceiling.

An array of colorful trails would glow from the screen and out into the crowd when rainbow colored cash registers began dancing across the screen as Pink Floyd's "Money" crooned through the speakers, the registers opening and closing with every beat.

My favorite though, was when the IMAX Theater showed movies about outer space; the stars, the moon, the planets, all working in unison. The infinite possibility of what's out there made all the drama and bullshit here on Earth seem so insignificant. It opened the door for me to a whole new universe. It was as if the creativity hamster in my mind was snatched off the wheel and put into a rocket ship and shot off into a different universe. It set my imagination free, free to explore beyond the realm of possibility.

And explore I did. Like the time we dropped some microdots (LSD) and went to the top of the parking garage at Tampa International Airport in the middle of night, straight chilling while watching the lights from the runway as planes took off and landed, which made for an enlightening point of view of the night sky.

Even when I was punished by the school system for getting into trouble for various infractions, I would explore it in a vastly different way than the rest of the students. Like the time my boy Mike and I tripped all night at Patrick's house then showed up at Hillsborough High's Saturday morning work detail because I got in trouble for spouting off my big mouth with one of my teachers, as usual. Mike didn't even have to be there, but he went anyway because that's how real friends roll, motherfuckers. We were like World Championship Wrestling's The Outsiders, Scott Hall and Kevin Nash. You know when we strolled in it was going to be a damn good time. It was going to be "Sweeeeeeet."

"Your name is not on the list," the grumpy old teacher crooned at Mike.

"Well, I am supposed to be here," Mike snapped back while pushing the clipboard down to make it look like he was shocked to not see his name on it.

"Well, I will write your name down here," The teacher grumbled before sending us on our merry way.

We spent the next three hours attempting to pick up trash in the parking lots and hallways, but our crazy train kept getting derailed because we kept goofing off and laughing at the sight of other students who were not in on our little acid joke.

I hadn't laughed that hard since we took acid and went for a walk through the neighborhood and saw a woman pushing her kid in a swing. There we were completely fucked out of our minds and this wholesome lady is trying to spend a pleasant evening with her kid and these two misfits can't stop laughing because of our inside joke of being on acid while no one else knew. What a trip those days were.

My drug portfolio, however, wasn't limited to just LSD. There was also weed, cocaine, XTC, heroin, Special K (horse tranquilizer,) and lots of booze. I'd smoke a blunt before class in high school. My first period OJT (On the Job Training) teacher, who was also the head coach of our famed Hillsborough High School football team, had to know I was high as hell every time I came to class. But Coach was cool about it. He would lecture me about being late then chuckle when I came in tardy half the time with a late note that my friend, who worked in the front office, would forge for me. He'd seen it all before, perks of teaching at one of the most disadvantaged schools in Tampa. I guess he figured at least I was actually in class and not out on the streets somewhere committing crimes.

Then there was the time when a few of my friends and I jumped the fence to Hillsborough High School's football field and smoked a bowl on the 50-yard line after watching the movie *Dazed and Confused* where they did the same thing. If you took that movie and combined it with the movie *Friday*, it would be like life imitating art and art imitating life.

Tampa was like New York City in the 80s. There were gangs such as the Crips, Latin Kings, The Outlaws MC, Skinheads, and Folk. Hookers and their pimps lined the streets of Nebraska and Florida Avenue every night. Heroin addicts would be shooting up along the sidewalks of the roach-coach motels as crack smokers hid in the alley ways. And as soon as the sun went down, the po-lice helicopters would start orbiting around the neighborhood like the moon orbits around the Earth every night.

Growing up in Seminole Heights was rough back then. Back before all the white yuppies in their khaki pants and boat shoes thought it was the hip cool place to drink their overpriced craft beers and paint all the houses in the neighborhood pink and yellow and say dumb shit like "ooh, we're so edgy cause we're hanging out in the hood."

Tampa wasn't always so gentrified. Back then, it was highly segregated into different areas. It wasn't done intentionally. It was just what people did naturally. Hispanics stuck to their neighborhoods that were built back when the Cubans and Columbians came during the great tobacco rush in the late 1800s. All the Whites that could afford to do so moved out to the suburbs in Carrollwood and Lutz during the 50s and 60s when the Blacks started rioting and burning down the inner city during the Civil Rights Movement. And Black people lived wherever the government said they could live, which was where they built the Robel Park projects and the surrounding areas. But for the poor white folk like us that couldn't afford to move out somewhere with posh living quarters, we stayed behind in the pile of ashes from the Civil Rights Movement that was still left smoldering with hate and paranoia.

No one seemed to get along. Blacks hated us because of what happened during the time of slavery, and we hated them because they were jumping and robbing us on the regular. And Hispanics were no exception either. The Cubans hated the Puerto Ricans, and the Puerto Ricans hated the Cubans. They both hated the Blacks. And they both really hated the Mexicans. Everyone hated everyone, but no one knew why other than something that happened in the past or happened to someone they knew. It was just the way things were. And the only way to survive in this ecosystem that we were born into was to flock together like herd animals.

Welcome to the jungle.

The funny part about our tiny white neighborhood in the hood though, was that it got caught up in the busing system, which was supposed to swap Blacks from the inner city with Whites from the rural areas because somewhere some suit-wearing genius with a map thought he could solve the world's problems by drawing a circle and waving a magical wand without ever stepping foot in those areas to see what the fuck was actually what. And just like that, *poof* went our Cinderella lifestyle, and a bunch of white kids were put on a yellow carriage with 420 horsepower and sent out to McLane Middle School in Brandon for 8th grade, which was surrounded by nothing but orange groves, strawberry fields, and cattle farms full of black and white cows. But then the clock struck midnight after that one-year detour, and we went right back to where we started in Seminole Heights.

I lived on Crest Street, which was about a mile from Hillsborough High School. It ran from Florida Avenue where Mauricio's bakery baked fresh Cuban bread daily for $1.25 and T'd out at the Hillsborough River. That's where my father stood next to the concrete wall that housed the sewer drain, and tossed my grandfather's ashes into the muddy water we grew up fishing in. The bench is still there. Everyone else is gone now. But I still find myself going there and sitting on that bench sometimes, staring across the river and remembering all the good times we had while it lasted.

Crest Street is also where I met my boy Mike, who lived across the rough concrete road with his dad, a full-time tow-truck driver and a part-time motorcycle mechanic for various motorcycle clubs. We were like Johnny and Pony Boy from the book/movie *The Outsiders*, except he looked more like Lenny from *Of Mice and Men*. He was 6 feet tall and jacked full of muscles from playing football in North Carolina his freshman year. But he was far from being mentally retarded.

After my brother graduated, Mike became my bodyguard during my sophomore year. And few would fuck with him because he was a good street fighter with a mean right hook. But the ones that did dare to dance with the devil like this guy Franky, well, it didn't take long for them to get knocked the fuck out cold and kiss the dirt faster than Hemingway with a handful of shotgun shells.

I got picked on a lot because my nose was too big and my body was too small, constantly being called Pinocchio, Toucan Sam, short and fragile, and Gonzo from the Muppet Babies. My slender frame was an easy target. So, I had to evolve in order to survive. What I lacked in physical attributes, I more than made up for with a slithery silver tongue full of humor and sarcasm and a venomous vocabulary that would make any Eastern Diamondback Rattlesnake look on with envy. Though, my mouth seemed to have been more of a curse than a cure, constantly drawing the ire of parents, teachers, girlfriends, ex-girlfriends, and anyone who tried to trample over me with a reckless disregard for my point of view of life from down here in the dirt.

Mike and I were hood rats who were always roaming around the streets looking to take advantage of our geographical location by scoring some "party enhancers." We were both wound a little tight because of the tension at home and in the neighborhood. An assortment of drugs and alcohol such as this wine called Mad Dog 20/20 would always help us unwind a bit. And we never had to look too far for the suds. If we wanted some booze, we'd go to the Texaco gas station a few blocks away on Nebraska and Osborne Ave or to the convenience store Princes on North Blvd and Columbus and buy a homeless guy a couple quarts in exchange for buying us a couple of 32-ouncers of Olde English 800, Mickey's, or St. Ides Special Brew.

From the outside looking in, the low-income Seminole Heights neighborhood looked like a bummer to live in, but it also made it very convenient to score whatever narcotics we wanted. That was one of the few perks of living there. It was sandwiched between two housing projects, and drugs flowed through it as smoothly and quietly as the Hillsborough River did.

If we wanted some LSD, we would cross over Hillsborough Avenue to Henry and Ola Park, where we knew this old hippy guy with long brown hair who'd always be wearing a tie-dye shirt who, for $100, would hook us up with a vile of liquid acid that we kept in an eyedropper container. Who would suspect a couple of 15-year-olds of having a hundred hits of LSD in a Visine bottle? We would then cut out an animal cracker or a sugar cube and drop a hit on it and sell it for $5. And for some hardcore friends, we would drop it right into their eyeballs.

If we wanted to cop a dime sack of weed, we'd peddle over to the Robels Park Projects. Though, we had to be careful because a lot of times it was some bunk ass shit like oregano.

And we also had to be careful because the cops would always bust our balls.

"What are you White guys doing down here?" they would ask with suspicious eyes.

"White guys come down here for one of two reasons; either you are looking for bud or a blow job. Now which is it?"

You didn't want to get on the bad side of the cops in the hood. They, too, were wound up a little tight because of the tension in the neighborhood and from seeing the constant violence that always accompanies the job. Mike and I found that out the hard way when we were running from the po-po after this bitch ass store clerk called the fuzz on us for using a fake ID to try to buy a bottle of Jose Cuervo Tequila.

After our friend David's piece of shit VW Bug wouldn't start, we bolted, ditching the ID in the alley way. They caught up with us soon after a good hike through a creek and down into the projects. They put me and my soaking wet Converse shoes in the back of the cop car and interrogated Mike near the front.

He kept talking loudly so I could hear him, and we could get our stories straight. But after being told repeatedly to stop talking so loudly, they slammed his head on the hood of the car, leaving a nice warm impression on his thick cheek bone courtesy of the hot engine bay. He never wavered though. The guy was tough as bricks. Mike was an intimidating figure. I guess that's why the cops always seemed to handle him a little rougher than my skinny ass. After our stories matched up, they let us go, and we found a payphone to call my brother who came and picked us up with his girlfriend in her jacked up 4x4 Ford Ranger.

Then there was the time Mike and I were sitting in a car in the middle of the Robles Park Projects in the middle of the night with this Black guy, one of the biggest coke dealers in Tampa everyone called "Uncle Pete," after a night of partying with him at the Seminole Indian Casino. Now if you wanted the good stuff, Uncle Pete was the one you called. His shit was straight fire. His shit was so good you couldn't get enough of it, and it didn't take us long to blow through the little white bitch he had on him. Any smart dealer knows when you are out in public not to carry large quantities on your person. You're just asking for trouble. But since we were out of the powder and wanted to continue snow skiing, we ended up there in Robles Park. Now it may not have snowed in Tampa since the seventies, but it definitely snowed every night at Uncle Pete's house.

Slunk down in the seat, the tall slender dealer nervously peered out every window in the car several times.

"You boys stay right here, I'll be right back," he said in a serious tone as he exited the car and walked into a house with bars on the doors and bars on the windows.

20 minutes or so went by.

"What's taking him so long," I asked out loud.

Mike replied, "don't worry, that's my boy, he'll be back."

And that's when the light flashed before my eyes.

"Get your fucking hands up where I can see him," a cop shouted from a herd of cops who had rushed up on us with their guns drawn, spotlights aimed right at us like a sniper's scope.

Fuck.

"What you white boys doing down here in the hood? They interrogated us with suspicious eyes as the sun started to come up from below the horizon. "You are either down here looking for dope or to get your dick to get sucked, now which is it?"

That was their favorite line, I guess.

But since we didn't have shit on us and it's not a crime to "drop off a friend at his house," they let us go.

The pigs were always harassing us like that. They would stop us for no other reason than the pigment of our skin, guilty only of being white in a black neighborhood. They were always asking us for ID and searching us without probable cause. So, we had to develop ways to get around them.

When you grow up poor you learn to be resourceful. You learn to get creative. Just like with the Visine bottle, we would empty the tobacco out of one cigarette, put a joint in it, then put it back in the pack with the cigarette filter over the top of it. That way, when the cops looked in there, everything appeared normal. Then there was the shaving cream can with the false bottom that we would store stuff in. But the 5-0 caught onto that one pretty quickly. It made no sense why kids not old enough to develop facial hair would be carrying around a bottle of it. The key though, was to always try and make the odd not look out of the ordinary. But that was hard to do when you were the only white guys walking around.

We were the odd.

But sometimes being creative wouldn't cut it. So, we also made connections to help us dodge the three little piggies who were always trying to huff and puff and blow down the big bad wolves' house of fun. As the saying goes, "it's not who you are, it's who you know." And we knew a lot of people from selling drugs and because of my older brother and his friends. We'd get free stuff from Bo's Ice Cream. We'd get free cookies at the Tampa Bay Mall. We'd get free food from ABC Pizza. Everywhere we went in the neighborhood we would get free stuff because we knew people. And they knew us. Everyone always had a smile on their faces when we ran into each other. And that's a damn good feeling to have when you don't have much at all.

Hell, even if we couldn't get stuff for free, we would sell enough weed and LSD to buy clothes at a "special" discount from our friends who worked at the Tampa Bay Mall on MLK Street such as these pants called JNCOS that had hidden compartments near the inside of the kneecap to stash our goods. Sometimes we just traded straight up with the managers who moonlighted as well-known Techno/rave DJs at night. They would sell their tapes along with others from DJ Santana, Huda Hudia, Rabbit in the Moon, and Baby Ann in their stores. It was convenient for all parties involved.

But the po-lice weren't the only road hazards we dealt with. Gangs of Black dudes were always riding around on bicycles like a pack of hyenas roaming the Serengeti, with one guy on the handlebars who was looking to jump off and catch you with a quick ass whipping before riding off into the sunset with your hard-earned prize possession.

My brother, who, as I've said, was a few years older and much bigger than me, found himself in a similar scenario. He wasn't on a bike, but one night he was walking home alone from a friend's house at the end of the street when six of them held him down while one sucker-punched him before stealing his wallet and shoes. And he was a star football player who was twice my size.

A few of our neighborhood friends rallied together. And let's just say, my brother got his stuff back and we never saw those cats on our street after that. What goes around comes around when you fuck around with the wrong the wrong motherfuckers. When you play stupid games, you win stupid fucking prizes. And that was the give and take, the back and forth of living there. But that's how we all became so tight. That's how we survived. We had each other's back.

When you live in a rough ecosystem, eventually you will have to become just as rough in order to survive. It's Darwin's theory put into practice. Only the strong survive. Kill or be killed.

I found myself on the receiving end of it as well. I was skateboarding on Central Avenue in front of Hillsborough High School when a gang of Black kids on bicycles came riding by and started calling me a "dumb cracker" and a "stupid white boy." To my best recollection, my mouth spouted back something to the effect of "fuck you."

That was stupid because they quickly circled around me. And it didn't take long before I felt a punch land on the back of my head. Luckily, I stumbled forward and accidentally sent one guy flying when I used my skateboard to brace for the impact. Then I turned and held up the Channel One skateboard with independent trucks and Fireball wheels like it was a baseball bat, as if I was really going to do something with it. Hell, I barely weighed 100 pounds. It was all smoke and mirrors. But I wasn't going to run or back down, and the magic trick cast the illusion it needed to, and the mind game worked. The thought of being smacked in the face with metal trucks by some crazy long-haired white dude was enough to get them to back off. It was like a pack of wild hogs staring down a rattlesnake.

I guess I had learned that don't back down spirit from my factory working father. He would always catch black guys jumping the fence to our backyard, looking for something to steal. He kept a Remington 870 pump-action shotgun under the bed and a Ruger .357 Magnum revolver in the nightstand, even though it made my mother, who was trained to save lives, not take them, a bit paranoid. We eventually got a red pit bull/rottweiler mix named Budweiser who we called Bud for short, and he put an end to the unwelcome company.

But there were still the drive-by-shootings to contend with, one of which happened at Pat's home. He lived four houses down from us at the last house on Crest Street next to the river. He got mixed up with some Folk gang members who wanted to send him a message using a 9mm. His crazy Vietnam veteran dad came out and returned fire.

Luckily no one got hurt.

Although murders did happen quite often. That's why Seminole Heights got the nickname "Murder Heights." Right after high school, our friend Philip, who I bonded with over our tattoos while we were at Hillsborough High School, was killed by a guy named George, who I'd known since our days at Broward Elementary and Oak Grove Junior High. Rumor was, it was all over drugs and a woman. Supposedly George walked right up to the vehicle and put a bullet in Philip's head during what was supposed to be a drug deal and walked off with $3,000 in ecstasy pills. George got 35 years and Philip got a headstone.

Then there were the two cops who were killed right down the road from where we lived in 1998 by this white trash guy with a mullet named Hank Earl Carr. The career criminal was picked up and handcuffed with his arms in front by detectives because his girlfriend's son was killed by Carr's AK-47, which he said was an accident. On the way to the police station for questioning, Carr used a handcuff key that was secretly stashed on him to get free and was able to overpower the two detectives in the front seat because there was no protective cage. He shot both of them with one of the detectives' pistols before hijacking another car and started heading north on I-75. That's when he shot and killed another cop who was trailing him before taking his own life while barricaded inside a Shell gas station three counties over. The horrific crime spree was splattered all over the local news, being played around and around the 24-hour NEWS carousel like OJ Simpson fleeing in a White Ford Bronco after murdering his ex and her waiter boyfriend.

So, like what any normal kids would do, Mike and I peddled over to where the kid was killed. The crime scene was only a few blocks from Mike's mother's house up near Nebraska and Sligh Avenue. Cops were scattered everywhere, like union soldiers on a civil war battlefield. The shock and sorrow in the civil servants' faces were highly visible, even to our young eyes. But there was nothing civil about their war, nothing civil about the war they faced every day.

Mike and I hung around till nightfall. On the way back home, the twirly bird shined its spotlight on us peddling through the streets as if we were actors in a Broadway show. It was strange though, none of it seemed surreal at the time. Violence was just a way of life in the Heights. It was as normal to us as Chick-Fil-A is to a soccer mom in an upscale suburb.

Welcome to hell, may I take your order?

Though hope was low and crime was high, we didn't let any of it stop us from having a damn good time. Most of the partying happened at Pat's house. He may have looked like a surfer with his bleach blond hair, tribal arm tattoos, and dark tan, but the only waves he surfed were the airwaves. His rave parties were notorious. Everyone from Hillsborough High would show up. Cars would be parked all down Crest Street and River Boulevard. There would be people on the roof, people in the pool, people on top of people, and people inside of people. He had his room decked out with a DJ table, strobe lights, and glow sticks. Kids would be blowing the fuck up on XTC while inhaling big balloons full of nitrous called "whipits" as techno music blared out through the speakers. Ravers would be strung along the floor all the way down the hallways, their Vicks Vapor Rub rubbed eyes rolling in and out of the back of their heads with smiles on their faces stretching as long as the Hillsborough River.

My preferred seating for the midnight matinee was always on the roof in order to space out at the solar system. I was always of the belief that you couldn't reach for the stars from inside the confines of mankind's home-made safe space. There was something peaceful about it up there, staring up at the stars and the moon, wondering, pondering the enormity of it all while thinking about how we are five billion people stuck to this giant rock full of molten lava that's floating in a big empty space, thinking how there's something greater out there that's bigger than all of us. Thankfully sitting up on top of Pat's roof didn't cost anything except for the $5 hit of acid… It was free. And it was freeing.

Man, what a blast into outer space it was.

Pat's house was the nicest in Seminole Heights and also had a great view of the river. A lot nicer than the basic house I grew up in, which my father and his four brothers also grew up in. Pat's house was one story with three bedrooms, two baths, and an in-ground pool made of black granite. It was one of those fancy architecture type homes with thick bushes surrounding it, a stone pathway that led to the front door, potted plants with rich soil throughout the front and back yard, and a winding hallway that snaked through the middle of the house to each bedroom.

And it was always filled with a crazy cast of characters. There was Troy, who was one of the best car thieves in Tampa. He was the first person to bypass the Club that people used to lock their steering wheels to prevent auto theft when it first came out. Hell, he even made the news when he stole a Dodge Viper and was filmed by a news helicopter driving it down the highway being chased by the police.

And there was Will, a native New Yorker who we called Casper because of the character from the movie *Kids* and because he was white as a ghost, damn near albino. He was a guitar player and loved to get hammered and explain free will to anyone who would listen. The Lizard King was what I called him because one night we were jacked up on microdots (LSD) and lying next to Pat's inground pool when we noticed some dead lizards laying at the bottom of it, and Will started singing the Doors' "The Celebration of the Lizard: Not to touch The Earth." He was a funny guy. Every Sunday, right when the sun began to come up, he would scream across the river at the Apartment complex, "Wake up, it's time to go to church," and "this is your alarm clock going off, eh, eh-eh-eh, eh."

Then there was my crew of friends Tom, David, and of course Mike. David was six months older than us and had a driver's license and a VW Bug that was held together with duct tape and a whole lot of prayer. We'd get drunk and smash into garbage cans and spray paint dicks on people's Christmas decorations and spray people with fire extinguishers we stole from buildings in downtown Tampa.

My crew was always welcomed at Pat's place, who lived there with his dad, Larry, and older brother. Now Pat's dad wasn't a DJ or a musician, but damn if he didn't party harder than anyone I've ever known. The Vietnam Veteran just seemed to be on a different level than everyone else, like he was riding high on a different frequency that we would never be able to reach no matter how many drugs we took. Every weekend around 3:30 in the morning, his car would come flying down the road like a Huey Helicopter. A squad of guys wearing Hawaiian shirts, a couple of hookers as thin as a drummer's drumstick, and Larry would jump out of his blue Mercedes with chrome trim and come busting through the door. They would stretch lines of cocaine so long across the dinner table that it looked like frets on a Gibson guitar.

Larry would always be holding a bottle of either Goldschlager that had tiny gold flakes swirling around the bottom of it or McCormick's Vodka that he gripped as if was a microphone while shouting words of wisdom such as "Ass, grass, or gas, no one rides for free," "He who has the gold makes the rules," and for those who had a little too much indulgence, "When you're done, you're done, and you my friend, are done."

He would also drop these mind-blowing bombs like napalm that stuck to our young minds such as "You ever thought how when you are born you fight like hell to come out of the pussy, then the rest of your life you spend fighting like hell trying to get back up in one?" and "have you ever thought about if the roles were reversed with fish and they would drop a line and a hook onto the land, then drag you in the water after you took the bait then mounted your body on their wall?"

We ate up his words of wisdom like groupies.

One night he came home and plopped down a $10,000 bag of blow on the table and asked, "Who wants a bump?"

"I do," Mike and I replied, holding up our 15-year-old hands.

Rave was never really my thing, so most of the time if I wasn't chilling on the roof, I would chill with Larry in his room in the back listening to the radio, which was either on the station 98 Rock or 102.5 Classic Rock. He would tell me stories about his time as an Army Ranger in Vietnam as bands like the Rolling Stones, Black Sabbath, and The Doors would be jamming through the radio. He'd tell me crazy shit about ambushing Charlie out in the jungle with claymore mines and coming back from missions with bullet holes in his uniform.

After coming home from the Army, he graduated from the University of Florida with an MBA. Then he became a millionaire when his construction company got a contract in the 90s to install cabinets in most of the middle schools in Tampa. And then for some reason, he bought a house in the middle of the hood instead of any of the nice upscale neighborhoods in North Tampa. I guess it was a good investment or just a place where he didn't have to worry about self-righteous neighbors getting all up in his business about his comings and goings at all hours of the night.

In the hood, people learn *real* quick to mind their own fucking business.

Except for this self-proclaimed neighborhood watch woman, who we called the "dog lady" because she would walk her show quality Doberman Pinscher up and down the street while picking up its poop by hand with a plastic bag. She was an oversized woman with an oversized ego. She just seemed to have it out for everyone in the neighborhood. She even called code enforcement on my parents a couple of times. I guess when you are 50 and single with no one to love or love you back, you just hate the world.

One time I was walking to Pat's house to cop some weed when five or six low-rider trucks came screeching around the corner. At first, I thought it was the Folk gang bangers coming back to finish Pat off, but when they jumped out, they were all wearing DEA vests. Apparently, the dog lady called the police and told them Larry was running a drug lab there. All they found was some cocaine residue, water bongs, and a little bit of weed. No charges were filed. Now had they come a few nights earlier, we'd all be in jail.

When Mike and I weren't partying at Pat's house or terrorizing the neighborhood, we were getting ourselves wrapped up in all kinds of shenanigans while out exploring all of Tampa. One night Mike and I were chilling with these two rich girls from North Tampa who went to our high school, a redheaded heroin addict named Kat and a blonde named Amanda. They were part of the International Baccalaureate (IB) program that was only available at Hillsborough High. That's a special program for super smart rich kids.

We had gone downtown next to the performing arts center and dropped acid and were chilling in this small outdoor amphitheater locally known as Trip Park. Mike and Kat were over there giggling about something. Amanda was lying on top of me with my arms tightly wrapped around her like Zigzag rolling papers wrapped around some expensive weed, and soon after our two bodies felt as if they were blending into one as I slid my trigger finger down her pants and into her pink flamingo.

But for some reason my attention kept drifting outside our little love bird's nest and across the Hillsborough River at the University of Tampa. The minarets on top of Plant Hall, the most iconic building on campus, had always reminded me of Moscow, Russia. I would always imagine what life was like over there on campus for the rich and powerful, knowing poor guys like Mike and I would never know. Guys like us don't make it out, and we certainly don't go to college. But it was still fun to dream.

Now, I don't know if it was the acid or what, but I kept picturing some aristocrat's rowdy children drinking champagne from silver platters and dancing in fancy Victorian-era dresses with circus bears that roamed in off the streets, caviar and hors d' oeuvres flowing through the party as the self-indulgent frat boys turned into horny beasts that ripped and ravaged and clawed those dresses off and turned the black-tie affair into a bloody orgy.

But my pleasant thought experiment was interrupted by this large white guy with a thick Irish accent and who was only wearing a pair of shorts which exposed swastikas tattooed all over his chest and arms.

"Can I kill you?" he asked.

"Um, no," I replied with a what-the-fuck look on my face.

"Why not?" he questioned, inching closer toward us. "I want to kill you?"

"Um, because that's not a very nice thing to do to such a morally outstanding citizen as myself," I mumbled back as we inched closer away from him, before hauling ass out of there faster than if the cops were tailing us.

Tampa was a crazy place full of crazy people back then. It was a free-for-all before all the corporate money took over and made it PG-13 for all the "family-friendly" types to enjoy. There were radio stations with Disc Jockey's like Bubba the Love Sponge who did crazy shit like have "No Panties Thursday" in which his female listeners would tie their panties to their car antennas and drive around town. And there were the women in T-Back bikinis, who would sell hotdogs along the side of the road next to Gandy Beach. It was all about sun, fun, and buns. No one gave two shits back then because there weren't any stupid cell phones to record the debauchery. People could be themselves without any fear of public persecution because they wouldn't have to worry about humiliating photos ending up on the internet with a giant red A the size of the book *The Scarlet Letter* scrolled across it for all the self-righteous hypocrites to point their fingers and snicker at.

Tampa was wild. And no place was wilder than Ybor City, which is a strip of bars on 7th Avenue. It is similar to Bourbon Street in New Orleans. Anything went there. It was come as you are. Gay, straight, crooked, it didn't matter. It was a sexual utopia. It was a place where inhibitions went to die.

Ybor City was the Wild, Wild West of the East Coast. Originally named for Spaniard immigrant Vicente Martinez Ybor, who helped build the cigar factories and Hispanic community there around 1885, it had since morphed into a strange ecosystem that became a utopian mecca for the odd and outcast. That's why my pals and I fit right in. Cigar shops and historical restaurants such as the Columbian Cafe and Carmine's now shared the tiny town with the northern pink flamingo district of clubs on 7th avenue called "Gaybor" and the south side district that was a mixture of hip hop clubs playing rap songs such as Warren G's "Regulators," Bone Thugs and Harmony's "Crossroads," NWA's "Fuck the Police," Biggie's "Juicy," and T-Pac's "California Love," and techno clubs complete playing songs such as DJ Sanatan's remix version of "Take my love," "Take me in your Arms," "This is Love," and Lords of Acid's Pussy as a rotating dance floor spun around and around the lines of candy kid ravers decked out in rainbow colored outfits with candy attached to it that seemed to stretched out as far as Mario Kart's Rainbow Road. And of course, one of my favorites was a small club concert venue called The Masquerade that put on big bands such as Jane's addiction, the Misfits, Foo Fighters, Tool, Nirvana, Marilyn Manson, Type O Negative, and NOFX.

And then there was a nightclub called The Castle. Oh, The Castle, an old two-story church someone converted into a gothic club. People would dress like vampires while dancing to songs by The Cure and the Cult. It came complete with its very own real-life 70-something-year-old senator prancing around in a pink nightie.

And every Halloween, Ybor City had a giant party called Guavaween. The promoters fenced the whole thing off and patrons paid a cover to get in. The radio station 98 Rock put on a big concert there every year. I convinced my parents to let me stay at Mike's house once, and his mom let us go while covering for me.

What an insane time. Women were dressed as half-naked nurses and naughty maids. Men were dressed as everything from Jesus to people-sized penises. Women would flash their boobs for thirty-cent beads likc they did at the pirate festival off Bayshore Boulevard called Gasparilla. Hell, even the band Veruca Salt flashed the crowd when they were on stage because the crowd kept chanting "show your tits, show your tits."

Godsmack was playing that night when Mike and I ran into my ex-girlfriend Lindsay with her new lesbian girlfriend Adrian and our best friend Jennifer in the back of the crowd. One thing led to another, and the next thing I knew, my friend Will took Lindsay into the porta john for a more intimate encounter, and then Adrian got mad and started blowing me in the middle of the crowd as I laid on the ground in my Crow outfit from one of my favorite movies. People started staring so I wrapped my black trench coat around her as tight as a blunt made out of a Swisher Sweet cigar. But my carefully crafted barrier didn't stop our friend Jennifer from seeing right through it and cock-blocking me.

"Is she sucking your dick?" she questioned with suspicious eyes.

"No," I shook my head with a smile.

"She's totally sucking your dick right now," she replied, grabbing Adrian off me.

And that was the end between me and my sweetest friend.

But my personal favorite place in Tampa Bay was Clearwater Beach. We had a Mexican friend Mike who lived out there. His parents were former roadies for big-hair bands in the 80s such as Ratt and Warrant. We would eat XTC all night then blasted off to the beach doing 110 MPH in Mike's 1990 Ford Mustang 5.0 as the sun came up. There was something magical about walking down Pier 60 and sitting in that cool white sand with the crisp cool breeze blowing in off the Gulf of Mexico while watching the colorful array of sunlight reflecting off the greenish-blue water. It was mesmerizing.

Growing up in Tampa in the 90s was unreal. It's still hard to wrap my head around it all. We always stayed as high as a Benjamin Franklin kite. The times were electric. Live bands were plugged in everywhere thanks to 98 Rock, who put on other shows such as the three-day camping event called Livestock. Artists like Slash's Snake Pit and Silver Chair were like gods to us kids as they jammed out in front of thousands of people.

It was a special time for me.

It was us against the system.

It was us against the corporations who wanted to turn us all into mindless workers for minimum wage while they make billions off the backs of the working class without so much as a thank you.

It was us against that authority.

It was us against our teachers who tried to mold us into obedient little ants to prepare us for those factory and cubicle jobs.

It was us against our parents.

It was us against the world.

Everything smelled like teen spirit, and we were out to rage against that machine. We were not going to be just another brick in the wall.

That's why I always dreamed of being up on stage like all my musical heroes that I saw in concert instead of getting lost in the crowd. They weren't like everyone else. They were on top of the world. They were as free as everyone in the crowd wished they could be.

The lyrics and riffs from their electric guitars seemed to flow right through us all as we danced around and around like madmen in front of the stage. Nothing else mattered at that moment in time. We didn't have a care in the world. We didn't care about material products or gold flake facial moisturizers. We had something way more valuable than any of that shit. We had something you couldn't buy or mass produce on an assembly line. We had a universal sense of togetherness, like a Native American tribe dancing around a fire. It was as if we were plugged into the same guitar amp, and our energy was wailed up into the stratosphere. We were flying high as the castle-shaped water tower that's a local landmark in Seminole Heights. We were floating on cloud 9.

Then it all came crashing down to Earth...

And that was a wrap.

WHERE WERE YOU WHEN THE WORLD STOPPED TURNING?

I **WAS SITTING IN WEB-DESIGN** class at Erwin Technical Center in Tampa, Florida, when the door slammed open. The impact jolted me half-way out of the black plastic chair. A white woman the size of a Boeing 747 with long, black fraying hair came flying through the doorway screaming hysterically.

"Turn on the TV! Turn on the TV! A plane just crashed into the World Trade Center!"

Professor Parker, whose gray-haired brain was trying to decipher what was going on, slowly walked over to the TV and pushed the power button.

Everyone in the classroom quietly looked on at the burning building.

"How did the pilot manage to fly into the tower accidentally?" Professor Parker asked out loud while scratching his balding head.

As the frantic woman attempted to reply, a second plane slammed into the second tower, sending an explosion of fire and debris through the air, completely killing any buzz I had left from the joint I smoked before class.

The image rocked me, it rocked me back to reality as if the plane had slammed into my chest, exploding with fear and panic, the jet fuel burning so intense with shock that it melted my steel core and sent my heart crashing down to a bloody death.

"Oh my God, oh my God, oh my God," my Puerto Rican computer partner, Naydaliz, said underneath her hands.

Professor Parker tried to console the class.

"Everyone calm down," he said with his hands raised. "Everything is going to be ok."

Chelsea, a blonde valley girl from West Palm Beach, Florida, trembled as she asked, "What's going on? I don't understand what's going on?"

No one answered. No one said a word. The class just stared around the room with intense looks of confusion and fear. No one moved. No one made a sound. Everything seemed as if the world stopped turning, as if everything was frozen in that moment in time.

In what seemed like 9 minutes and 11 seconds later, a crackling sound came over the intercom. A male voice began to speak in a low trembling tone.

"We have just received word that America is under attack. I say again, America is under attack. Two hijacked planes have hit the World Trade Center, and one has hit the Pentagon. Remain in your classroom until further instructions."

Chelsea cried out, "Who would want to kill us? Somebody say something!"

Again, there was no reply. Just blank empty stares.

Naydaliz mumbled into her shaking hands, "My children. I have to get to my children."

In what seemed like another 9 minutes and 11 seconds later, the somber male voice came back over the intercom.

"We have been advised to release all students. School is canceled for the day. You are free to leave."

I flew out the door like jumbo jet, jumped down two sets of stairs that led to the parking lot, hopped in my gray jacked-up Ford Ranger 4x4 sitting on 33-inch tires and raced home. I rushed into my room and loaded up my 12-gauge Remington pump shotgun and a Remington bolt action 243 and carried both of them to the living room. I laid them both next to the brown couch and pushed the power button on the TV box.

Patiently waiting, gripping the remote tightly, I stayed glued to the live NEWS station's every word. Something about the brutality of seeing those planes slamming into the World Trade towers over and over again reeled me in as if I were a speckled trout feasting on live bait out in the flats off the coast of Florida.

And when the NEWS is playing reality TV that is as real as it gets, live in real time across a screen that looks like a war zone here at home, it's hard not to get pulled in. There is no escape; no going to the kitchen to make a sandwich, no napping, and for damn sure no changing of the channel. America hasn't seen this sort of live action in real time since the Gulf War in 1991. But this, this wasn't over there, this is right here on our own soil, it is right here in our face. And what a terrifying sight it is to come face to face with it on live TV.

Every television station in the universe was showing the chaos and destruction happening in New York City, but few details emerged. Over and over, I watched the planes full of human beings crashing into the Twin Towers next to images of bloodied firefighters and police officers rushing out of the buildings as they collapsed. The grave images became engraved in my mind.

I switched over to a local TV station reporting that MacDill Air Force Base could be a possible target because it's the home of the U.S. Central Command (CENTCOM) and the Special Operations Command (SOCOM.)

Fuck, the enemy could be anywhere.

The movie *Red Dawn*, in which Russians use civilian airliners to drop paratroopers into U.S. cities kept playing over and over in my mind. I called my brother, but he was still half asleep and didn't seem too concerned. Everyone else was at work. Hour after hour I waited for more details.

What should I do?

Where should I go?

I sat and waited, glued to the television.

After what seemed like 9 hours and 11 minutes later, President George W. Bush came on the television to address the nation. I watched intently.

"Good evening,

"Today, our fellow citizens, our way of life, our very freedom came under attack in a series of deliberate and deadly terrorist acts. The victims were in airplanes or in their offices: secretaries, businessmen and women, military and federal workers, moms and dads, friends and neighbors. Thousands of lives were suddenly ended by evil, despicable acts of terror...

"A great people has been moved to defend a great nation. Terrorist attacks can shake the foundations of our biggest buildings, but they cannot touch the foundation of America. These acts shatter steel, but they cannot dent the steel of American resolve. America was targeted for attack because we're the brightest beacon for freedom and opportunity in the world. And no one will keep that light from shining. Today, our nation saw evil — the very worst of human nature...

"Tonight, I ask for your prayers for all those who grieve, for the children whose worlds have been shattered, for all whose sense of safety and security has been threatened. And I pray they will be comforted by a power greater than any of us, spoken through the ages in Psalm 23:

'Even though I walk through the valley of the shadow of death, I fear no evil for you are with me...'

"Thank you. Good night. And God bless America."

I lay my head down and attempted to sleep, hoping it was all just a bad acid trip. But I awoke the next day to all the TV stations still replaying the attack on a loop like a broken record. Hour after hour, the towers kept crashing down over and over and over again. But I couldn't look away. I couldn't help but think about all the families affected by this, by all the families getting that message on the answering machine, "Babe, I am on a plane that's been hijacked, just know I love you, I love you so much. Please tell the kids and my parents that I love them too – [cries] – Bye."

I remained hooked to the television screen. But the shock and sorrow soon gave way to anger. It began to fester as the day went on. Everyone I talked to was in a "stand by to see what happens next" mode. My mind shifted from the attacks to those who were responsible for those innocent people's murder. I wanted revenge. I wanted to kill whoever was behind this.

They must pay for what they have done.

In what seemed like 9 days, 11 hours later, the anger reached its breaking point as reports surfaced that some guy named Osama Bin Laden and his terrorist network Al Qaeda were behind the attack on the World Trade Center.

I now had a target. But my patience was growing thin sitting on the couch. A fire erupted underneath that pile of melted steel. It began to rage inside as the clock ticked on.

And then George W. Bush came back on TV to give another speech, and what I heard sent my moral compass flying in a completely different direction.

A reporter asked the President, "if the FBI knows of a credible threat, can you assure the public that you would take the precaution of locking down any system involved, whether it's buildings, airports, water systems, to prevent more deaths? And, most importantly, is there anything you can say to Americans who feel helpless to protect themselves and their families from the next wave of attacks, if there are more to come? What can people do to protect themselves?"

Bush replied, "Sure. Today, the Justice Department did issue a blanket alert. It was in recognition of a general threat we received. This is not the first time the Justice Department has acted like this. I hope it's the last. But, given the attitude of the evil doers, it may not be. I have urged our fellow Americans to go about their lives, to fly on airplanes, to travel, to go to work."

Go about my life? How can I just go about life like nothing ever happened?

I couldn't just rid myself of the rage I felt toward those responsible for this heinous act.

I couldn't just rid myself of the pain I felt for the innocent men, women, and children who exploded as the planes slammed into the twin towers.

I couldn't just rid myself of the thought of human beings on the top floors, feeling the building shake below, and then being gripped by fear as they sprinted as fast as they could down the stairs; jumping, sweating, panicking, hoping, and praying to whatever God was listening to let them see their families again.

I couldn't just rid my conscience of the image of a man leaping from atop the World Trade Center because he had no other option.

I couldn't rid my mind of over 300 police officers and firefighters being crushed to death while they selflessly attempted to rescue anyone they could.

I couldn't rid my heart of the pain I felt for the families who stood there frozen in horror as they frantically tried to call their loved ones over and over only to get a voice message.

I couldn't rid my soul of the thought of all those families getting that gut-wrenching phone call from the morgue saying they will have to come down and figure out a way to pick up the pieces and go on.

I couldn't.

I couldn't wait any longer.

GET UP, STAND-UP

WEARING A PAIR OF Chuck Taylor high tops, ripped up blue jeans, and a black t-shirt with Johnny Cash giving the establishment the middle finger, I nervously walked toward the U.S. Army Recruiting office, passing a pale redheaded Air Force recruiter in blue slacks and a light blue collared shirt, an angry Marine dressed in camouflage, and a chill Coast Guardsman who nodded and said, "What's up?"

"Hey," I replied, pulling my black shoulder-length hair behind my ears and opening the door to the Army recruiting office.

Pictures of soldiers jumping out of an airplane, a bearded man in scuba gear coming out of a river with a black rifle, and a pretty blonde nurse with a stethoscope around her neck lined the walls. The office was packed full of civilians waiting to sign up by an overwhelmed group of soldiers in woodland camouflage uniforms moving at a frantic pace.

A tall, muscular recruiter with bulging neck veins noticed me from behind a line of civilians and stood up as he shouted, "CAN I HELP YOU, SIR?"

"Um, I'm interested in joining the Army," I said, trembling.

"Well, you have come to the right place," the Hispanic soldier replied, still with a raised voice as if I was standing across the street instead of two feet in front of him. "We have some OUTSTANDING signing bonuses of up to $5,000 and money for college through the Montgomery GI Bill and tuition reimbursement. My name is Sergeant Ortiz. And your name is?"

"Jack, Jack Ruger."

"Nice to meet you, Jack. So does any of that interest you?"

"Um, not really. I am just interested in going to war to help in the fight against the terrorists who were responsible for 9-11. I'm not trying to make it a career. I am not interested in getting married to the Army. I just want to take her to the big dance, have my way with her, and drop her off at her boyfriend's house when I'm done.

Sergeant Ortiz replied, "Well, the Army Reserves are usually the ones that get called before the National Guard because they get attached to active-duty units. The Guard is state-run and is more for hurricane duty. With the Army Reserve, you only have to serve once a month, two weeks out of the year. We have a unit in St. Petersburg called the 420th MP Company. They are a combat unit and deployed during Operation Desert Storm. And if you don't want the money for college, you can do a three-year active reserve contract with five years in the inactive reserve."

"That would be perfect, but I'm not the cop or college type," I replied. "Are there any infantry units? And I don't want to be tied to the Army for eight years."

The recruiter shook his head in a stern response, "No, there are no infantry units in the reserves. But the combat MPs have medics, cooks, and mechanics assigned to them. They aren't like the cops you see on base. These guys ride around in Humvee gun trucks doing convoy escort, base security, and guarding of enemy prisoners of war. And unfortunately, everyone signs an eight-year contract."

Not knowing jack shit about any of this, it took me a hot minute to think about things. Being a mechanic sounds cool, I thought to myself. My boy Bryan was a U.S. Marine Corps mechanic already. I've always looked up to him as a big brother and when he came home on leave with his Marine buddies, I was just in awe of them. They were tough and they had balls.

When we went to Clearwater beach, one of the jarheads, who was jacked full of muscles, walked right up to these girls carrying a couple of coolers and snatched it out of their hands and said "hey, let me help carry that for you." And they didn't scream for the police or bitch about inequality. Nope, they just smiled at him and said, "Thank you."

And another Marine named Timmy and I were drunk as shit along with Bryan's brother Adam at a 7-11 on Waters and North Blvd in Tampa around midnight to pick up some more beers when he saw these two cute girls pumping gas. He walked right over and got into the driver's seat and was like "what's up?" At first, they were a little freaked out, with the girl in the passenger turning up the radio to try and drown him out as he attempted to talk to her friend pumping gas, but he turned it back down and said, "Hey don't touch my radio." She was like, "Your radio?" And somehow, someway he ended up convincing the girl pumping the gas to cook him spaghetti the following night after she told him she was Italian.

Despite all the flowery bullshit you hear about how a woman wants a nice guy, the reality on the street was vastly different. Women were always receptive to aggressive advances. Not many women in Tampa want to date a pussy. These guys were legit. They were full of testosterone and good times. And I wanted to be just like them.

So, I looked up and said to the recruiter, "Let's do it. I want to be a mechanic.

The recruiter responded, "Alright, alright. We can make it happen. I just need you to fill out some paperwork."

Full name: Jack Frank-Norman Ruger.

Age: 19

Race: White

Hometown: Tampa, Florida

Height: 5'9'

Weight: 117 LBS

"Oooh," the recruiter said with a concerned look. "Let me check my weight chart. Yeaahh, oh, ok. Yeah, it says you are two pounds underweight, but you qualify for a waiver to get in. It shouldn't be a problem."

Eye color: Brown

Hair color: Black

"Where did you go to high school?"

"I went to Hillsborough High School."

"Oh wow, that's in the hood," Sergeant Ortiz said with a look of pity.

"Yeah, tell me about it," I replied. "Whites were the minority. And the majority didn't like us. I got jumped a lot for being a 'stupid white boy' and during 'cracker day.'"

"What's cracker day?" he asked with a look of confusion.

"It's where if you're white, and you show up to school, you are getting your ass kicked."

"Damn, sounds like you had a pretty rough time growing up."

"A little."

"Did you graduate high school?"

"Barely. I had to be put into a special program called "Impact" to make up all the classes I failed from skipping school and getting suspended all the time. During my senior year, my GPA was .666666, and was put in a freshman homeroom because I didn't have enough credits to be in a senior one.

"Does it say High School Diploma on your certificate?"

"Yes."

"Ok, you should be good to go. Did you attend college?"

"No, just tech school for web design for a semester, but I just dropped out."

"Are you married?"

"Heck no. I was dating this girl for a while, but she stole my money and my heart when she took that money and flew her ex-boyfriend here from California."

"Damn, that's fucked up," he replied shaking his head. "It's good you are single. That kind of stuff happens a lot in the military. You are better off this way. I need a list of your employers for the last five years. Are you employed?"

"No, I just quit the graveyard shift at 7-11. My first job was flipping burgers at Wendy's when I was 15. Then I became a dishwasher and a cook at a Greek joint called ABC Pizza when I was 16. I did that until I was 18 when the manager grabbed my girlfriend's ass at work, and we got into it."

"Have you ever been convicted of a crime?"

"No."

"Have you ever done drugs?"

"I've done a few," I replied with a smirk.

"Like what?"

"LSD, XTC, weed, cocaine, Special K,"

"Any other drugs I should know about?" the recruiter chuckled.

"I also snorted heroin once. After running away from home, I was staying with these junky friends of mine I knew from high school at the Tampa Bay Mall. The one guy's girlfriend worked at the cookie shop, and she let us borrow her purple Volkswagen Bug. We ended up pawning her saxophone that was in the trunk and went and bought a couple packs of smack with it. The two junkies shot it up while my buddy Mike and I just snorted it. They laid in a coma, but I got paranoid and ended up vacuuming the house. Funny part of the whole thing was we told his girlfriend the saxophone was stolen, but she was more pissed off that her spare tire was gone, which actually did get stolen."

Sergeant Ortiz looks up from whatever he was writing with a look of astonishment, "I'll put you down as a 'noooo.'"

He leaned in and whispered, "If anyone asks, just say you've never done anything. They won't find out unless you say something."

I leaned in and whispered back, "Ok."

"Can you pass a urine test?"

"Oh yeah. I haven't smoked in a month."

The recruiter took a sip of coffee, "What do your parents think about you joining?" he asked.

"They don't know," I replied, looking down at the carpet. "I don't really talk to them much since their divorce. My dad was a hard ass. We bumped heads a lot.

"What about your mom?" the recruiter replied.

"My mom and I never really got along either. She was always wrapped up in the hospital life. She spent most of her time talking on the phone with her nursing friends and watching shows like ER. I haven't really talked to her since she dropped me off at my grandmother's house and moved to Virginia."

The recruiter paused for a moment, then continued with the interrogation.

"Do you have any siblings?"

"Yes. My big brother lives with my dad and works at the same box factory here in Tampa. And my little sister lives with our mom in Virginia. Says she wants to become a registered nurse just like her when she graduates high school in a few years."

"Hobbies?"

"Hunting, fishing, four-wheeling, skateboarding."

"What do you hunt?"

"Deer, hogs, squirrels, and rabbits."

"Where do you hunt around here?"

"Sometimes in Ocala National Forest, but mostly a place over in Lakeland called Green Swamp."

The recruiter continued writing down every word I said as if he was a stenographer at my court hearing. The questioning continued.

"You have any pets?"

"I have a cat named Tiger. Had him since I was 12. He would follow me to the bus stop every morning."

"Cute," the recruiter replied. Do you have someone to keep it while you are gone?"

"Yes."

"Any tattoos?"

"Yeah, I have the words 'All is fair in true love and war' on my rib cage and a red tail hawk across my back."

"Are they gang-related?"

"No. They're mostly just nature tattoos."

"Are you affiliated with any gangs?"

"No."

"Have you ever denounced the U.S. government?"

"No."

"Have you ever filed bankruptcy?"

"No."

After spending an hour collecting everything about me except my underwear size, which I was sure would come soon enough, the recruiter scheduled me to take the Armed Services Vocational Aptitude Battery test (ASVAB). I took it a few days later and scored a 55, just good enough to be a mechanic. Guess I should have paid more attention in school and I could have become a rocket scientist or something, but this wasn't the Air Force, and I never aimed that high because, well, it's hard to aim high when you grow up a low life. Hell, the only thing I've ever aimed at was an animal unfortunate enough to walk through my rifle's crosshairs. *Boom.*

Shortly after the ASVAB scores came back, I was scheduled for a day at the Military Entrance and Processing Station (MEPS). Sergeant Ortiz rolled up to my house in a black Mitsubishi Spyder Eclipse convertible around 5 a.m. He jumped out of the car looking like he just left Gaybor in a pair of really short black booty shorts and a bright orange fishnet t-shirt with a spider-web in the middle. (Don't ask, don't tell.) His muscles were protruding so much it was a wonder the skintight t-shirt webbing didn't get ripped apart like a fly caught in an R-rated version of Charlotte's Web.

"Hey Ruger, we need to talk real quick," the concerned recruiter said in a serious tone. If anybody asks, you never did drugs, ok. There is no record of it, so they won't know unless you say something."

"Ok," I replied with an uneasy feeling, as if I was becoming the fly wrapped up in the shady recruiter's web of lies. But my young mind knew nothing of this process, and I put my trust in his judgment, because after all, the guy was a sergeant in the world's greatest Army and who would suspect he would do anything to break the rules. Besides, how would it look if I was already trying to buck the system before I even signed the paperwork. So, for the first time in my life, I kept my mouth shut.

We arrived at MEPS at 5:45 a.m. to the sound of someone yelling. Sergeant Ortiz pointed me in the right direction, and I sprinted up to the mass of people standing in front of the building. They began to split everyone up into four lines based on which branch of service they were joining. Then they filed us in like a herd of cattle.

Once inside, we were measured, weighed, prodded, and sent to piss in a cup for a drug test by a group of angry men and women in woodland camouflage uniforms. After that we waited for a couple of hours to see a doctor. They filed eight guys into a cold room with white tile flooring and dark brown walls. The smell of bleach drowned out the stench of the military's fresh new meat. It was silent except for a few impatient moans and groans. We weren't allowed to talk. We weren't allowed to look at each other.

Then came the sounds of footsteps from a short Asian man in a long white coat as he walked in and said, "Oh tay guys, strip dowwn into yo boxers and nutting else, no socks, no shirt, no nutting. Now, eech of you line up against dat wall. Bend knees like duck and place hands above head. Now walk like dis to utter wall and back. Ok, go."

I bobbed up and down like a fishing cork floating across the ripples of the ocean's surface all the way to the Great Wall of China and back. A couple of the other guys fell over, and one complained of pain in his hip.

"Oh tay, put clothes on and come in one at a time," Dr. Hong Kong Phooey said after we were done.

Then, after about six guys and 15 minutes later, it was my turn in the meat market. The doctor commanded me to bend over the table and drop my pants.

"Pool yo cheeks a part," he said with a creepy smile.

What is going on right now?

What fresh Hell have I gotten myself into?

The thought was interrupted by a sharp pain shooting up my rectum. My back straightened out like a breadstick, and my eyes opened as wide as two pizza pies. I felt like such a meatball standing there.

"Oh tay, Mr. Ruger. You good, no sign of hemorrhoids."

Any sign of what's left of my manhood back there? I thought about asking out loud, but I was in such shock that I just did the walk of shame out through the waiting room; head down, feet moving fast.

A few hours later, I sat down in front of a computer with my recruiter and another soldier. We went through a checklist of items to ensure my name, social security number, and military occupational specialty (MOS) matched all 50 billion pages that were printed out and stacked as high as the Statue of Liberty. Ok, maybe it really wasn't that tall, but I am sure a small forest was wiped out in order to complete the mission.

In the end, the paperwork all looked good to me. I took a deep breath and nervously put my signature and initials on every page. And just like that, I signed my life away to become a "63 Bravo; Light-Wheel Vehicle Mechanic" in the 420th Military Police Reserves. Only one thing was left to do; get sworn in.

They took eight potential recruits and sat us in a room with several American flags. An Army Captain came in looking like Captain America and commanded us to get up and stand up straight with our hands by our sides.

"Raise your right hand and repeat after me," he said with a stern tone.

"I, state your name, do solemnly swear or affirm that I will support and defend the Constitution of the United States against all enemies, foreign and domestic..."

I replied "I, Jack Ruger, do solemnly swear that I will support and defend the Constitution of the United States against all enemies, foreign and domestic..."

"... that I will bear true faith and allegiance to the same..."

"That I will bear true faith and allegiance to the same."

"... and that I will obey the orders of the President of the United States, and the orders of the officers appointed over me"

"And that I will obey the orders of the President of the United States, and the orders of the officers appointed over me."

"... according to regulations and the Uniform Code of Military Justice. So help me God."

"According to regulations and the Uniform Code of Military Justice. So help me God."

"Congratulations, you all are now officially members of the United States Military," the captain said proudly. "Today marks the first day in a long journey that will take many of you around the world and into harm's way. Godspeed. You are dismissed."

I left MEPS and walked about a mile to my friend Pat's house, where he now lived with his girlfriend Tina. I knocked on the white door of his blue Victorian-style house with a screened-in front porch. The door creaked open, and he appeared from a cloud of cherry-scented incense.

"Yo dude, what are you doing here?" the surfer looking dude said half-stoned.

"I just signed up for the Army. I was down the road at the entry station. Physical, contract, oath; it's all a done deal. I thought I would stop by. But you can't tell anyone. No one knows I joined. I haven't even told my family."

"No shit," he said with a look of shock. "You joined the fucking Army? But you hate authority. You are the last person I would have thought would join. Wow. When do you leave?

"January 8."

"Can you smoke?"

"Hell, yeah, I can. I have plenty of time to clean out my system."

"Come in, come in," he said, waving his hand.

Jim Morrison and Tampa Bay Buccaneer posters lined the baby blue walls. Alice in Chains' "Rooster" was blaring on the radio. Pat reached underneath the wooden coffee table, pulled out a three-foot-Bob Marley water bong packed with vibrant green and orange hydroponic weed that was glazed with tiny crystals and handed it to me.

"Go easy," he said with a devilish laugh. "That's the good stuff."

I put the bong to my lips and set fire to the weed, inhaling a deep breath of smoke as the water bong made the sound of someone sucking the last few sips of their drink through a straw. The THC quickly entered my bloodstream and began relieving all the built-up tension. I leaned back, sinking into Pat's fluffy purple couch while exhaling a large cloud of smoke as all the built-up anger and stress faded away with it. A calm feeling came over me for the first time since 9-11. It felt good to unwind. It felt good to finally relax. But shortly after, the reality of what I had just done began to sink in. My palms became sweaty as my heart raced faster as I began to think about getting killed in battle.

Gripped by paranoia, I gripped the yellow water bong tight and held it against my chest, staring up at the white ceiling fan and thinking...

What the fuck have I just gone and done?

THUNDERSTRUCK

JANUARY 8, 2002
COLUMBIA, SOUTH CAROLINA

FORT JACKSON WAS BUILT like a Ford automotive factory in 1917 in order to take large numbers of model civilians as if they were parts to a Model T car and build them into a well-oiled fighting machine during WWI. Originally called Camp Jackson, the United States Army assembly line was shut down after the war due to lack of demand. But thanks to horrible human beings like Adolf Hitler and some really stupid Japanese Kamikaze pilots in the 1940s, it has been open for business ever since.

Over 36,000 soldiers are processed through the training facility every year. There have even been a few famous names such as Leonard Simon Nimoy (Spock from *Star Trek*) and singer songwriter Jim Croce ("Operator" and "Bad, Bad Leroy Brown") that have also graced these hallowed grounds at some point during their military careers. Now the largest training facility in the country, the post trains 50 percent of all U.S. Army recruits. Named after President/

General Andrew Jackson, Fort Jackson also trains 60 percent of all females that enter into the Army.

That's why it has the nickname "Relaxin' Jackson" because the Drill Sergeants aren't allowed to use a vulgar vocabulary that includes the phrases "stop being a pussy," and "I bet you suck dick for a living." It's far different from military movies I watched growing up such as *Full Metal Jacket.*

The Drill Sergeants are also not allowed to physically push trainees as hard as they would an all-male basic training such as Fort Benning, Georgia where they train the infantry and other combat occupations. Instead, they make special provisions for females such as not being so hard on them and creating a separate set of physical fitness standards with slower run times and fewer pushups per two minutes, leading me to the question, "will the enemy also do the same?"

Nope.

So much for equality, huh?

Fort Jackson is the politically correct, PG-13 version for non-combat jobs such as mechanics and medics. But even though the standards are lowered to accommodate women, there is still nothing "relaxing" about it. Especially for a guy who spent the last six years drinking, smoking, and running his mouth instead of his legs.

The indoctrination into this new world, into this rough new reality is an eye-opening wake up call. Dreamers need not apply.

After a nine-hour ride in a black Ford E350 van from the Military Entrance and Processing Station in Tampa, Florida, I arrive at Fort Jackson just before dark. A row of Drill Sergeants in woodland camouflaged uniforms are waiting under a blanket of snow flurries and are in no mood to fuck around. As soon as the side door to the van opens, the verbal bombardment begins.

"Get out the van. Get out the freaking van right now and move inside in a single file line! Move, move, move."

Nine recruits of every make and model rush out the door and hurry into a room full of telephones lined against the wall.

"You have 30 seconds to call home and let someone know you made it here safely," the Drill Sergeant yells with such ferocity that the veins in his neck nearly explode like a plane crashing into the World Trade Center.

I phone my dad and blurt out the speech written on the wall above the phone.

"Hey Dad, I made it safely to Army Basic Training, I have to go. Bye."

My stomach sinks like a boat anchor as I place the phone handle back down. It sinks even farther knowing my father still doesn't believe I joined the Army. But I don't have time to dwell on it. Once everyone is done calling home, they quickly funnel us into a room with other recruits for a "shake down" to make sure no one has any contraband such as tobacco or drugs.

I watch as pack after pack get thrown on the amnesty table.

I sure could use a drag from one of those Camel Light's to calm my nerves right now, I think to myself.

After they search us like prisoners for about two hours, the angry pack of jackals filter us into a room full of medics in camouflage uniforms who are waiting with syringes in their hands and evil intent in their smiles. They shoot us up with everything from a Meningitis vaccine to some experimental Pneumonia shot. Some recruits try to refuse to be a part of the experiment, but the argument is pointless. The Drill Sergeants demand we sign the release or face the possibility of being kept up all night. I didn't realize I signed up to be a guinea pig. But I am not going to argue with them. This isn't the place for challenging anything. "Lay low and do what you're told" is what my recruiter said was the key to making it through. "Stay, in your lane."

The Drill Sergeants waste no time stripping our keyboards of the question mark key.

"Never question what you're told to do," they hammer into us with the volume from their voice's boombox cranked all the way up. "Just do it. People will die if you don't do what you are told. We will tell you the who, the what, the where, and the when, but you don't need to know the why."

Boom.

Our vocabulary is now limited to "Yes, Drill Sergeant," "No, Drill Sergeant" and "Hooah! Drill Sergeant," whatever that means. Apparently, it is some sort of primal communication. *Hooah* is the preferred method of understanding in the Army. "Do you understand, hooah?" Even if we don't understand the question, all we have to say is "hooah," which means not upsetting the vicious beast screaming at me.

"Do you understand it now, hooah?"

I don't want to get on Drill Sergeant's bad side, so I tip-toe the company line. They seem angry enough, no use stoking the fire when it's already steaming hot in here. Besides, it's only going to get worse on its own. I don't need to help it along.

After we bed down for the night, rumors begin to swirl that these Drill Sergeants are like kittens compared to our real Drill Sergeants. Apparently, we aren't technically in Basic Training for another six days. The recruiter just so happened to leave this extra week called "reception" out of his mathematical formula when he tallied up the number of weeks. Similar to advertisers using $4.99 instead of $5, I guess keeping it a single digit of 9 weeks just sounds better than the double digit of 10 to unsuspecting 19-year-old civilians.

Now I am not a very smart man, but even I can figure out that some things just don't quite add up to the bullshit people are selling, hooah.

Note to anyone joining the military: Never listen to a damn thing the recruiter says prior to you signing the dotted line. They're like used car salesmen in camouflaged uniforms trying to meet their monthly quota.

During the rest of the six extra bonus days in the frozen tundra of South Carolina, they funnel us through the GI Joe action figure factory like we are Coke bottles on a conveyor belt as Pink Floyd's "Another Brick in the Wall" plays over and over in my head as we go through multiple stations, being stripped of our individuality, sandblasted by a Native American barber who damn near takes the skin off my scalp, wrapped in camouflaged uniforms, issued dog tags, labeled with name tags, and capped off with a camouflaged hat before being shipped out to be filled up with the cold-hearted confidence to kill another human being.

At the end of the reception week, we board a long white school bus with a bluebird on the side that takes us to our permanent barracks. On the way, Drill Sergeant Safewright, who's a white guy with chubby red cheeks and who's the size of a chiseled phone booth, sits in the middle of the bus.

"How's everyone doing?" he calmly asks

"Good, Drill Sergeant!" everyone yells back.

"Anyone have any questions?" he asks with a devilish smile.

"What's the first few weeks like, Drill Sergeant?" one recruit toward the front asks.

"It's not that bad, mostly drill and ceremony," he replies in a soft tone.

Another recruit asks, "What's the rifle on your chest for?"

"That's a Combat Infantry Badge. I got it during Operation Desert Storm."

"What is the patch on your right shoulder?"

"That is the Big Red One combat patch," he says looking down at it. "That was the unit I deployed with."

We ride along for 15 minutes or so like we are going on some kind of Sunday picnic. But as soon as the bus stops in front of our red brick barracks, Drill Sergeant Safewright flips a switch faster than the safety on an M16.

"Get off the bus, get off the fucking bus right now" he screams. "Get off my fucking bus. Move, move, move."

Fuck.

All of us thunderstruck recruits go stumbling toward the exit. Green duffle bags full of gear and uncoordinated FNGs (fucking new guys) tumble out the door and onto the snowy grass. It's chaos in every direction. A pack of angry male and female Drill Sergeants are waiting in a perfectly set up ambush. They open up on us with a thundering barrage of verbal bombs that sends my mind into a blurry daze. The rabid pack of jackals place their large circular brown hats right up against everyone's faces with saliva slinging wildly from their lips as they spit real shit about the realities of war.

A Drill Sergeant climbs up on a wooden platform in front of the barracks with a microphone. Facing out at the field of recruits scrambling for our lives, he begins to bark orders. "Line up in a straight line. I want everyone in four rows of eight. Do you understand me?"

"YES, DRILL SERGEANT!"

"Move!"

We form up and he instructs us to spread two arm lengths away from one another.

"On my command, you will dump everything out of your duffle bags, hooah. When I call out an item, you will hold it up in the air, hooah. Once a Drill Sergeant comes by and verifies that you are holding up the right item, you will place that item inside your duffle bag. Do you understand, hooah?"

The crowd of scared recruits yell back, "YES, DRILL SERGEANT!"

"Good. Now turn your life upside down and start dumping it out. Pick up one set of PT pants. Hold them up! One pair of black gloves, hold them up. Higher, I can't see them!"

My brain feels like scrambled eggs from that drug commercial as I scramble for anything that resembles whatever he is screaming about. This is your brain. This is your brain on drugs (crackling sound of an egg hitting a hot frying pan).

A female recruit next to me struggles to keep up. The Drill Sergeants, sensing weakness, circle around her like hungry vultures.

"What is your problem, recruit?" one of them yells in her face. "Where are your gloves?"

"I don't know," she cries.

"What do you mean you don't know, Private? Were you not issued any? Did they just disappear? Did OJ Simpson take them?"

"I don't know, Drill Sergeant," she screams back, frantically searching through her stuff.

"Well, you better find them real quick, Private. Maybe they're in the grass. How about you look for them down there?"

They make her get in the "front lean and rest position," which is a fancy way to say the push up position.

After ripping her apart, the flock of death turns its attention to a rather large male recruit in front of me moving like a wounded walrus walking in circles on an iceberg as bloodthirsty polar bears close in on him.

Drill Sergeant Carver, a tall and slender black guy who reminds me of the Drill Instructor from *An Officer and A Gentleman* played by Louis Gossett Jr. charges toward his prey.

"You better start moving your butt, Private," he yells, pointing his finger in his face.

"I am moving as fast as I can, Drill Sergeant."

"Private, I've seen pond water move faster than you. You better find a way to move those mash potato legs like they are rushing toward a buffet. The enemy won't give you a head start, and neither will I. I bet if there was a cheeseburger in there you would move faster. Now, where are your brown trousers? You are three items behind."

"I don't know, Drill Sergeant," the recruit cries out as a dark shadow runs down his leg.

"Did you just pee yourself, Private?" Drill Sergeant Carver asks with a confused look.

"Yes, Drill Sergeant," the recruit replies, his eyes doing the same thing down the side of his face.

"OUTSTANDING, our first diaper change of the day," Carver says with a smile.

He signals some soldiers over to escort the soggy bottom boy down the walk of shame and into the barracks, which becomes known as the trail of tears.

My 19-year-old brain can't help but look over in horror. It's a terrible idea though.

I done swerved into someone else's lane.

And it doesn't take long for Drill Sergeant Carver to catch my harmless glance out of the corner of his eagle eye and circle around to me, landing right in front of my feet.

"What are you looking at, Private? Do you see something you like?"

"No, Drill Sergeant," I reply.

"Bullshit, Private. You were looking at something? You must find something interesting over here. How about you get down in the front lean and rest position, see how interesting things look from down there."

"It doesn't look interesting at all," I mumble as I get down in the pushup position.

"What did you say, Private?"

"Nothing."

"Nothing? I'm sorry. Are we friends? Are we drinking buddies? How about 'nothing, Drill Sergeant?' You must think this is some kind of joke. You must be some kind of terrorist sympathizer because an American soldier sure as heck wouldn't address a Staff Sergeant in the greatest Army in the world with such disrespect."

"Are you a terrorist sympathizer, Private Ruger?" another sergeant joins in.

"No, Drill Sergeant," I scream back.

"Are you some kind of Communist Sympathizer?"

"No, Drill Sergeant!"

Carver leans down and whispers in my ear, "I know your type, Private. You think this is some type of joke. Well, this ain't no joke. Our country is at war in case you haven't noticed. And people like you are going to get someone killed. See how you will be laughing when your buddy gets his head blown off because you are out dicking around. Now start beating your face."

I begin doing pushups and it doesn't take long for my hands to go numb from the icy grass. A tingling feeling in the tips of my fingers feel as if Drill Sergeant Carver is smashing each one with an ice pick. The borderline frostbite drifts up from my hands and through my sleeves, twisting my insides up as if it is a pile of loose guts lying on an iceberg. I begin to shiver as the scope of it all zeros in on me with sniper-like precision. Staring down the barrel of such a frigid new reality, I shake worse than a wounded walrus caught in the crosshairs of a polar bear's meal plan.

The only thing as harsh as the Drill Sergeants at Fort Jackson is the wind chill factor. It's brutal, especially when it's breathing down the neck of a Floridian like a pissed off polar bear.

Drill Sergeant Carver yells down at me, "Recover."

I jump back up, clicking the heels of my black leather combat boots together.

What fresh hell have I gotten myself into?

We sure as shit aren't in the Sunshine State anymore are we Toto?

IF I COULD TURN BACK TIME

THE CARE-FREE 90S ARE officially over now, gone like the World Trade Center. The Drill Sergeants have replaced my mixed tape of Nirvana's "Come As You Are," Hole's "Doll Parts," Rage Against the Machine's "Killing In The Name Of," Alice in Chains' "Down in a Hole," Pantera's" Cemetery Gates," Live's "Lightning Crashes," Eminem's "My Name Is," Snoop Dog's "Gin and Juice," Dr. Dre's "Ain't nothing but a G thang," The Cranberries' "Dreams," and Alanis Morissette's "Ironic" with Army tunes such as "I hear the choppers hovering/they're hovering overhead/they come to get the wounded/they come to get the dead," and "a little bird, with a little bill/sat upon, my window sill/so I lured him in/with a piece of bread/ then I smashed, his little head."

My collection of movies, *Mall Rats*, *Fight Club*, *Friday*, *Fear and Loathing in Las Vegas*, *Empire Records*, *Dangerous Minds*, *Chasing Amy*, *Half Baked*, and *Dazed and Confused* have been replaced with training exercises and classes covering map reading, infantry tactics, communication, the soldier's handbook, Code of Conduct, Uniform Code of Military Justice, the seven Army core values of Loyalty, Duty, Respect, Selfless Service, Honor, Integrity and

Personal Courage, (LDRSHIP), and first aid that simulates fellow soldiers getting their legs and arms blown off while others lay paralyzed with sucking chest wounds caused by a 7.62x39 mm bullet holes tearing through their lungs.

My favorite TV shows *Friends, Fresh Prince, Martin, Roseanne,* and *Family Matters* have all been replaced with death-by-PowerPoint presentations covering chemical and biological warfare with instructions on how to react to a nuclear bomb blast and how to deal with chocking on your own vomit during a mustard gas attack.

The streets of Tampa and the yearly parties of Gasparilla, Guavaween, YBOR City, 98 Rock's Livestock concerts and the LSD playground at Adventure Island and Busch Gardens have all been replaced with a serious military training facility with areas named Anzio, Omaha, and Remagen, which reflect the deadly battles of WW2.

My broken alarm clock has been replaced with a trash can being beaten with a stick by a loud angry man at 0500 hours every morning.

My watch with the civilian time of 9:00 p.m. has been replaced with the military time of 2100 hours.

My ripped- up jeans and black T-shirts have been replaced with camouflaged jackets and trousers.

My Chuck Taylor shoes have been replaced by black leather combat boots that I spend 20 minutes each night attempting to shine (to no avail) with a shoeshine kit, during which time all I can think of is the movie *Goodfellas* where one of the gangsters says, "Go home and get your fucking shine box."

My carpeted room full of burning incense has been replaced with bleached tiled floors and a giant gray footlocker.

My comfy waterbed has been replaced with a rock-hard bunk bed.

My warm solitary shower has been replaced with a chilly open bay full of hairy butted naked men. (Don't ask, don't tell)

My friends and family have been replaced by recruits from all walks of life, but mostly bottom of the beer keg type of people.

They're definitely not the head of the hop. Most come from rough neighborhoods such as myself. I've yet to meet anyone from the Hamptons or Malibu.

No. The Army is a poor man's game, even more so since they ended the draft. Now, it's mostly kids searching for a better life. Who in their right mind gives up a life of luxury for a life without it? Hell, for some of these recruits, this place is a step up, it's their golden ticket, Willy Wonka style. Most already deal with getting shot at in places like Brooklyn and Oakland. Death is already a way of life for them. At least now they get three good meals a day, a roof over their heads, free healthcare, and free college money. Not a bad life if you don't mind getting yelled at.

But for some whose deadbeat parents weren't around or who were always at one of two jobs, this lack of personal freedom can be a difficult adjustment. And what a difficult adjustment it is. One guy wasn't seeing eye to eye with the Drill Sergeants, so he tried to kill himself by shoving a pencil in his eye. He didn't write home much after that. There's not much to write home about anyways.

There was also a couple of people who jumped the fence and went AWOL and several who said *fuck this* and flat out quit. They were shipped out to God-knows-where by what I image were Oompa-Loompas in camouflage uniforms. Fort Jackson is starting to feel more and more like Willy Wonka and the Chocolate Factory as the number of recruits keep decreasing as the days goes by.

A lot of those people are flight risks to begin with and need to have their wings clipped – like this one guy from another unit, who, rumor has it, somehow got ahold of some smuggled PCP, then wigged out in the barracks believing he could fly like R. Kelly as he jumped out of a second-floor window. He didn't die but was broken up pretty badly.

Now I am not sure what ever happened to Ol' Crash after that. Hopefully, he was able to land back on his feet after such a horrific injury. I'd like to think the Army didn't give him his walking papers while he was still unable to actually walk, but instead just transferred him out of aviation and into a ground unit like mechanized infantry. Whereas fly boys usually frown upon crash landings – in the world of ground pounders, that sort of *gung-ho* destruction – I figured out – is highly encouraged.

You have to stay grounded in Basic Training if you want to make it out of here in one piece. Which is a new concept to me, because as many times as I was confined to my room as a kid for getting into trouble, this is the first time that I'd ever been ok with being grounded. I keep my head down and my feet moving forward.

But I do feel these people's pain though. The initial shock of Basic Training is sobering. It's like changing schools in the middle of the year or going off to camp for the summer. I don't know anyone, and I am completely out of my comfort zone. And it doesn't take long for regret to creep in and the fight or flight response to take hold. Homesickness can be just as paralyzing as mustard gas. And it doesn't help that the Drill Sergeants sing cadences like, "I miss that Burger King, that double whopper with cheese. I want to go home, home, home, home. I miss that finger lick'n', that Kentucky Fried Chicken, I want to go home, home, home, home."

The worst though, is when I lay in my bunk at night and stare up at the plain white ceiling. That's when there is nothing to distract me from those gut gripping thoughts about home swirling around my thick skull.

Fuck, I think. *I just want to be back with my ex-girlfriend Katie and her bar tender dad, snorting blow off their family photo that hung on the apartment wall, and playing backgammon all night long.*

I want to be back home celebrating my 20th birthday.

I want to be back hanging out with my friends celebrating getting piss drunk and pissing out of the window of David's beat up old Volkswagen Bug as we drive down the road to Denny's for a "Moons Over My Hammy" and a "Grasshopper Blender Blaster."

I want to be back in Green Swamp in Lakeland with my brother hunting deer and hogs and drinking Bud Light around a campfire at night while listening to Garth Brooks, Brooks and Dunn, Tim McGraw, Faith Hill, and Mindy McCready.

I just want to be anywhere but Basic Training really. I want to turn back the clock.

But there is no turning back.

Time marched on.

Time marches on.

Your left, your left, your left right left. Your left, your left, your left right left.

WINDS OF CHANGE

RED PHASE: WEEKS 1-3

BASIC TRAINING IS BROKEN down into three phases; Red, White, and Blue. The first three weeks are called Red Phase because it starts off red hot. The Drill Sergeants stay on our ass as they turn up the heat to a sweltering pace that melts away everything we once were.

The seasoned soldiers are master craftsmen at molding mindless civilians into a working piece of art, pounding us into the pavement with the precision of a blacksmith's ball peen hammer, hammering away until our hands can no longer handle the heat for the day.

Day after day, week after week, they spend forging us in the fire. Then they take their glowing hot piece of steel and begin upsetting, bending, shaping, and molding us into their liking.

From sun up to sun down they march us from one side of a large field to the other while singing cadences such as, "I used to drive a Chevrolet, now I am rucking every day," "Hey there Captain

Jack, meet me down by the railroad track, with that rifle in your hand, I'm going to be a shooting man," and "a C130 rolling down the strip, we're all leaving on a one-way trip."

Marching in formation is the initial way the Army beats the selfish way of thinking out of recruits. No matter our race, gender, or sexual orientation, here we all march to the beat of one drum, one team, all in perfect step. And when someone gets out of line, whether it's this uncoordinated dipshit with a couple of screws loose who keeps turning left when everyone else turns right or the one female recruit who is just as screwy keeps eating cupcakes from the chow hall, (we are technically allowed to have them, but it is highly frowned upon,) the Drill Sergeants stick us back in the fire, making us all suffer together with a face full of snow-covered cement from the anvil-like pavement until our hands go numb and our arms can no longer push our battered bodies back up off the ground.

By making all of us pay for one person's screw up, peer pressure takes effect and causes everyone to turn up the heat even more as the mob mentality lashes out in anger at the loose screws, thus screwing the screwups back down into place. It's an effective way to buff out those rough edges on the fringes and sharpen the tip of the spear. It's psychological warfare at its finest. Lucky for me, I am used to getting into trouble and yelled at. So, it doesn't psych me out as much as everyone else.

Although, marching around all day every day is taking its toll on my psyche. I can't stand Drill and Ceremony. All that *rah, rah, rah* chanting bullshit reminds me a little too much of a high school homecoming football parade. I didn't realize I signed up to be a cheerleader. *Go team go.* It's worse than working in a box factory for 30 straight years. It's the same boring thing hour after hour, day after day. I don't know how my dad and brother can do it. It makes me want to take some PCP and jump off the roof of the barracks as R. Kelly's song "I Believe I Can Fly" blares across the sky.

What happened to all the guns and grenades the recruiter promised me? Where is the combat stuff? Where is the action? Where is the glory like in all those movies and books parading around the frontal lobe of America? Is all this really necessary? Can't we just skip all this bullshit? Can't we turn the pages of all this pageantry and get right to the good stuff?

Not so fast my friends. This critical step is important to understanding the bigger picture. Everything is done for a reason. I promise no word is wasted. No sentence is squandered.

"Fire for effect," as the artillery guys like to say.

You see, we have to train for the worst-case scenario together. We have to hope like hell for the best together. This way we understand each other and what it all means in this battle called life.

"The more you sweat in training, the less you will bleed in battle," is what the Drill Sergeants beat into our brains.

I'd like to beat it out of here to be honest with you. I bet you would, too. I bet you're beating yourself up right now for buying this book.

Boom.

But don't worry, the way things are going, it's looking like we both might get our wish because it's not looking too good for me. It doesn't seem like I am going to make it that far into the hearts and minds of society by doing my part for the war effort as I find myself sitting here on Sunday in a pool of despair, with only my journal to keep me company. Since I am one of a handful of recruits that isn't religious, I get to clean the barracks instead of attending church services. However, since we get it cleaned quickly, it gives me time every Sunday to jot down a few notes in a journal I decided to start. And nothing right now is as note worthy as the pain I am in.

After the last few weeks of 2-3 mile runs every other day, the impact coupled with the bone chilling cold has taken a toll on my warm weather shins. Every step I take, every move I make feels like those master craftsmen smacking the inside of each leg bone with a ball-peen hammer. I try to push through the pain, but it's become too much.

After two days of complaining to the Drill Sergeants, I am signed up for sick call and put on a "Blue Bird" bus that circles around and around the base picking up recruits and taking them to where they need to go, such as the finance office or the hospital. I board the bus and sit near the back with some recruits in their Physical Training uniforms and flip flops. I strike up a conversation with this skinny kid with spaced-out eyes that seem to drift off to another galaxy when he talks.

"Where are your shoes?" I ask, staring down at his feet.

"The Drill Sergeants took them," he says in a somber tone. "I am on suicide watch. I've been in the rehabilitation battalion for three months because I was having trouble adapting."

A trembling voice behind him chimes in.

"I've been here for almost six months because I dislocated my ankle," the red headed female says.

Then another voice pops up from behind the seat. And then another, and then another as if I'm in some sort of twisted game of whack-a-mole.

"I've been here for two months because I couldn't pass the physical fitness test," a chubby guy says.

Then it dawns on me, this is where all those recruits went that the Oompa Loompas in camouflage uniforms hauled away.

Fat Kids Camp, they call it. That is where most of these recruits are from, which is where they send people who can't pass the one-mile run in 8 minutes or less during the first week of reception or can't meet the weight standards. The others are sent to the rehabilitation battalion. Most seem like lost causes though; a bunch of broken and defective doll parts Uncle Sam doesn't really know what to do with except throw them in a recycling bin and pray they can salvage what they can. The military is going to need all the bodies they have to send to Afghanistan soon enough.

Talk of which week I am in quickly comes up from the broken parts bin. A male recruit the size of the marshmallow man from the movie *Ghost Busters* claims he made it to Blue Phase... I don't believe for a second that he ever made it past the chow hall. He starts babbling about what was going to happen and the psychology of the whole process as if he was awarded the Expert Basic Training Badge, which I just made up and pinned on him.

The group of damaged goods begin talking shit about everything from the Drill Sergeants to the training process. Their Negative Nazi energy fumigates the bus like a cloud of toxic gas, causing the occupants to become stupid and highly contagious. It's worse than any bad trip on acid I've ever had. I start getting even more bummed out than I was before I got on the bus.

Holy shit, I think to myself. I have to get away from these assholes. They are like a pack of miserable zombies trying to grab my soul and bring it down to whatever graveyard they crawled out of.

The emergency exit starts looking real tempting. One pull of the lever and I could be out of here. "Airborne!" Luckily for me, my stop comes up next.

"Good luck," I say with wide eyes and a fake smile as I rush off the bus.

After an x-ray and a two-hour wait in the hospital waiting room, which is full of nurses in camouflage uniforms, I finally get called in to see the doctor, who comes in wearing a white robe around his woodland camouflage uniform.

"Have a seat," The Full Bird Colonel tells me. "I see here you are having some pain in your legs?"

"Yes sir," I reply, pointing to the inside of my calf.

He reaches down and presses down on the tender bone.

"Ouch," I squeal as I squirm in the chair.

"Hmm," he mumbles, turning to his desk and writing something down. "Have you had feelings of suicide?"

"No sir."

"Do you want to quit Basic Training?"

I think about it for a second, flashing back to being stuck on that bus with those zombies for months. Then I think about having to go back home after that and face my father as a failure. He always said I would grow up to be a nobody. And I'd rather shove a pencil in my eye than give him the satisfaction of being right.

"Hell no, sir," I shout.

"Ok, I just have to ask," he says with a smile. "We get a lot of recruits who want to get out of training by coming in here."

"I know. I just met half of them on the bus on the way here. No way in hell do I want to be stuck with those nut cases."

The old fart chuckles and says, "Well, the prognosis looks good. I think it's just a bout of shin splints. Here is a prescription for Ibuprofen and Bengay plus a one week no-running profile."

On the way back I make sure to sit in the front of the bus and slink down in the seat like it's a foxhole. No making conversation, no making eye contact, and certainly no making noise alerting the enemy to my position.

After returning to the barracks, I hand the doctor's note to the Drill Sergeant on duty. He looks at me and shakes his head. Drill Sergeant Carver isn't any happier.

"What the heck is this Private? he yells, snatching the paper out of my hand. "Light duty? There's no light duty here."

"That's what the Colonel wrote," I reply, pointing down to the piece of paper. "See it says it right there, Drill Sergeant."

"I can read, Private! Get out of my face."

I do an about face (180-degree turn,) then march up to my bunk.

And the Army keeps rolling along.

Your left, your left, your left right left. Your left, your left, your left right left.

TILL I COLLAPSE

WHITE PHASE
WEEKS 4-6
ARMY GENERAL ORDERS

1. I will guard everything within the limits of my post and quit my post only when properly relieved.

2. I will obey my special orders and perform all of my duties in a military manner.

3. I will report violations of my special orders, emergencies, and anything not covered in my instructions to the commander of the relief.

ONCE WE LEARN TO live for something greater than ourselves, we are ready to move on to the next phase, where we learn to push ourselves mentally and physically past where we ever thought was possible, grinding from sun up to sun down day after day, running farther and faster day after day, pushing up and down harder and higher day after day. We then sit through classes and training day after day.

Day after day in white phase we go through training covering basic rifle marksmanship, how to operate and clean a M-16, and how to clear a rifle malfunction using SPORTS – Slap, Pull, Observe, Release, Tap, and Squeeze. We learn about proper night vision goggles (NVGs,) operation and training, land navigation covering map reading and compass headings, and more first aid.

During white phase the gaggle fuck of new recruits also starts coming together more and more as a platoon as things begin to take shape, slowly morphing into the competent soldiers the Drill Sergeants have been diligently attempting to mold us into with their callous hands.

It's no longer just about the I in individual. It's about the team. It's about the people around us. And thank God for them. Because if it wasn't for Private First Class Edward, a 38-year-old white guy nicknamed "Grandpa" who gave up a cushy computer job and a wife and three kids to come into the Army for his country on the accelerated promotion plan with his degree, and my battle buddy Roony, a goofy 19-year-old New Yorker with the accent to prove it, I would probably have given up by now.

Edward is always there like a father figure whenever our young heads start to blow too much steam. And Rooney's always quick with a joke to make us laugh. He busted up his ankle on a run and was placed on crutches about the same time as I busted up my shins. Since I was his battle buddy, we had to walk next to each other off to the side of the platoon as we marched to chow. As the Drill Sergeants shouted out "Left, left, left, right, left," Rooney would say, "Gimp, gimp, gimp right gimp."

Just looking at the guy cracks me up, with his thick brown Army issued glasses the Drill Sergeants call BCGs (Birth Control Glasses) because they are so hideously ugly that no woman would want to reproduce with whomever is wearing them. I tell him we should drop him into Afghanistan because Al-Qaeda would die laughing after taking one good look at him and the war would be over before we know it.

Laughter is always a welcome break from all the doom and gloom. It's like a beacon of light beaming in and breaking up the darkness. It's easy to break down here physically and then mentally. And if you let it all get to you, well it will break you into a thousand pieces. And that's a picture of you that's not worth a thousand words trying to explain to your friends and family back home how you couldn't hack it.

Now, it may seem like a dark way to look at the world, using dark humor as a coping mechanism, but picture this, they're just words. It's ok to laugh at them, assholes. I bet there are way more serious things for the alphas out there to worry about than the alphabet.

The jokes never last long though, as the reality of war soon sets back in. White Phase also includes a history lesson of all the major battles in U.S. history such as D-Day during WW2, the Tet Offensive during Vietnam, and the Highway of Death during Operation Desert Storm. They bring in several veterans to speak to us so we can learn respect for all those that came before us.

Some wore Korean Veteran hats and WW2 patches. Some seem to look right through us while others just have a thousand-yard stare gazing off to the side of the room. Some speak angrily while others tremble as they talk; their eyes watering as they recall what they went through, with one witnessing the boat ramp lowering down to the surface of the water as the sight of the beaches of Normandy came into full view, the ocean water stained with the blood of dead and dying soldiers as Nazi machine gun fire came raining down on his position. The bodies of his buddies, dropping right in front of his young eyes as their chests were riddled with bullets, ripping apart his youthful innocence and leaving it for dead on the ocean floor.

"War isn't a video game with unlimited lives," the WW2 Veteran says. "People die and they don't come back. I lost several of my friends there. And I think about them every day. Every day."

A Drill Sergeant steps in and shouts, "Just like all those that came before us, you will carry on the great tradition of being the greatest fighting machine on this planet. This isn't some Hollywood movie folks. This is the real deal. And people will die if you don't take it seriously. And in case you didn't watch the news before you came here, we are at war now."

For the next three weeks we train intensely in Vietnam Era tactics, jungle warfare, hand to hand combat, pugil stick fighting, team building exercises, rappelling from Victory Tower, M-16 qualification, and conquering the confidence course – a series of obstacles in which we have to navigate through the woods, over wooden logs, and under barbed wire as we low crawl through the dirt and mud.

But nothing during basic training has had more of a profound effect on me than the Bayonet Assault Course, as it transforms me from a harmless milk snake nicknamed Milk Dud (my striking posture was more dud than actual danger) into a deadly Eastern Diamondback Rattlesnake.

Our bus arrives in front of a dense forest of pine trees at 0900 hours. Rooney leans over to me and says, "fock dude, there is still ice on the ground. This field jacket ain't gonna keep shit warm."

A light fog hovers over the underbrush of palmetto bushes with the sun attempting to sneak a peek through the broken clouds to see what is about to go down. The scent of fresh pine permeates through the air.

Drill Sergeant Safewright instructs the platoon to exit the bus and form up in front of the narrow pathway leading to the course. Everyone struggles to get off the short bus with their M-16s, bayonets, load bearing vests (LBV) with 2 ammo pouches, and 2 canteens strapped on the back. The Blue Bird motors off as a Drill Sergeant begins to scream.

"This morning, your task will be to negotiate the Bayonet Assault Course," he says, ice crunching underneath his boots as he paces back and forth. "Your target will be green rubber dummies and white rubber tires that are strategically placed in between multiple obstacles. Your job is to disable the enemy using lethal force by butt-stroking to the head, butt-stroking to the groin, and thrusting the bayonet into the target's midsection.

The conditions today could be hazardous to your health, so use what's under that Kevlar helmet of yours. There will be uneven terrain, watch out for holes. It's wet out there, so take your time across the obstacles. It will be warming up here soon, so there may be snakes out there. Leave the wildlife alone. You don't mess with them; they won't mess with you. These knives are sharp, don't be a retard and attempt to touch it or poke your buddy with it. DO YOU UNDERSTAND, HOOAH!!!"

"YES, DRILL SERGEANT," the platoon of freezing recruits screams back.

"You will take all instructions from the tower. Do you understand?"

"YES, DRILL SERGEANT."

"Now, on my command, each squad will fall out and make 4 lines in front of the log walls. FALL OUT!"

Everyone starts screaming as we rush through the pathway to a field with 4 logs stacked 4 high,

"Kill em all!"

"Get some!"

"Yeeeaaaahhhh!!!"

A Drill Sergeant yells out through an intercom.

"On my command, four soldiers, one from each squad will move forward across the log wall. Once across, you will low crawl away from the wall and pull security for your fellow soldiers. Go ahead and fix bayonets."

We attach our bayonets and move in front of the wall. Rooney and the squad are behind me.

"The wall is now live," the Drill Sergeant screams over the intercom.

"Squad leader, what is the first command?"

"Live wall, Drill Sergeant!"

"Good, move them out."

We approach the wall, slowly sliding up and over it and flattening down against the red clay ground on the other side.

Drill Sergeant Carver is standing there as I crawl forward, head down in the dirt, M-16 snug around my wrist. I slide on the frigid grass for about 5 yards when I look up and see his long, black, mocking grin.

"Are you ready to get violent soldier?" he yells.

"Hell yeah, Drill Sergeant!"

"Good. Cause shit's about to get crazy."

A soldier on the lane next to me didn't crawl far enough away from the log wall. The Drill Sergeant on the intercom starts screaming at him.

"Hey, you, Mr. Smart Guy on lane 2, you are too close to the wall. Unless you want your buddy's bayonet to give you a colonoscopy, I suggest you move forward."

As he slides away from the wall, explosions begin rocking the ground. White smoke grenades fill the field.

"Move out, move out," Drill Sergeant Carver screams.

We get up and sprint 50 yards toward the first target, a green rubber dummy with a pole sticking straight toward me. I smack it to the side with my M-16, then I stab it repeatedly, screaming, "KILL, KILL, KILL!"

Drill Sergeant Safewright steps in and yells "stop pussy footing it Ruger and stab it like a man. Get pissed off. Pretend that's Jodie and you come home from deployment and find him fucking your girlfriend. Remember Private, the one with the most aggression always wins the fight. Five to one, when one enemy comes at you, you go back at him five times harder. Violence of action. Now stab the motherfucker."

"Yes, Drill Sergeant!"

I picture every bully from every year I was in school. I see their taunting smiles laughing at me. I hear their voices mocking my nose for being too big and my body for being too thin, hurling the names Gonzo from the *Muppet Babies* and Pinocchio at me. The bear inside me awakens from hibernation. A warm glow flows through my chest and down through my arms as I stab the green dummy over and over, all the built-up anger from so many years of being picked on roars from deep within and flows up through to my hands.

"Kill, Kill, Kill," I scream, repeatedly stabbing the target in the throat, silencing those voices forever.

"There you go, Ruger, that's what I am talking about. What makes the green grass grow Ruger?"

"BLOOD, BLOOD, BLOOD MAKES THE GREEN GRASS GROW, DRILL SERGEANT!"

"You're goddamn right it does. Move out."

The line of four soldiers sprints another 30 yards to the next target. Machine gun fire rattles off in the distance as we jump down in a ditch with rubber tires in it.

Grabbing my rifle with a firm grip, I butt-stroke the top of it with every ounce of anger I have.

"KILL, KILL, KILL!"

We climb out of the ditch and jog about 30 yards to another set of green enemy targets. Huffing and puffing by this point, I summon up every ounce of energy I have left, and butt-stroke the target before slowly crawling up a slippery slope, the damp clay mud turning my green woodland uniform red. Ammo pouches dig into my hips with every thrust, the skin slowly peeling back, but I feel no pain. Machine gun fire gets louder as we continue to crawl down the other side of the hill and into a lane filled with water and covered by barbed wire.

When I jump down into it, the liquid mud sends a freezing shock to my exhausted bones. I squirm underneath the obstacle on my back, my canteen jabbing into my lower spine as I slide back and forth. Focusing on the barbed wire above, I try not to cut myself on the razors edge as I wiggle like a worm down through the lane. I make my way through the trench, exhaust fumes flowing from my face like a steam engine about to blow. Struggling to breath, I stumble 25 yards to join the other three soldiers at the finish line, yelling,

"VICTORY! VICTORY! VICTORY!"

We are all cold, tired, wet, and covered in mud. But damn it feels good. I've never felt so alive. It feels so liberating, to finally be able to let loose, to fight back, to take control. From this day forward, I will no longer take anyone's shit. I will not run. I will not lie down. I will not bitch out. Just like the Drill Sergeants have taught us, when one enemy comes at us, we hit back with five times the amount of firepower. And every time my mind feels like it wants to give up, every time my body feels like it wants to give out, every time my heart feels like it wants to give in, every time I start to think I can't overcome the odds, I will channel that rage and push through the pain like a 5.56 FMJ penetrator bullet screaming at 3,000 feet per second. I will never surrender; I will never fucking quit. I will keep marching forward with a purpose. I will keep fighting with every ounce of strength within me. I will keep fighting with everything I have, until I collapse.

Your left, your left, your left right left. Your left, your left, your left right left.

RING OF FIRE

OUR INDOCTRINATION INTO BLUE phase starts with a fun filled field trip to the gas chamber that concludes our chemical and biological warfare training. For weeks we've been learning about Anthrax, Ricin, Sarin, Mustard Gas, Smallpox, Cyanide, and a multitude of others that you need a fucking degree in chemistry or biology in order to fully comprehend, or to even pronounce correctly for that matter. But it doesn't take a genius in statistics to understand the severity of the situation, i.e., to understand there is a high probability that we will encounter these sadistic instruments of war on the battlefield. That's why we've also been training religiously in the proper use of our protective masks, attempting to get the octopus looking contraptions on our faces and tighten the six straps on the back of our heads while getting the proper seal within the allotted 9 seconds or less after the Drill Sergeants yell the dreaded *GAS, GAS, GAS* – a task most of us have been unable to achieve.

Chemical and biological weapons. What a horrible way to die; a slow and painful death choking on your own fucking vomit. At least with small arms fire, you can duck. With mortar rounds, you can dig. But with shit like anthrax and mustard gas there is nothing you can do but hope like hell you get your pro-mask and chemical suit on in just enough time to stab yourself with a god damned syringe. *Good fucking luck.*

Just the thought of chemical weapons is so nerve racking that my nerves already feel as if they've been hit with a nerve agent. You'd think after all the chemicals I've ingested over the years this would be a walk in the park, but nothing scares the shit out of me more than this twisted style of warfare. Even non-lethal CS gas is nothing I want to fuck around with.

But there is no way around it. You just know deep down in your heart of hearts; the gas chamber is gonna suck. Unless you're the poet Sylvia Plath, who killed herself by sticking her head in an oven while inhaling a big hit of gas, then this just might be your ticket to the promised land.

Puff, puff, I think I'll pass.

That just doesn't seem like the correct path to liberation.

Your mileage may vary.

But for this guy who's still standing here on planet Earth, it is like someone with a fear of spiders being forced to walk into a room full of spiders, all creeping and crawling across the walls as their hairy little paws come creeping and crawling on your shoulder and down your spine and up around your neck and then creeping and crawling into your mouth, nose and ears before their tiny tentacles finally claw their way down into your scratchy throat.

Fuck.

This is going be one hard pill to swallow.

After getting off the Blue Bird Bus the Drill Sergeants march us down what I call the trail of tears…

"Here we go again, same old shit again, marching down the avenue, three more weeks and we'll be through, I'll be glad now how 'bout you?

Wearing our protective masks, we file inside a cinder block house and line up against the wall. Two Drill Sergeants decked out in full chemical gear are standing behind an old wooden table directly across from us, dancing and waving as a glass bottle sitting on a hot plate in front of them is billowing a thick cloud of green CS gas throughout the room.

One Drill Sergeant is standing next to the exit. He stops each recruit one by one and instructs them to pull off their mask and shout out their name and social security number, making sure that each recruit gets a good mouthful before sending them out the door on their merry little way.

Everything was flowing smoothly until this one arrogant guy in our squad, Private Princeton, tries to be slick as shit by pulling his gas mask back and saying his name and social security number real fast without opening his eyes and attempting to bolt out the building prematurely. The Drill Sergeant isn't having any of it. He grabs Princeton, who's trying to do his best Elvis-has-left-the-building impersonation, pulls him back in, lifts his mask up and gives him a love tap on the chest, nothing malicious, but hard enough so he inhales a big whiff of CS gas, then slings him out the door. Only now has Elvis left the building.

I want to laugh at the situation, but situational awareness tells me this ain't the dentist office and this sure as shit ain't laughing gas. There isn't anything funny about the gas chamber, especially as I look out through the goggles of my pro-mask and down the line to see that my ticket is getting closer to getting punched.

I inch closer and closer down the wall until it's my turn to stop in front of the dreaded death door. As soon as I pull my mask up and say three letters I am peppered in the face with a stinging sensation, as if someone poured a bottle of Holy Shit's Habanero Hot Sauce into my eyes, nose, throat and lungs. I yell as much of my information as humanly possible and stumble out the flimsy wooden door. Tears flood out my face as snot drips down my nose and onto my lips.

I struggle to breathe and steer this stumbling bottle of fireball whiskey in a safe direction. Screams from somewhere followed by a yank of my arm helps guide me to a ring of soldiers standing around a water barrel coughing like crazy as they frantically try to baptize themselves in holy fuck water. I rush to flush out the burning gas with splash after splash, but it does little to help remove the sting.

You can lead a soldier to water they say, but no matter how much they drink, that pain ain't going away. The shit just burns, burns, burns Johnny Cash. To hell with this ring of fire. To hell with this ring of fire.

Fuck.

That sucked.

After we survive that pleasant experience, we are ready to move on to the rest of Blue Phase. Or what I call the fun phase. For the next three weeks we participate in weapons training to include throwing live hand grenades, shooting M203 grenade launchers, firing anti-tank rocket launchers (AT-4s), qualifying with M-16s, and my personal favorite, experiencing the destructive power of the M249 Squad Automatic Weapon (SAW). There is just something about looking down range at targets hundreds of meters away and then holding down on the trigger as round after round of 5.56 mm penetrator rounds rattle off.

Bang bang bang bang bang bang bang...

I couldn't help cracking a smile to be one of a few select recruits to get to experience it.

Bang bang bang bang bang bang bang...

Now, I've bumped a lot of cocaine in my life, but none of it comes close to the quality of high you get while firing a fully automatic machine gun. The blast, the adrenaline, the smell of the gunpowder... it all takes me to someplace higher than I've ever gone before...

Bang bang bang bang bang bang bang...

What a fucking rush.

Drill Sergeant Safewright catches my grin and drops by my lane with a couple hundred extra rounds and says, "Here's some more finger candy, Ruger. Shoot the shit out of it."

I unleash some more rounds.

Bang bang bang bang bang bang bang...

Fuck yeah.

Blue Phase is also fun because the Drill Sergeants have eased up on us now, probably due to the fact that we are handling live ammunition. You don't want to get down too hard on a recruit that has the ability to light your ass up like Gomer Pyle did in the movie *Full Metal Jacket*. But whatever their reasoning is, I welcome the tension unwinding a bit.

During this phase, Drill Sergeant Safewright's personality seems like he flipped his safety switch on his M16 from automatic back to the safe position. He even seems to take a special liking to me, in a non-don't ask don't tell kind of way there, numb nuts. Maybe it's my tattoo that spells out "It Is All Fair In True Love and War" on my rib cage that I got the day before I signed up for the Army, or maybe it's just my eagerness for combat, which I've caught a lot of shit for from many recruits who have questioned my tattoo and eagerness for war, which confuses me because I thought I joined the Army and not the goddamn Girl Scouts. Do they not have a television back home? Did they not see we are currently at war?

People are strange, Jim Morrison. People are strange indeed.

Hell, I enjoy the combat phase so much, I even ask Drill Sergeant Safewright if I could switch to infantry, but he said it was too late to turn back now. He's a cool motherfucker though.

One night he drops into our room.

"Hey Ruger, you know what a fun bag is?" he asks.

"No, Drill Sergeant" I reply, confused by the question.

"A woman's tits," he says grinning. "Do you like fun bags, Ruger?"

"Hell, yeah Drill Sergeant," I reply laughing. "I love me some titties."

"Good," he says with a grin as he pops smoke and disappears down the hall.

Rooney and Edward look at me with confused faces.

"What was that about?"

"I haven't a clue," I reply, shrugging my shoulders.

But that wasn't the only funny moment we had with Drill Sergeant Safewright. The next day a few soldiers and I have some clothing and gear that needs to be replaced. Drill Sergeant Safewright loads us up on a "Cattle Truck," which is a F-350 single cab with a flatbed in the back surrounded by aluminum railings that we pile into, and drives us to the other side of the base. We hop down, and he marches us from the parking lot toward the warehouse while singing a different tune since there are only males with us.

"My girl is a vegetable, and she lives in a hospital. And I'll do anything, to keep her alive. My girl has her own TV, some call it an EKG. And I'll do anything, to keep her alive."

And a new version of an old tune...

"A little bird, with a little bill, was perched upon, my windowsill. So, I lured him in, with a piece of bread, then I smashed, his fucking head."

After arriving at the supply warehouse, Safewright finds a large note that is attached to the tiny door.

"Sorry we are closed for a half day," it reads.

Safewright flips his safety switch to fire as he takes the ammo can he is holding and slings it full force at the door.

"What the fuck is a half day?" he yells at the note. "There is no fucking half day in the Army. The enemy doesn't have fucking half days."

He flips his switch back to safe as he spins around with his signature grin and calmly says, "well folks, you won't be getting your gear today because this new soft ass Army is on a half day."

Drill Sergeant Safewright is a fucking badass who doesn't care for bullshit. I respect that. I look up to him, in a non-don't ask, don't tell kind of way there, asshole. He's a combat infantryman with the attitude to prove it. I hope all my sergeants are like him. You can tell he doesn't want to be here, even telling us he wants to be with the men in a line unit. Says he was pulled out of an infantry unit in Germany and forced to become a Drill Sergeant. And to add insult to injury they put him in Relaxin' Jackson and not Fort Benning with the rest of the combat occupational specialties. I get it. He wants to be part of the action, not babysitting a bunch of bitch ass POGs (Position Other than Grunt).

Hell, the Staff Sergeant even said he got into a lot of trouble trying to get out of it by mouthing off to all the training NCOs (Noncommissioned Officers) during the Drill Sergeant training course.

Mouthing off? I can respect that too.

I don't blame him though. Who wants to be on the practice squad when the Super Bowl is happening? And that's what war is. It's the Army's Super Bowl. It's our World Series. It's our Stanley Cup. And I have sat on the bench enough in my short-lived sports life. I am ready to play in the big game, coach. I am ready for war.

But the closest we will be getting to a battlefield anytime soon is a final three-day Field Training Exercise (FTX) that simulates a combat experience.

The whole battalion of soldiers start off by marching 12 miles from our barracks in full battle rattle; weapon, Kevlar helmet, load bearing vest with six ammunition magazines, two canteens of water, night vision goggles (NVGs), a rucksack full of socks, shirts, toothbrush, toothpaste, entrenching tool, sleeping bag, and a change of uniforms. We marched along the dirt roads in two separate columns, one on each side with the Drill Sergeants in the middle. For hours we march deep into the night, stopping every so often for a water break as we take up security positions on each side of the road, eventually making our way to a makeshift base in the woods that is surrounded by razor sharp wire.

For the next few days, we dig foxholes in the heat of the March mornings, then go out on simulated patrols, practicing ambushing the enemy, and defending our base from attacks in the middle of the night. Sleep is minimal. Four hours at best as our position is constantly attacked or approached by strangers.

"Halt!" We say with a fist up. "Who goes there? Move forward to identify yourself."

And the sleep we do get isn't nothing to dream about. There are no 5-star accommodations here. It's more of a 5-billion-star resort as our windowless room in the foxhole comes complete with a nice breeze drifting through it and a panoramic view of the night sky if you catch my drift. But the downside is the rooms are not soundproof and our sweet dreams are always interrupted by the sounds of mortar rounds and machine gun fire. And a sleeping bag in the dirt isn't the most comfortable mattress out there and there is no room service or housekeeping to come and fluff our pillows.

But it does come with a decent continental breakfast in the tasty form of T-Rats that taste like Styrofoam eggs and rubbery sausage. *Yum, yum, yum.* For lunch and dinner, we get to eat MREs (Meals Ready to Eat) which are prepackaged foods designed with a 5–7-year shelf life. They taste like shit, but the good thing is they plug your colon up like the Hoover Dam so effectively that even beavers marvel at such great feats of engineering. And it's nice not to have to worry about taking a shit for a while. Can't exactly stop in the middle of a firefight to go unload a heavy payload.

Never get caught with your pants down. That's the key.

The three days of training is long and draining; mentally and physically. But the war game is essential to prepare us for actual combat. There is no reset button in war. You don't get to respawn like you do in video games. So, you better learn from your mistakes now.

"The more you sweat in training, the less you bleed in battle" the Drill Sergeants keep telling us.

And it doesn't take Rooney and I long to start sweating because we die nine times the first day and forced to do pushups for our fuck ups. Shit, it feels like I really die when pissed off Drill Sergeant Carver catches me pissing 15 yards from our foxhole in the middle of the night. Dude scares the shit out of me, creeping up on a motherfucker like that when he's trying to relieve himself under the peacefulness of the night sky's star-spangled banner. Never get caught with your pants down there, numb nuts. *Didn't we just talk about this?* But what am I supposed to do, piss in the foxhole? Last I checked, it does not have the proper plumbing to dispose of said bodily fluids.

The second time it feels like I died for real was when we are out on patrol and come across these red and orange triangular signs. Before we even realize that we had stumbled into a chemical area, Drill Sergeant Safewright comes charging full speed at us with an erupting canister full of CS gas attached to a long ass tree branch, shoving it in our face, with that old familiar pain resurrecting itself from the grave.

"You're dead," the combat infantryman says, laughing. "You're dead too. You are all dead."

Fuck.

I thought we were done with that ratchet shit, Sylvia?

But here it is when we least expect it, choking me up tighter than my throat while thinking about never seeing my family again after facing real chemical weapons. I get all choked up thinking about that shit.

But it's a valuable lesson learned.

War is brutal.

Don't ever get soft and never let your guard down.

Never.

Always be prepared for the worst, even when you least expect it.

And always, always, always, expect the unexpected.

The day you become complacent is the day of your replacement, from the war, from this world.

Stay alert, stay alive.

Stay Alert, Stay Alive

After the FTX comes to an exhausting end, we pick up our gear, fill in our fox holes and march another grueling 12 miles back to our barracks. As we arrive, we are greeted by a Lieutenant Colonel standing next to a ring of fire blazing up out of a 55-gallon drum barrel while Survivor's "Eye of the Tiger" blares out from a boombox. We all stagger over to him and form up in a half-moon shape. He pretends to pull a sword out of the fire, which is a really bad optical illusion because we are not morons, we can see the sword was obviously hidden behind the barrel. But, I suppose, it is more of the symbolic gesture from the Army's court jester that matters the most.

"Welcome, ladies and gentlemen," he says calmly. "You have officially completed Basic Training. Congratulations. Though, this is just the beginning because many of you will be going into harm's way in the near future. But we have armed you with the necessary skills needed to succeed in battle. We have sharpened you into a deadly weapon, just like this sword."

I try to pay attention to the comedy show as everyone swerves in formation like trees in a gusty wind because we are all tired as fuck. I am pretty sure everyone checked out about four miles ago. We can barely stay awake, let alone pay attention to some high-ranking officer, who is jacked up on coffee and plenty of sleep, stroking his sword in front of us.

Officers love to hear themselves talk as they ramble on about nothing for hours to make their dick feel longer than it really is. Some might even say they are a bit tone deaf when it comes to the plight of junior enlisted soldiers. But either way, his fancy speech, complete with all its cheap props and complementary music, is definitely falling on deaf ears tonight. Hell, ol' Lieutenant Colonel Julius Caesar might be the one going into harm's way if he doesn't wrap up his theatrical tragicomedy real soon as grunts and moans echo out through the formation.

After another thirty excruciating minutes being forced to experience the shittiest Shakespeare skit in history, a tremendous relief comes over everyone as we are finally released and get to throw our heavy rucksacks onto the barracks floor and take a nice hot shower.

But not even a bay full of butt naked dudes or the stinging pain from the quarter size blisters oozing out of my feet after I pulled off my black leather combat boots can dampen the mood, nothing can dampen the sense of pride I feel right now, nothing can dampen that feeling of exhilaration.

We are finally done.

Basic Training is finally over.

I did it.

I fucking did it.

I made it all the way through.

I made it all the way through the Drill Sergeants' ring of fire in which they spent weeks forging us in.

I've gone from a solid block of shit to a chiseled soldier. I've gone from being 117 pounds of skin and bones to 135 pounds of muscle. I've gone from barely being able to run a mile in 8 minutes to running two miles in 14 minutes and 21 seconds. I've gone from floating in a shallow pool of nothingness to standing up straight with my feet solidly on the ground, standing next to a solid group of soldiers as we become a part of something that is deeper and more meaningful than all of us, as we know deep down, most of us will play an important role as instruments of war in the deadly battle for America's freedom.

After getting out of the shower, I shave my face, slowly wiping away all the shaving cream with warm water, slowly washing away everything I once was. I turn the water off and look up from the sink, staring at the man in the mirror, staring at the transformation, staring at what I've become.

The metamorphosis is complete.

Let the march to war begin.

Your left, your left, your left right left. Your left, your left, your left right left.

PATIENCE

ONE YEAR LATER
MARCH 1, 2003

HURRY UP AND WAIT.

That's the Army way.

Whether it's being at a 0700 formation at 0630 or rushing through chow just to sit around for an hour while some goofball lieutenant prepares a pointless mandatory briefing, everyone is always in a hurry to get to what we call the "waiting room." And if you show up late, some pissed off sergeant will be sure to do his best to send you to the ER by making you do pushups until your fucking arms fall off. And even if they do fall off, they will just strap them back on with some hundred-mile-an-hour tape, give you some Ibuprofen, and then make you do some more.

"To be on time is to be late, to be early is to be on time."

That is the gospel our Cuban First Sergeant loves to recite religiously. First Sergeant Garcia pulls no punches. I guess that's why the former Army boxing champ is such a stickler for punctuality.

"To be on time is to be late, to be early is to be on time."

"Top," as his junior sergeants refer to him because he is top of our company's Non-Commissioned Officer (NCO) food chain, is highly respected in our unit, almost God-like. He sticks up for his soldiers and in return, they would all go out on a limb for him. I guess that's why the former Drill Sergeant's words always stick in our minds when he speaks. He drills it home.

"To be on time is to be late, to be early is to be on time."

The First Sergeant talks softly and carries a big stick. He is a straight shooter. In order to stick around the Army long enough to reach such a high-ranking status, you have to be. You have to stick to your guns because low ranking soldiers will see right through your bullshit, they will sense your weakness, and they will walk right the fuck all over you if you don't. They will show up late for morning formation. They will show up late for physical training (PT.) They will show up late for a mission. They will show up late for a firefight. Shit, they will show up late for their own fucking funeral.

And the dark haired catholic First Sergeant would be right there at the soldier's wake still spreading the gospel as the coffin came rolling in.

"To be on time is to be late, to be early is to be on time."

God damn.

As much as he recites it, I'd bet both my middle fingers that he has it tattooed on his dick and makes his wife read it out loud after he pops a Viagra. Can a brother get an Amen?

Boom!

Hurry up and wait.

That's the Army way, my friends. And that's all I have been doing since I joined the Army over a fucking year ago. For some reason I thought the whole process of going to war was a lot faster without much time in between. Nope. Time has moved like pond water.

Now you know what life in the military is really like. Which is far from the glorified movies such as Tom Cruise's *Top Gun,* Charlie Sheens's *Navy Seals,* and Ben Affleck's horrendously lame love triangle of a bomb called *Pearl Harbor,* which was way worse than watching the actual bombing of Pearl Harbor.

Boom!

Hurry up and wait.

Now that is the real war story. Trying to survive getting bored to death by a Hemingway sized shotgun blast of useless information that was created by Army officers just to fill time, just to fill space. Sitting through their pointless PowerPoint presentations is just as dry and mind-blowingly dreadful as reading any of old Ernest's novels, if I am being earnest. Now is it really necessary to describe a mountain for 10 God-forsaken pages? We get it dude. It's a mountain. With trees and rocks and grass. There I described it all in one sentence. Get to the fucking point. Shit, I can see why Hemingway called that book *A Farewell to Arms.* It makes me want to rip my arms off and beat myself to death with them without any Ibuprofen to help soften the blow.

Boom!

But for most readers I guess it's a welcome calmness that eases them into the story, eases them into the darkness. Which is a similar phenomenon that the "waiting room" does for most soldiers. It's a welcomed break from the overly serious training regimen. It allows them to relax for a bit and bullshit with other soldiers, telling tall tales and dirty jokes to help break up the constant doom and gloom of the reality of life in the military during war time. "Smoking and joking" they call it. Hell, we even use the time to rip on one another and other branches, from which many have switched over.

"Hey, you know what Marine stands for? Muscles Are Required, Intelligence Not Expected."

"Oh yeah, you know what Army stands for? Ain't Really Marines Yet.:

"And Marine stands for My Ass Rides In Naval Equipment."

"Better than serving in the Chair Force."

"Chair Force is still better than being called a seaman your whole career. Aim higher Navy, you might actually be able to hit that target in the bullseye like a seasoned porn star. Ha! I don't charge extra for those money shots."

"And don't get me started on Uncle Sam's bastard child – The United States Coast Guard. The Army has to go on patrol, and we might not make it back, while the Coasties have to go to lunch, but they don't have to come back."

And it's about that time when the First Sergeant usually screams out for us to get into formation.

"Fall in!"

And just like that, it's back to reality.

Now, while most soldiers enjoy hanging out in the waiting room, I've been in a hurry to get to war ever since those planes hit the World Trade Center. But it's been nothing but hurry up and wait ever since.

At the end of basic, I was jacked full of adrenaline, like a surfer riding a 30-foot-high wave at Mavericks. There was this feeling, this air of confidence I've never felt before in my life. It was a proud feeling of accomplishment, the kind of feeling that has been far and few between in my short life.

I couldn't wait to see my family again, so they could finally look at me in my dress uniform with some sort of pride instead of the drug addict loser I'd been for so many years before, the one that caused my parents to split up.

But instead of riding that wave of momentum to go fight Al Qaeda in Afghanistan, I found myself caught in the crossfire of my parents' civil war. One of the joys of being a child of divorce. You get to be the red flag in the middle of their tug of war, being pulled back and forth, back and forth, back and forth… until they finally pull your sanity across the line.

"In war, the first casualty is always the truth." – U. S. Senator Hiram Warren Johnson

And that is never truer than in the hypocrisy of a parental propaganda war, with both sides always on the offensive, always quick to point their offensive fingers at the other side in a blitzkrieg of blame and shame while never taking responsibility for their own actions as they try to teach their kids about taking responsibility for their own actions. Both sides become overly engaged with engaging the enemy in a shock and awe campaign to win the hearts and minds with a bombardment of wicked words that they don't ever stop to place a comma in the middle of their run on sentences in order to pause for one goddamn second to take the time to see the damage that their actions are causing to the non-combatants caught in the crossfire.

But it's hard to get people to see the world from another person's perspective. It's hard to get other people to care about other people. We are not created that way are we Darwin? That's not how our DNA is written. We are designed to be selfish creatures who only care about our own survival. It's called the selfish gene. It's called self-preservation. The grizzly bear doesn't care if other bears eat or not. It's so busy filling its stomach that it doesn't have the stomach for much else.

Humans are no different. We are animals too, despite claims to the contrary.

It sucks parents are this way. But what can a kid do?

You can't ignore the situation.

You can't go to war with your parents.

I always try diplomacy first, my version of appeasement, which worked so well with Hitler during WW2, didn't it? But I don't see any other choice. You don't get to choose your parents. They are who they are.

During family day at the end of basic training, I scheduled separate times to spend with both of my parents in hopes they wouldn't run into each other, causing an all-out firefight. But, as with dealing with any war-like factions, the best laid plans never go according to design because people are hard headed and only care about what they want no matter the collateral damage it causes, showing up unannounced with their chest puffed out to achieve some sort of glory, some sort of moral victory over the other side.

Getting caught in the middle of that tangled mess torpedoed what was supposed to be my big day, my proudest moment. Instead of walking tall with my head held high, I was left with a sinking feeling that caused my own puffed out chest to sink back down into the darkness faster than the *Lusitania* after taking a direct hit from a German torpedo during WW1, killing all the joy that was left on board.

I never felt so deflated in my life, like a kid who had all the air let out of his bounce house. There was no more air about me. There was no more air in my tires. There was no more pep in my step... I was completely flattened.

And just when I thought I couldn't sink any further down into that abyss, family day was over, and I got shipped down the road to mechanic school. While Rooney and Edward got to get on an airplane to go to their medical school in Fort Sam Houston, Texas, we mechanics got to pick up our duffle bags and follow our new Drill Sergeant as he marched us four blocks down the road where we spent the next three months marching to class with a 30-pound tool box on our shoulders every day.

Every day, for eight hours, we sat through PowerPoint presentations covering the Humvee's diesel engine, brakes, shock absorbers, coil springs, three-part tire assembly (wheel, tire, and runflat,) tie rods, half shafts, glow plugs, computer system, batteries, and electrical wiring.

No more trips to the rifle range. No more throwing grenades or blowing stuff up. No more bayonet assault courses or rappelling from a tower. No more cool Drill Sergeants. No more fun. Nope, just some white guy with angry short man syndrome who never served in combat and a crazy black Drill Sergeant who served in Vietnam that would show up to formation every morning with a stuffed monkey doll on his back while playing a ukulele and singing, "gotta get this monkey off my back, gotta get this monkey off my back."

The closest thing to combat I got was when I called out this Hispanic female Drill Sergeant during a Q&A with the Battalion Commander. She had made me carry a footlocker up three flights of stairs by myself, which caused me to get a fucking hernia, and then made me stand in the back of chow formation every time, which barely gave me enough time to eat. None of the other Drill Sergeants did that. She kept questioning my mental fortitude, saying there is nothing wrong with me, which was ridiculous. I am not a quitter or a poser. Hell, I finished the last three weeks of mechanic school while marching miles and miles with my guts poking through my stomach's muscle wall like a turtle poking its head out of its shell; all while refusing the doctor's advice of checking out and having surgery at home. I even carried a 30-pound rucksack during our final two-day field training exercise, which simulated recovery missions of vehicles that were broken down in enemy territory.

Guess she had something to prove being a female in the Army. She had to put me down in order to lift herself up. Guess it makes her feel bigger than she really is. Some of the higher-ranking females seem to overcompensate in the testosterone department to prove they are capable of being more badass than the men. It's the same as the male soldiers with "angry short man syndrome" who overcompensate by being overly pissed off to try to make up for the height discrepancy. I don't know. I was not interested in entering a big dick contest, with men or women. Forget all the bullshit, I just want to go to war and do my part for my country. I don't give one fuck about all this other bullshit. I am not trying to make the Army a career. I am not trying to compete with anyone other than the enemy.

But whatever her reasoning, I guess she got in trouble for it after the Q&A because she cornered me in the stairwell the next day with a face full of tears demanding to know how I could say those things about her. Luckily, I had my battle buddy there and we sent the incident up the chain of command. She never messed with me after that.

Boy, I was glad when mechanic school finally ended. Though, the downside was I had to spend the next few months recovering from hernia surgery. You never realize how much you use your stomach muscles while taking a shit until you have your lower extremities sliced open and sewed back together with what I am pretty sure is a used tennis net that the Air Force surgeon at MacDill Airforce base claims is a mesh. And that wasn't even the shittiest part. For some reason, days before the surgery, the gray-haired Colonel stuck his finger up my ass in his office, causing my eyes to become as big as two pizza pies. I'm starting to sense a theme here with these military doctors.

Don't ask, don't tell.

What the fuck, over?

The surgery itself wasn't that bad. It was quite comical to be honest. The anesthesiologist numbed me from the waist down, pumped my IV full of what he referred to as "a margarita," and placed a net across my chest so I couldn't see what they were doing. But me being the drugged-up clown I am, I kept trying to peak over the Berlin Wall.

"Hey, Dr. OZ what are you doing over there behind that curtain," I said laughing.

The nurse, who looked like the Wicked Witch of the West, didn't seem too amused and raised the net higher.

"Hey, where are you guys going," I said laughing. "Don't leave me. Ah, Stella, STELLA!"

That's about when Dr. Feelgood came cruising back by.

"I got you another margarita," the airman said with a smile that was as long as the yellow brick road as he flicked something into my IV.

"You the man," I replied, pointing my finger at him as my mind began spinning like a tornado, floating in and out of consciousness in a dream-like state. All I remember after that was seeing my dad through what looked like a very narrow telescope with everything else blacked out as I slowly crept back into reality. Slowly, the view got bigger and bigger until life came back into full view.

But that's when the drugs began to wear off, and I was left with nothing but that oh-so-familiar-pain. That stinging sensation of a thousand razor sharp bee stings. And I thought the gas chamber was painful. Nothing compares to the experience of the aftermath from hernia surgery. I would have to lean over the side of the toilet and try to suck in all the air so the stomach muscles wouldn't tighten as those turds took a nosedive off my colon's diving board and into the kiddy pool. You never realize how many muscles you use just to drop a deuce. Thank goodness for the painkiller Darvocet. It was my battle buddy that helped me get through it all.

Fuck, I was glad when that finally healed.

But the celebration was short lived because on January 14, 2003, I got the call to arms from my Puerto Rican team leader, Sergeant Rodriquez.

"Hello?" I said through the speaker of my house's rotary phone, the cord getting tangled up in a plant sitting next to it.

"Is this Private Ruger," a stern voice replied.

"Yes, it is," I said, my thoughts beginning to spin like the dial on the landline phone.

"Hey, this is Sergeant Rodriquez," the former body builder said with a voice that was as serious as a snake bite. "Our unit has been activated. You have three days to report to the reserve unit here in St. Pete."

"Where are we deploying to?" I questioned back with a mix of excitement and fear.

"I can't tell you that," he quipped back. "It's classified. Be here in three days or they will send MPs to find you."

Three days. Three fucking days. That's all the notice I got. That's all the time I had to get my life together and say goodbye to my family and friends, for what could be the last time. That thought was a tough shot of tequila to swallow as that worm squirmed around in my stomach.

And to make things worse, it looked like my favorite football team, the Tampa Bay Buccaneers, might actually win the Super Bowl for the first time ever and I wouldn't be able to be there to join in the celebration because I have a Super Bowl of my own to go play in. And I am not talking about a bowl full of that green ganja either.

After spending a few days at our reserve unit, packing up all of our tools, parts, weapons and everything else we might need, we boarded a giant Greyhound bus and headed to Ft. Stewart, Georgia, where we spent the next month training in the freezing forest of pine trees and palmetto bushes to prepare us to go fight in the desert.

What the fuck, over?

The mandatory training included weapons qualifications using the Squad Automatic Weapon (SAW,) M16, M9 pistol, and my personal favorite, the Mark19 fully automatic grenade launcher on which I qualified as an expert. The training also included first aid, chemical and biological weapons, calling in artillery, calling for a nine-line medevac, vehicle training, convoy operations, enemy prisoners of war, enemy weapons, and general tactics.

We also got a multitude of vaccines; smallpox, anthrax, and God knows what else. That was fun, especially watching all these big bad soldiers pass out in fear of a god damn needle. One admin guy had to be strapped to a wooden chair to have his shots administered. Now *that* was amusing because he damn near squirmed his way out the seat as his eyes damn near squirmed out of his skull.

It wasn't that bad, though. Shit, I have several tattoos that lasted hours. This was nothing compared to that. I guess some people's pain threshold is a little different. I myself enjoy pain. It makes me feel alive. It reminds me that I am not in the coffin just yet. Tattoos, running, pushups and a woman's nails running down my back, leaving a trail of blood? *Fucking yes!*

But the shit ton of mundane paperwork we had to do? Now *that* was painful. And not in a fun way either. We had to go over and over what seemed like a million pages of paperwork; record of emergency data, family care plans, Tricare Health Insurance, obtaining active-duty ID cards, ensuring we get combat and hazard-duty pay, and ensuring our finances were in order.

Etc., etc., fucking etc.

One by one we filed into a room with a large lumbering finance officer who looked like Lurch from the *Addams Family* and whose personality was more sterile than a hospital room.

"Please fill out your name, rank, unit, branch and everything that is highlighted," the second lieutenant said with absolutely zero facial expressions. "You're a reservist, right?"

"Yes sir," I replied.

"How much do you pay rent? You will get that back under your basic allowance and housing."

"I don't pay any rent sir. I was living with my family."

"Don't worry Private, I will take care of it. I will make sure you get the max $1200."

"*Hooah,* sir."

I wanted to argue with the guy about the morality of how he planned to perform this magic trick, but 1) my Drill Sergeant always said never question what you are told to do, just do it, or people will die. And 2) the guy was an officer, and I was just a private. And 3) who the fuck argues about receiving free money? Especially poor motherfuckers like me. Dude is doing me a solid. That's mad cool of him. And when you come from the streets, you never question a hook up. You just smile, nod your head, and say "Appreciate ya."

My dad always said, "If it's free, it's for me."

After we completed every task with the finance magician, we were filtered along into the next room. Now, up until that point, the gravity of the situation I found myself in hadn't completely sunk in yet. Everything was happening so fast that my mind hadn't had a chance to process that I was actually going to war. But then a soldier asked me the question.

"In the event you are killed in combat, who do you want to be the beneficiary of your $250,000 life insurance policy?"

Wait, say what? Who do I want, what? If I die?

Fuck.

I never really thought about death so seriously up until that moment. Yeah, I've dealt with people close to me dying, but never was my life ever in jeopardy. Hell, even during basic training, the danger still felt like it was a world away, especially after being pumped so full of confidence that you begin to think you're invincible, with the arrogance and anger always pushing that not-so-happy ending so deep down into the abyss that those dark thoughts never get a chance to surface. It seemed more like a game than real life.

Leaving Earth has always felt like an abstract concept to me, like one of those fancy paintings hung on the wall of those pretentious art galleries where people drink expensive wine and scoff at the work with their noses held high in the air.

When you look at anything in the abstract, the focus isn't very fine, out of focus of sorts one might say, most often so blurry you can hardly make out what the hell it is. *But this?* This was becoming crystal fucking clear, as if it was being broadcasted across my frontal lobe in high definition. All the fine details. All the king's men. All walking along the watchtower with their M16s.

That's when the fight or flight response kicked in as the thought of eating shit and dying sent an electric shock of fear blazing through my veins like a ring of fire in that Johnny Cash song – playing round and round on a record player.

And it burns, burns, burns.

Survival mechanisms are a hell of a thing, aren't they?

Life was all one big funny joke before I sat down in that electric chair. But that was the moment my whole outlook on life changed. What if I never see my friends and family again? What if this is it for me? What if I don't come back? What would I say to them? Would I say I love you? Would I say I am sorry? Would I say maybe some other time? Would I say maybe next week? So many questions ran through my mind after that question mark key was pressed down upon my psyche at such a young age.

At 21 years old, I should have been out drinking with my high school buddies, raising our shot glasses high in the air as we shouted "cheers, you assholes." Instead, I was staring down the barrel of a piece of paper.

"Sign here," said the sergeant. "In the event you are shot in the face and die, all your belongings along with the $250,000 life insurance policy will be given to your brother, who you have made the beneficiary."

Boom!

Those words hit me in the chest like a 7.62x39 mm round fired from an AK-47. And that's when I knew. That's when I knew what

I would say to everyone back home that I cared about if it turns out to be the last thing… I ever say to them.

This is what I would say; *thank you.*

Thank you for all the crazy fun memories. Thank you for being there. And thank you for caring about some loser like me. There are no words to describe what it feels like to have people that have your back no matter what. Just know the goodness in my heart is real. And it's all because of you. I am honored to have experienced this life with such good-hearted misfits. The good and the bad. It's been one hell of a ride. And if I do die in combat, please know that it is for a worthy cause I wholeheartedly believed in. It will be a better death than being a drug-addict-nobody who died for nothing. At least now I will die for something. Something greater than myself. Something for the greater good of America. This is all for you. I will fight for you. I will die for you, so you and your family can live in a world of freedom, where you will no longer have to worry about planes being flown into buildings.

Boom!

It felt like walking down death row after walking out of that office. A seriousness became embedded in me, becoming the Ying to my class clown's Yang, becoming the dark wolf howling at its white twin when the moon is full and the blood bowl is empty.

I was in such a hurry to get to war that the consequences never really sank in. Part of me is still ready to go, still ready to fuck some shit up, still ready to get a kill just like I did all those years growing up hunting in the Florida Swamps, so let's not get it twisted. But now, now there is also a part of me that is all like wait, hold up a minute. Maybe we should pump the brakes just a god damn bit. But this train is full steam ahead.

Fuck.

Hurry up and wait, right?

That's the Army way.

Now why isn't that in the recruiting brochure? Why isn't that the recruiting slogan? "Be all you can be while you hurry up and wait."

Fuck, it feels like nails on a chalkboard screeching from one ear to the other sometimes, thinking about all that deep shit. That's what happens when you have too much time on your hands instead of getting your hands dirty. Got to stay busy. Got to keep your mind occupied. Got to build a wall around your frontal lobe to keep the enemy from breaching the peace.

Hurry up and wait.

Are you bored yet? Does it seem like time is just dragging on? Does the universe seem like it's moving like pond water? Are you questioning all your life choices yet? Are you contemplating sending this book back to the store for a refund? *Good.* Then now you know how it feels to really serve in the military.

Hurry up and wait.

Hell, they gave me three days to get all my shit together and report to our unit in St. Pete then we rushed like hell to get to Ft. Stewart, Georgia, and guess what? We completed all of the training and paperwork in about a month. Shit, my squad of mechanics even knocked out all 52 vehicles, getting them to pass inspection with plenty of time to load 'em up on a train bound for a port in Texas. That's just how the Army rolls, motherfuckers.

We did all that frantic-stress-induced hurrying, working long hours in the motor pool 7 days a week, just to sit around waiting on a mission for another two goddamn months.

What the fuck, over?

Apparently, we were supposed to be attached to the 3rd Infantry Division, but somehow our unit got magically bumped from that. We sat around waiting for a new mission, spending more time on base at the bowling alley and the night club Sports USA than we did training. We had the whole base to ourselves too as the 3rd Infantry Division was already in Kuwait.

The good part about the extra waiting though was we got to watch the Bucs beat the Raiders in the Superbowl. The shitty part though was I've been a lifelong Bucs fan, and they finally won their first title, and I was stuck somewhere in the middle of bum fuck Georgia, unable to celebrate the victory with everyone in the streets back home.

I spent years painstakingly attending games that my mom got tickets for a from working at the hospital (they couldn't give away tickets back then) and watching horrendous teams year after year losing in their orange and white uniforms called creamsicles because they look like the ice cream. Players like Trent Dilfer, Brad Johnson, Eric Rhett, Paul Gruber, Jacquez Green and Vinny Testaverde played in the "Old Sombrero" stadium that got the nickname because it looked like a giant Mexican hat.

Hell, we used to enjoy watching all the fights in the stands more than we did the games. There was one time this power drinking bodybuilder was getting out of hand when two female cops thought they were going to be Billy Badasses and go up the steps to bring him back down to reality. But it didn't take him long to get both of them in a headlock.

Needless to say, the two biggest cops I've ever seen in my life, ran up the steps and had him hog tied and carried off faster than any running back on the Bucs roster. The running joke for the rest of the season was the team ought to hire those guys to play.

Now you know why it pained me to miss such a momentous event as the Superbowl. We were just sitting around doing nothing, they could have at least let us go back home to partake in such a historic moment. But the Army had other plans for us to partake in a historic moment of our own. The celebration would have to wait.

Hurry up and wait, right?

You bet your sweet ass sitting on a plastic chair at the DMV.

Stop trying to fight it, soldier.

Stop trying to find answers to such ridiculous questions like what in the fuck is the actual hold up? It's just the Army way. The faster you accept that, the smoother the journey will be. You can swim for miles upstream wandering down that rabbit hole. But it's best just to hop on a leaf and float on down that river.

Eventually we do get attached to another unit; the 800 Military Police Brigade, which was transferring from Kosovo to Kuwait.

Everyone called them the 1-800 MP Brigade, and joked, "You can call, but they won't answer."

On the bright side, we got our mission. And we got to keep the 3rd Infantry Division's broken TV patch sewn on our left shoulder because our commander ordered us to keep it on, even though we are attached to a completely different unit. It's a smart on his part, because it would act as a sort of camouflage to help us blend in with active-duty forces. No one wants to be associated with an Army reserve unit, let alone one with a black cat for a unit patch. Active-duty guys looked down on the reserves. We were not considered "real soldiers" in their eyes, and thus they treat us as second-class soldiers. I can just picture them now yelling things at us like "hey look at those pussy patch reservists," and "Hey dickface, don't cross our path with those black pussy cats on your shoulder, y'all are bad luck." But either way, they are going to get our help whether they want it or not because we are going over to join in the fun of taking out Saddam Hussein and his Republican Guard.

Hurry up and wait.

MOUTH FOR WAR

WE ARE GETTING CLOSER now.

President George W. Bush issued his final war ultimatum to Saddam. Several of us were out bowling when he came across every TV screen in the building. And everyone stopped what they were doing and tuned into his every word.

"My fellow citizens, events in Iraq have now reached the final days of decision. For more than a decade, the United States and other nations have pursued patient and honorable efforts to disarm the Iraqi regime without war. That regime pledged to reveal and destroy all its weapons of mass destruction as a condition for ending the Persian Gulf War in 1991.

"Since then, the world has engaged in 12 years of diplomacy. We have passed more than a dozen resolutions in the United Nations Security Council. We have sent hundreds of weapons inspectors to oversee the disarmament of Iraq. Our good faith has not been returned.

"The Iraqi regime has used diplomacy as a ploy to gain time and advantage. It has uniformly defied Security Council resolutions demanding full disarmament. Over the years, U.N. weapon inspectors have been threatened by Iraqi officials, electronically bugged, and systematically deceived. Peaceful efforts to disarm the Iraqi regime have failed again and again — because we are not dealing with peaceful men.

"Intelligence gathered by this and other governments leaves no doubt that the Iraq regime continues to possess and conceal some of the most lethal weapons ever devised. This regime has already used weapons of mass destruction against Iraq's neighbors and against Iraq's people.

"The regime has a history of reckless aggression in the Middle East. It has a deep hatred of America and our friends. And it has aided, trained, and harbored terrorists, including operatives of Al Qaeda.

"The danger is clear: using chemical, biological, or one day, nuclear weapons, obtained with the help of Iraq, the terrorists could fulfill their stated ambitions and kill thousands or hundreds of thousands of innocent people in our country, or any other.

"The United States and other nations did nothing to deserve or invite this threat. But we will do everything to defeat it. Instead of drifting along toward tragedy, we will set a course toward safety. Before the day of horror can come, before it is too late to act, this danger will be removed.

"The United States of America has the sovereign authority to use force in assuring its own national security. That duty falls to me, as Commander-in-Chief, by the oath I have sworn, by the oath I will keep.

"Recognizing the threat to our country, the United States Congress voted overwhelmingly last year to support the use of force against Iraq. America tried to work with the United Nations to address this threat because we wanted to resolve the issue peacefully. We believe in the mission of the United Nations. One reason the UN was founded after the second world war was to confront aggressive dictators, actively and early, before they can attack the innocent and destroy the peace...

"Today, no nation can possibly claim that Iraq has disarmed. And it will not disarm so long as Saddam Hussein holds power. For the last four-and-a-half months, the United States and our allies have worked within the Security Council to enforce that Council's long-standing demands. Yet, some permanent members of the Security Council have publicly announced they will veto any resolution that compels the disarmament of Iraq. These governments share our assessment of the danger, but not our resolve to meet it. Many nations, however, do have the resolve and fortitude to act against this threat to peace, and a broad coalition is now gathering to enforce the just demands of the world. The United Nations Security Council has not lived up to its responsibilities, so we will rise to ours.

"In recent days, some governments in the Middle East have been doing their part. They have delivered public and private messages urging the dictator to leave Iraq, so that disarmament can proceed peacefully. He has thus far refused. All the decades of deceit and cruelty have now reached an end. Saddam Hussein and his sons must leave Iraq within 48 hours. Their refusal to do so will result in military conflict, commenced at a time of our choosing.

For their own safety, all foreign nationals – including journalists and inspectors – should leave Iraq immediately.

"Many Iraqis can hear me tonight in a translated radio broadcast, and I have a message for them. If we must begin a military campaign, it will be directed against the lawless men who rule your country and not against you. As our coalition takes away their power, we will deliver the food and medicine you need. We will tear down the apparatus of terror and we will help you to build a new Iraq that is prosperous and free. In a free Iraq, there will be no more wars of aggression against your neighbors, no more poison factories, no more executions of dissidents, no more torture chambers and rape rooms. The tyrant will soon be gone. The day of your liberation is near.

"It is too late for Saddam Hussein to remain in power. It is not too late for the Iraqi military to act with honor and protect your country by permitting the peaceful entry of coalition forces to eliminate weapons of mass destruction. Our forces will give Iraqi military units clear instructions on actions they can take to avoid being attacked and destroyed. I urge every member of the Iraqi military and intelligence services, if war comes, do not fight for a dying regime that is not worth your own life.

"And all Iraqi military and civilian personnel should listen carefully to this warning. In any conflict, your fate will depend on your action. Do not destroy oil wells, a source of wealth that belongs to the Iraqi people. Do not obey any command to use weapons of mass destruction against anyone, including the Iraqi people. War crimes will be prosecuted. War criminals will be punished. And it will be no defense to say, "I was just following orders.""

"Should Saddam Hussein choose confrontation, the American people can know that every measure has been taken to avoid war, and every measure will be taken to win it. Americans understand the costs of conflict because we have paid them in the past. War has no certainty, except the certainty of sacrifice.

"Yet, the only way to reduce the harm and duration of war is to apply the full force and might of our military, and we are prepared to do so. If Saddam Hussein attempts to cling to power, he will remain a deadly foe until the end. In desperation, he and terrorist groups might try to conduct terrorist operations against the American people and our friends. These attacks are not inevitable. They are, however, possible. And this very fact underscores the reason we cannot live under the threat of blackmail. The terrorist threat to America and the world will be diminished the moment that Saddam Hussein is disarmed.

"Our government is on heightened watch against these dangers. Just as we are preparing to ensure victory in Iraq, we are taking further actions to protect our homeland. In recent days, American authorities have expelled from the country certain individuals with ties to Iraqi intelligence services. Among other measures, I have directed additional security of our airports, and increased Coast Guard patrols of major seaports. The Department of Homeland Security is working closely with the nation's governors to increase armed security at critical facilities across America.

"Should enemies strike our country, they would be attempting to shift our attention with panic and weaken our morale with fear. In this, they would fail. No act of theirs can alter the course or shake the resolve of this country. We are a peaceful people – yet we're not a fragile people, and we will not be intimidated by thugs and killers. If our enemies dare to strike us, they and all who have aided them, will face fearful consequences.

"We are now acting because the risks of inaction would be far greater. In one year, or five years, the power of Iraq to inflict harm on all free nations would be multiplied many times over. With these capabilities, Saddam Hussein and his terrorist allies could choose the moment of deadly conflict when they are strongest. We choose to meet that threat now, where it arises, before it can appear suddenly in our skies and cities.

"The cause of peace requires all free nations to recognize new and undeniable realities. In the 20th century, some chose to appease murderous dictators, whose threats were allowed to grow into genocide and global war. In this century, when evil men plot chemical, biological and nuclear terror, a policy of appeasement could bring destruction of a kind never before seen on this Earth.

"Terrorists and terror states do not reveal these threats with fair notice, in formal declarations – and responding to such enemies only after they have struck first is not self-defense, it is suicide. The security of the world requires disarming Saddam Hussein now.

"As we enforce the just demands of the world, we will also honor the deepest commitments of our country. Unlike Saddam Hussein, we believe the Iraqi people are deserving and capable of human liberty. And when the dictator has departed, they can set an example to all the Middle East of a vital and peaceful and self-governing nation.

"The United States, with other countries, will work to advance liberty and peace in that region. Our goal will not be achieved overnight, but it can come over time. The power and appeal of human liberty is felt in every life and every land. And the greatest power of freedom is to overcome hatred and violence and turn the creative gifts of men and women to the pursuits of peace.

"That is the future we choose. Free nations have a duty to defend our people by uniting against the violent. And tonight, as we have done before, America and our allies accept that responsibility.

"Good night, and may God continue to bless America."

END OF THE LINE

*H*URRY UP AND WAIT.

Not anymore. The wait is over. No more training. No more war games. No more football. No more bowling. No more bullshit. It's game on now, motherfuckers. It's go time. George Bush laid out the path for Saddam to get with the program by getting rid of his weapons of mass destruction program or get the fuck out of Iraq because we are coming to get his WMDs that he used on his own people, one way or the other.

You would think it would be an easy decision for the dictator to make, seeing how he has firsthand knowledge of the United States military might after we bombed his ass out of Kuwait during Operation Desert Storm. And they had the 5th largest army in the world at the time, with close to a million soldiers, 15,000 battle tanks, and armored vehicles dragging around close to 4,000 artillery pieces.

With that much armor, it's easy to see how a person can become hardheaded to a fault. It insulates you from reality. It gives you a false sense of security. I guess that's why he decided to draw a line in the sand and prayed to Allah that we wouldn't cross it, just like we didn't cross into his regime after freeing the Kuwaitis from his brutal assault in 1990. But he underestimated the balls our president has. George Bush senior may not have had the *cojones* to take Saddam out, but his son does. And I am proud to follow his orders to take out such a brutal dictator.

And that's when the Shock and Awe Campaign began. And not long after it started, George Bush came back across the television screens. Let the bodies hit the floor motherfuckers.

SEEK AND DESTROY

"MY FELLOW CITIZENS, AT this hour, American and coalition forces are in the early stages of military operations to disarm Iraq, to free its people and to defend the world from grave danger.

"On my orders, coalition forces have begun striking selected targets of military importance to undermine Saddam Hussein's ability to wage war. These are opening stages of what will be a broad and concerted campaign. More than 35 countries are giving crucial support—from the use of naval and air bases, to help with intelligence and logistics, to the deployment of combat units. Every nation in this coalition has chosen to bear the duty and share the honor of serving in our common defense. To all the men and women of the United States Armed Forces now in the Middle East, the peace of a troubled world and the hopes of an oppressed people now depend on you. That trust is well placed.

"The enemies you confront will come to know your skill and bravery. The people you liberate will witness the honorable and decent spirit of the American military. In this conflict, America faces an enemy who has no regard for conventions of war or rules of morality. Saddam Hussein has placed Iraqi troops and equipment in civilian areas, attempting to use innocent men, women, and children as shields for his own military—a final atrocity against his people.

"I want Americans and all the world to know that coalition forces will make every effort to spare innocent civilians from harm. A campaign on the harsh terrain of a nation as large as California could be longer and more difficult than some predict. And helping Iraqis achieve a united, stable and free country will require our sustained commitment.

"We come to Iraq with respect for its citizens, for their great civilization and for the religious faiths they practice. We have no ambition in Iraq, except to remove a threat and restore control of that country to its own people.

"I know that the families of our military are praying that all those who serve will return safely and soon. Millions of Americans are praying with you for the safety of your loved ones and for the protection of the innocent. For your sacrifice, you have the gratitude and respect of the American people. And you can know that our forces will be coming home as soon as their work is done.

"Our nation enters this conflict reluctantly—yet our purpose is sure. The people of the United States and our friends and allies will not live at the mercy of an outlaw regime that threatens the peace with weapons of mass murder. We will meet that threat now, with our Army, Air Force, Navy, Coast Guard, and Marines, so that we do not have to meet it later with armies of fire fighters and police and doctors on the streets of our cities.

"Now that conflict has come, the only way to limit its duration is to apply decisive force. And I assure you, this will not be a campaign of half measures, and we will accept no outcome but victory.

"My fellow citizens, the dangers to our country and the world will be overcome. We will pass through this time of peril and carry on the work of peace. We will defend our freedom. We will bring freedom to others, and we will prevail.

"May God bless our country and all who defend her."

WAR ENSEMBLE

WE ARE GETTING CLOSE now. We are getting fucking close. The 180 soldiers from my unit woke our asses up at the crack of dawn today and rushed over to Hunter Army Airfield near Savannah, Georgia with all of our gear, weapons, and duffle bags stuffed full of clothes to depart on a plane destined for the Middle East.

Destination: Unknown.

And for those keeping score at home, you guessed it, we are still sitting around waiting while the plane we were supposed to take off on has a flat tire fixed.

But here we are. Sitting on deck at our World Series. Waiting for our turn to step up to the plate.

Most of my unit is spread out along the walls of the airport terminal. An American flag stretches across the entire side of the beige cinderblock building.

My battle buddy and fellow mechanic, Specialist Vega, is lying next to me on a dark-blue-carpet floor. We're wearing our Desert Combat Uniforms (DCUs,) our backpacks resting underneath, our protective masks attached to our round legs in a green square carrying case; weapons in hand.

Vega, who's the son of a businessman and a former student at the prestigious private school, The University of Tampa, has a black machine gun known as a squad automatic weapon (SAW) stretched across his lap. The liberal college boy's left foot is crossed over the right with his hands wrapped around the back of his head. I am lying exactly the same except I have an M-16 across me and my feet are independently flat on the floor.

For being total opposites, we've become pretty tight friends since our unit was activated in January. We are the Ying to the other's Yang. And to the dismay of our parental team of squad leaders, we give each other a hard time the way brothers do. He calls me a "dumb redneck" and I call him a "know it all college boy who doesn't know anything at all." And when we get to debating each other on a wide variety of topics such as politics, societal issues, and the stupidity of mundane life in the Army, well, it doesn't take long for it to spread to other soldiers with the lighting quick speed of a highly contagious virus as they get sucked into our vortex, quickly choosing a side and offering their thoughts and opinions. And with the amount of testosterone strutting around like a rooster in a cage full of hens, the big dick contest can turn into a cock fight rather quickly. It's all in good fun though, because we, for better or worse, are stuck with each other. And when the bullets start flying, we will have to lean on one another to get out alive.

One of our other motor pool squad members and wrecker operator, Specialist Lee, who is two inches from legally being considered a dwarf and two pounds from violating the Army's overweight policy, paces back and forth in front of us with his M203 (M-16 with the grenade launcher attachment) slung downward around his back. The 4x4-driving redneck's normally boisterous demeanor now seems as deflated as a flat tire, his trailer-park face looking down as if he's looking for loose change, occasionally running his hand through his dark red hair and mustache. The loud mouth's usual glowing tan is as white as the stars on the Confederate Flag.

First Sergeant Garcia, a military policeman, former Marine, and previously an Honor Guard for military funerals, comes creeping by with his squinting vulture eye, searching for the slightest uniform infraction so he can swoop in and make roadkill out of us.

The squad leader of our motley crew of mechanics, Staff Sergeant Jackson, a 6-foot-8 black guy from Alabama who has the strength of an elephant but the mind of a mouse, comes towering over us with a yellow notepad in his right hand and a M203 slung upward on his left shoulder. He lightly taps my desert combat boot with his and says with a deep voice and an ivory smile,

"Hey, Ruger, don't be dozing off now. We can be leaving any minute. Stay alert, stay alive."

"You said that three hours ago, Sergeant," I reply laughing.

"You heard what I said, Private," he says with a serious tone, not at all amused by my brand of sarcasm.

The bible thumping soldier does this kind of shit a lot though. He comes around like Tarzan, beating his chest and throwing his verbal turds at us every time one of our higher-ranking handlers comes strolling through our section of the zoo.

"Me Sergeant. You Private GI Jane."

But that's the way the Army works. Shit always rolls downhill. I am three ranks under Jackson and the third lowest to the bottom, so it doesn't take long for shit to stack up in my cage.

As I go to sit up, a female voice comes across the intercom.

"We are now boarding for the 420th Military Police Company. Please proceed to terminal 13. Thank you, God bless."

Another fellow mechanic, Specialist Sheen, a former French Foreign Legion soldier who looks like a hockey player with three missing teeth and faded tattoos on his legs and forearms, comes rushing in from a side door smelling like a carton of Marlboro Red cigarettes.

First Sergeant Garcia stands in front of the door leading to the runway and yells, "Squad leaders! Get your soldiers and get them on the plane! Let's go! Get your shit on! Move! Move! Move!"

We all rush to put on our green Vietnam-era-flak vests, rucksacks, and weapons. The motor pool's sexy little white computer clerk with bleach blonde hair, Specialist Arabella, struggles trying to pick up her bags and carry her 17-pound squad automatic weapon at the same time.

Somewhere along the way, some number cruncher, probably one of our goofy lieutenants we call "butter bars" because of the color of their rank insignia, which signifies that they are the lowest ranking officer and usually fresh out of college with no military experience, thought it was a great idea to mass distribute heavy weapons to the unit without physically looking at each person to see if they could handle it. It looks good on paper to have more machine guns. It looks good on paper to all of the equality warriors back home taking notes to see women being treated equally as men, but after taking one look around at most of the female soldiers, any idiot can see the practicality of them carrying all this heavy shit bears little resemblance to some sheet of politically correct paper that everyone wants to magically turn into reality. That's not how real life works. Watch any National Geographic documentary about wolves in Yellowstone National Park and you will see what reality really looks like. All that *Kum Ba Yah* bullshit may be fine on a college campus, but not out here in a world that is about to get real as fuck, a world that doesn't give a shit about your feelings, a world that doesn't give a shit about your political views, a world that doesn't give a shit about your gender, and a world that certainly doesn't give a fuck about you.

But what do I know? I don't have a fancy college degree. I am not some famous actor or reality tv star. I am not anyone important.

I am just a Private in the United States Army.

Keep your head down, mouth closed, and stay in your lane like my Drill Sergeants used to say, right?

I go over and grab Arabella's squad automatic weapon and hand her my M16 as her motor pool team leader, Sergeant Young, a tall, fit as hell African American goddess with a smile as thick and sweet as black forest cake, walks over and grabs one of Arabella's green duffle bags and throws it on her back. My Puerto Rican team leader, Sgt. Rodriquez, rushes over and grabs her other duffle bag and slings it around his Ninja-Turtle shaped body, messing up his perfectly pressed uniform in the process.

Now I know what you're thinking. How can you put women down then go over and help them back up? Well, first off, I may be an asshole, but I am not a dick. I am not trying to put women down in order to keep them below me. Quite the opposite. I am trying to bring them up to my level with a dose of reality, a bar that is not set very high to begin with, but still, you should have to be able to achieve the same physical fitness standards for combat. The enemy doesn't give a fuck, they're not going to give you a head start or say, "Oh, she's a female, let's give her a break because she's struggling to carry all her gear." They are going to fucking kill you. There are no safe spaces here.

And second of all, she is a soldier in my squad, and I look out for all of them regardless of what they look like, just like I did back in my old neighborhood. Because for better or worse we are stuck with each other and will have to lean on one another to get out alive. We are a team, not individuals. You are only as strong as your weakest link. And you never break the chain. Never.

Maintenance Squad files through the double glass doors that lead to the runway. The First Sergeant is standing by the steps directing everyone like an air traffic controller.

"Platoon Sergeants, I need a detail of about 30 soldiers to form up at the rear of the bird. Let's make it happen. Everyone else, get on the plane."

Staff Sergeant Jackson looks at the squad.

"Vega and Ruger, go with the detail."

"Yes, Sergeant," we reply.

We line up in a straight line near the back of the plane and begin loading the pile of 360 duffle bags in some sort of twisted version of Chubby Checker's song "The Twist" by grabbing a green bag, then handing it to the soldier next to you. Grab a green bag, then hand it to the person next to you. Now I've grabbed a lot of green bags in my life, rolled them up tight and passed them to the person next to me, but this is not nearly as much fun.

Puff, puff, pass this bullshit motherfuckers.

Fuck.

Vega looks over at me and says with his thick eyebrows low and his cheeks high, "What the fuck man, it's nothing but headquarters soldiers back here. How come I only see five like MP's?"

"I know man. It's bullshit. It's always the mechanics, cooks, medics, and supply soldiers that end up getting stuck doing all the work. Headquarters is the bitch platoon of the company for sure."

Vega starts singing:

I've been working on the railroad

All the livelong day

I've been working on the railroad

Just to pass the time away

Can't you hear the whistle blowing

Rise up so early in the morn

Can't you hear the captain shouting

Dinah, blow your horn

Dinah, won't you blow

Dinah, won't you blow

I chime in. And not long after the whole line of soldiers started singing it as well. But it didn't take long until our slave master sergeant that is in charge of the duffle bag detail tells us to knock it off. There is one thing the Army doesn't like, and that's soldiers having fun. As long as you're miserable then the higher ranks are happy. But as soon as you show one drop of happiness then they come in ready to crack the whip.

But Vega and I just crack jokes as a way to blow off steam from dealing with so much bullshit as low-ranking soldiers. We can't help that. It just so happens to be contagious. But it's a sign of mutiny to those in power, I guess. And they will squash it faster than a Sumo wrestler squashing a toilet bowl on taco Tuesday.

Boom!

Welcome to the shit show my friends.

After doing the twist for about 30 minutes, we finish loading all the duffle bags and make our way to the loading ramp.

I struggle to make it up the steel stairs, my arms feeling like wet spaghetti noodles after tossing all those green stocking stuffers. As I reach the entrance to the American Airlines 747, an attractive blonde flight attendant greets me with a half-smile and squinted eyes. It's one of those awkward looks your friends give you after your family member dies and they don't know exactly how to go about expressing their grief. I'd imagine it's also what it feels like walking down death row while looking into the eyes of a priest standing by the door that leads to the electric chair.

The flight attendant tries to fight back her emotions, but the crackling sound in her throat and the water in her light green eyes give her away. As I pass, she touches my shoulder and says, "Thank you so much, good luck out there."

Fuck.

My throat tightens.

Holy shit, we are really going to war.

And that's when the guitar from Lynyrd Skynyrd's "Free Bird" begins playing in my head.

If I leave America and die in Iraq tomorrow, will any of my Tampa friends remember me? I am a high speed 5.56 mm bullet traveling on now, and there's a war I am about to see.

Everyone struggles to make it down the aisle with all their gear, their weapons, and gas mask carrying cases smacking everyone's seat along the way, to the dismay of everyone sitting in an aisle seat. I finally make it to my seat in the back of the plane. Vega sits to my right in the window seat. He pulls out a book about Buddhism and starts reading, occasionally looking out the window at the activity bustling around the tarmac.

PFC Robinson, the last member of the maintenance squad, is sitting to my left humming along to his fellow Jamaican countryman Bob Marley's, "No Woman No Cry" as if the Brooklyn native is telepathically communicating with all 10 girlfriends the skinny player left behind. The rest of the squad is somewhere up front.

The mood on the plane is somber with just a few whispers echoing off all the blank faces to break up the sound of silence.

The winged coffin has the feeling of sitting at a wake before a funeral.

NOTE TO SELF

PRIVATE FIRST CLASS RUGER
MARCH 2003

SITTING IN A PLANE that is headed to a war zone full of T-72 Tanks, Scud Missiles, RPGs, AK-47s, and chemical weapons such as anthrax and mustard gas is a heavy thing to experience, it's a heavy thing to face at the ripe old age of 21.

On the surface you put on a brave face paint that camouflages your fear from the rest of the unit. It helps show them that you are ready to fight, that you are ready to kill if need be. It shows them that you won't freeze with fear when the bullets start flying.

And a part of me is ready. I've killed all my life; deer, hogs, rabbits, squirrels.

Never once did I freeze when it came time to pull the trigger. That's just what we did growing up. That's just what we did when hunting in the mosquito-filled swamps of Florida while facing the dangers of banana spiders, alligators, water moccasins, pygmy and eastern diamondback rattlesnakes, all while trekking through two feet of water in 90-degree heat and 95 percent humidity.

Humans will be no different. They are the ultimate species to hunt. And I won't hesitate to pull the trigger when the time comes.

But as I sink down farther into that Boeing 747s seat, another part of me gets a sinking feeling in my stomach that I imagine is the same sinking feeling all those worms got after being hooked on the end of my fishing pole and lowered down into that murky lake of fire.

I pop the painkiller Darvocet that I have left over from hernia surgery and swig a shot of Nyquil.

Thirty minutes go by, and the plane still hasn't moved.

What the fuck is the actual hold up, over?

Who knows, Private? Who knows?

Hurry up and wait, right?

Stop trying to fight it.

Just hop on the leaf and float down the river.

I start to drift in and out of consciousness as the engines finally fire up. The plane makes its way around the tarmac as I put on my headphones. The plane stops on the runway.

My eyelids drift down as my little sister appears next to my older brother. They are sitting on white plastic chairs in the backyard of our parents' Seminole Heights home in Tampa. The same home we all shared together before the divorce. My cat, Tiger, comes over and jumps into my lap, rubbing the top of his calico-colored head up under my cheek. My childhood friends, Pat, Bryan, Adam, Luke and Mike are there. As is my ex-girlfriend Katie, the good Katie, the one I fell in love with before she broke my heart with that other guy. The one I shared so many great memories with, getting high and drinking Bud Lights on Clearwater Beach the summer after I turned 18. She's standing there looking amazing as ever in those blue jeans and flowery tank top, her black hair flowing down to the small of her back. She smiles at me.

Oh, she smiles at me.

"We're all so proud of you, Jack," she says with a soft whisper, her brown eyes sparkling like the ocean off the Gulf of Mexico on a sunny day.

A whistling pot on a burning stove begins screeching from inside the house. I frantically rush toward it, but a jolt throws me back into a blurry reality as we shoot down the runway like a bullet fired from a .357 Magnum revolver. Jim Morrison's voice comes across my headphone's speakers singing "The End" as I see the opening scenes of *Apocalypse Now* playing across my frontal lobe's movie screen.

This is the end

My beautiful Tampa Friends

This. is. the. end...

FAR FROM HOME

MARCH 22, 2003

AFTER BEING SANDWICHED ON a plane for 22 hours with stops in Canada—where there was 12 feet of snow on the side of the runway, Ireland—where the grass was definitely greener on the other side of the pond, and Cyprus—where the whole city of white houses with pink clay roofs was surrounded by a dark blue sea—we finally land somewhere in Kuwait City.

And it doesn't take long for our new setting to set in. As soon as the plane's door opens, a heat wave comes blowing down the aisle like a supercharged hair dryer and hits me right square in the face with an intensity so oppressive that it makes what the poet Sylvia Plath felt in the 1950s as she opened her oven and reached in to take out the muffins she baked to please her husband Ted Hughes like the good subservient wife all women were forced to be back then, feel like a breath of fresh air.

Boom!

But the heat isn't the only harsh condition we have to contend with right out the gate. After I stumble out of the exit with all my gear, I am blinded by the light. And I am not talking about that 1970s song either. I am talking about the scorching sun that seems so enormously close that you could bake muffins on it. The alien-looking light, beams down from the sky with an intensity so oppressive that it makes a 'roided up cop shining his enormous black flashlight in my blood-shot eyes after pulling my white ass over in the Robles Park Projects seem like, well, a walk in the park.

Boom!

I put my black sunglasses on to block out the light show, but there is no blocking out the strange new world in front of me. *We are definitely far from fucking home aren't we, Toto?* This place looks nothing like anywhere I've ever been. Hell, it looks like nothing I've ever even read about.

What a strange new ecosystem we've been dropped off into. And here I thought Florida was a weird habitat inhabited by even weirder creatures who proudly proclaim that the sunshine state is a sunny place for shady people.

But this. This shit is stranger than any fiction ever written.

It's strange going from seeing clear blue skies off the Gulf of Mexico while walking along Pier 60 on Clearwater Beach to dusty clouds of sand filling the air next to the Persian Gulf.

It's strange going from a swamp environment full of pine trees, Cyprus stumps, palmetto bushes, river otters, rattlesnakes, alligators, and mosquitoes to a desert full of camels, goats, striped hyenas and camel spiders.

It's strange going from a city such as Tampa that consists of White, Black, and Hispanic people to a country full of Arabs.

It's strange going from the pirate-themed beach town called Treasure Island which is full of free-living souls with parrots on their shoulders, booze in their mugs, and not one fuck to give about anything to a desert oasis where the dryness of the local liquor and morality laws are matched only by the suffocating environment where they are enforced.

It's strange going from such a care-free city, where pretty much anything goes, to a world where you can get stoned to death for what we would call a "Friday night" back home.

It's strange going from seeing guys with long hair wearing blue jeans and long sleeve flannels wrapped around t-shirts with the names of bands across them to seeing a bunch of Middle Eastern men wearing man dresses.

But the strangest of all, is going from seeing half naked women wearing T-back bikinis on Gandy Beach to seeing women covered from head to toe like a car cover, a car cover that all those rich dudes put over their fancy Porches when they park them on a city street, trying to keep their prized possession hidden from those with immoral thoughts of molesting property that doesn't belong to them.

It sure is strange going from the strip club capital of the world called Tampa, where women are free to express their bodies however they choose to a world so oppressive that it seems more closely aligned to the Scarlet Letter time period in the 1850s than it does to the modern era of the free world.

Now people may complain about how bad it is living in America, but for those living outside the safety of our walls, for those living outside the reach of our constitution, for those living outside our TV boxes and history books, this place makes America seem like, well, a breath of fresh air. It makes America seem like a walk in the park. It makes America seem like a beacon of light, a beacon of light beaming so bright that it becomes a de facto lighthouse for the oppressed, guiding all those who dare to brave the storm of the high seas to safely make their way to the land of the free.

And that's why we are here, to ensure America stays that fucking way. So that these Arab men will never think about flying another plane into one of our buildings ever again.

That's why, when I step out of the plane, I step out with a purpose and make my way down the ramp.

But as usual, I am quickly greeted by Staff Sergeant Jackson with his used car salesman smile and dictator style of leadership which is as oppressive as the Soviet Union's Joseph Stalin.

I try to stall him with a joke.

"Hey Sergeant Jackson, which way is the beach villa with all the women and booze? Is it that way?"

He laughs with his fake and absurdly loud "Ha...Ha...Ha..." followed by "Ruger, you and Vega all are on bag detail."

"Hooah," I reply out loud.

"Fucking surprise there," I say to myself.

After tossing and turning another 360 green duffle bags in what's becoming a recurring nightmare, Vega and I find our bags with our names and last four of our social security numbers spray painted on the side of them. We grab 'em and make our way to the shuttle bus, struggling to carry our rucksacks, weapons, load bearing vests with ammo magazines, Vietnam era flak vests, Camelback (water hydration system), gas masks, two green duffle bags and Kevlar helmets. We look like the goddamn Hunchbacks of War walking down the runway.

First Sergeant Garcia starts yelling off in the distance.

"Listen up! The first four buses are for the MPs; platoons 1 then 2 then 3 then 4. The last bus is for headquarters platoon. That means all medics, mechanics, and cooks will be on this bus along with the captain and me. Does everyone understand?"

"Hooah" the company screams.

"Good, now move out!"

PFC Robinson and I make our way to the back of the white rectangular tourist bus with a flat front end and sit in the two seats next to the bathroom. Robinson and I have also become fast friends. The 22-year-old is different from all the black dudes from my old neighborhood that hated us solely because of the color of our skin, who jumped and beat us up solely because we were white. The Jamaican descendant doesn't have that same preconditioned hatred for all white people that many African Americans have, like

Sergeant Jackson, who seems to be on a mission to get back at Whitey any way he can because of what some white people did to him based solely on the color of his skin. Robinson doesn't give a shit though; he's cool as fuck. The PFC accepts me for who I am, and I do the same for him. He likes everyone really. Especially women. The Bob Marley fan's favorite color isn't white or black, it's pink. And he isn't afraid to dip his pen in the company ink as he already has tagged and bagged several female soldiers in our unit. And he doesn't put a car cover over the spoils of his conquest either. No, my friends, Robinson shows it off like poor kids from the Bronx show off their new pair of sneakers.

"Yo Ruger, what's this smell like," he said, placing his finger up to my nose when we were back at Ft. Stewart.

I just shook my head with a smile and replied, "It smells like pussy."

"You're damn right, son," he replied back with his signature grin. "I'll teach you how to be a real player."

Specialist Vega comes crashing down the aisle and plops down in the window seat in front of us. Now Vega couldn't be more opposite than Robinson in the lady's department. He tries to be sweet and romantic. But women aren't receptive to it. They don't want a man to make them muffins, they want a man who's aggressive. I know this because I used to be this way until I had my fucking heart ripped out.

Shit, I even tried to be sweet and romantic after Katie and I broke up. There I was in Ybor City, hitting on this cute bartender when she told me, "I don't want flowers and candy from some weak ass dude who asks for permission, I want a man who will throw me up against the wall and take it."

"Take it?" I replied with a confused look.

"Yes, take it."

"Wait, what?" I thought to myself. "But what about all that feminist… Oh never mind."

You got to love all the crazy straight forward Tampa chicks, who have their pick of the litter as it's a male dominant ecosystem. Only the strong survive there, Darwin. Only the strong survive. It's much like the Army. Even the ugly female soldiers get hit on because the odds are in their favor as there are maybe 30 women out of the 180 soldiers in our unit. They are transformed into supermodels overnight by the Fairy Godmother herself. Their mustaches disappear as their love handles appear to become flat as a washing board with one stroke of the magic wand. It's a strange phenomenon that happens during deployment. Almost like an oasis appearing in the desert to those dying of thirst. And there are some seriously thirsty dudes in our unit.

But not the female soldiers. They are swimming in a pool of potential suitors because there is no competition. There is plenty of meat to go around. Nobody is starving for attention here. It would be like if Vegas' goofy ass was sent off to the playboy mansion for a year, where he was only one of a few males that the playmates saw on a daily basis. Vega would have his pick of the litter. They would be staring at him like a pack of starving lionesses staring at a retarded antelope that has no clue what's about to attack him.

Fuck.

I can hear the angry pitchfork mob coming to burn my village down now. Oh my god Jack, you said the R word. That's offensive to mentally challenged antelopes. Now how in the fuck is it offensive to the mentally challenged? They don't even know what the hell is going on. It's only offensive to a bunch of weak ass bitches who walk around through life thinking flowers and candy are going to solve all the world's problems. They can all get fucked for all I care...

Now, speaking of mates to play with.

Robinson looks at me and nods his head upward as PFC Jameson, a young female cook with long black hair and tits the size of Persian melons, comes walking down the aisle, (no not that aisle) and sits in the seat across from me.

Shit. Now that's not going to go over well with the home crowd either. I can hear it now. I can hear Specialist's Lee's conservative ass on one shoulder telling me that I need to tell her to start acting like a lady by covering those things up in public, and Specialist Vega's liberal ass on the other side telling me I shouldn't describe a woman's anatomy like that because it's disrespectful to everything feminists have fought for.

But fuck, man. This ain't no romance novel.

What, am I supposed to lie? Am I supposed to write some flowery bullshit to appease the masses? Am I supposed to say, "Oh this lovely young lady with a lovable personality came cruising down the aisle with a little pep in her step, her perfectly straight hair flowing through the wind as all the men on the bus looked away out of respect?"

Fuck no. And Fuck everyone.

I ain't Taylor Swift. There ain't no tear drops on my guitar here. I don't give one fuck what anyone else thinks. That bullshit may sound great on a college campus, but out here in the real world of the deployed, we don't have the time nor the inclination to indulge in fairy tales.

The truth is every straight male on that bus wants to motorboat the fuck out of them titties. They're all just too scared of rejection to be that forward, to make that first move, to move that first "chest" piece forward if you will.

Boom!

And this my friends, is how 21-year-old male soldiers in the Army think. This is how we talk when the political correctness police ain't around. Don't blame me, blame God, he's the one that made us this horny goddamn way.

But Jack, what about how women think? Aren't you going to write from their point of view?

Fuck no. How the fuck would I know anyways?

I am not a woman. If you want to know how a woman thinks then go ask a woman. And good luck getting a straight answer there. Have you ever asked a woman what she wants to do this weekend? It's always "I don't care, whatever." Or better yet, have you ever asked a woman what she wants to eat for dinner? How about pizza? "No, I am not in the mood for that." How about steak and potatoes? "No, the starches make me bloated." How about you starve then!!!!!!!!!!!!!! "No, I hate how skinny I look when I don't eat." How about I eat you for dinner? "No, the head chef doesn't give very good head." How about Sushi? For the love of God, it's got to be sushi. Sushi is always the answer. "Yeah, I can go for a tiger roll with some spicy mayo."

My God, that was a terrible experience. And that's the god-awful truth.

Shit man, even if I did write from a woman's perspective, could you imagine the political correctness mob that would come storming in with torches and pitchforks screaming, "how dare this white man, spewing such toxic masculinity by telling the world how a woman thinks? Who does he think he is? That's gender appropriation. Rip his balls off. Yeah. Rip his balls off. We need them to staple between the legs of a woman who identifies as a man!"

And that my friends, is why I say, *fuck everyone*. You can't please anyone but yourself. And that's the god-honest truth. In the words of the great Al Pacino character Tony Montana from the movie *Scarface*, "All I have in this world is my balls and my word[s] and I don't break them for no one."

Now, if you can't handle the truth, then maybe you need to go watch *A Few Good Men* because you aren't going to find any here.

We are filthy fucking animals. But then again, we aren't trained to be wholesome house pets, are we? Our mission isn't to bring love and harmony to the Middle East, is it? No motherfuckers, we are here to fuck shit up so you can sleep peacefully at night inside your gated community and not have to worry about evil men flying a goddamn plane into your frontal fucking lobe. But I get it. You want your freedom cake nice and clean so you can eat it too without spilling any of it on your designer dress. You want your steak; you just don't want the bloody truth of how it ended up on your plate dripping all over that fancy suit and tie of yours. You want us to deliver you peace, you just don't want to know how soldiers go about doing it. Out of sight, out of mind, right?

Well, *fuck you*. That's not how I roll. I am like a tiger roll dipped in spicy mayo.

Just because I have an Adam's apple doesn't mean I work in a candy apple factory. I am not here to sugar coat shit for you.

And besides, the Caucasian persuasion formerly known as Specialist Jameson is no angel herself. Back at Fort Stewart, Georgia, she got drunk and expressed a little too much enjoyment for one night. And after a female Master Sergeant, who was twice her size, thought she was going to be Billy Badass and get the cook into a choke hold and squeeze all the joy out of the lower ranking soldier, Jameson flipped the script by flipping the MP over her shoulder, slamming her to the ground, and falling on top of the much older woman, cracking her sternum in the process. The Master Sergeant got out of the deployment and Jameson got demoted down to my level, PFC. But, hey, as the saying goes "you're not a true soldier until you have an Article 15,"—which is an official military action for disciplinary reasons. She is well-respected among the junior enlisted after that, male and female.

Now speaking of a different type of playmate, one of our medics, PFC Thompson, whose zit-covered face looks like a minefield, comes hurrying back and sits next to Vega. Thompson was my bash brother back at Ft. Stewart. The "toxic twins" they called us after we got fucked up one night at Club USA, the base's only drunken watering hole. We were out with the whole company drinking shot after shot off the sea of trays full of Jack Daniels, Patron, "buttery nipples" and "sex on the beaches" that were floating around the club like a crowd surfer at a concert. "Party like there is no tomorrow" and "party like a rockstar" isn't a cliché in the Army. It's a goddamn reality.

And nobody parties harder than soldiers before going to war. Death is a high probability in our line of work. Nothing is guaranteed, certainly not tomorrow. We've been let out of that domesticated cage that most Americans are confined to. That's why we drink, fuck, and howl at the moon like wild animals. We go to strip clubs and drink enough whiskey to float the whole Navy around. We make rock stars look like choir boys.

Sex, war and rock and roll motherfuckers...

After three hours of demolishing our livers at Club USA, the DJ started playing the song "Closing Time." Everyone headed out the door, poured themselves into a cab, and headed back to the WW2-era barracks we were staying in. But Thompson and I somehow missed the memo about coordinating proper transportation back to the barracks and found ourselves stranded. We didn't panic though. We were goddamn soldiers after all, so we started humping it back, stumbling through the streets at 2 a.m., singing Army cadences and screaming at the moon as if it was the women who cheated on us.

We wrapped our arms around each other's shoulders as we shouted, "Four miles? No sweat. Five miles? Better yet."

But it wasn't long after that when a military police car flashed his red and blue lights from behind us.

An officer jumped out and yelled, "Hey, you two, what the fuck do you think you're doing?"

"We are marching back to our barracks," we both grumbled.

"What unit are you with?" he asked with suspicious eyes.

"The 420th MP Company," we yelled.

And in perfect unison, like two squared away soldiers marching in perfect step together, we both said at the same time, "We are MP's."

"Hell, why didn't you say so?" the officer replied. "Hop in, I'll give y'all a ride back."

I couldn't believe the Army cop bought it. His tone changed from aggression to friendly faster than we could hop in the back of the car. And that's the trick about cops. It's a boy's and girl's club, my friends. They take care of their own, even when they break the law.

Now normally, I would be against such acts of hypocrisy, but we were in no position to protest. And after being on the other end of the police so many times while growing up in Tampa, it was nice to get the red-carpet treatment for once, to be able to pull that curtain back to get a glimpse into what life is like on that side of the badge.

And besides, who were we to turn down such a generous offer of free transportation back to the barracks?

After buckling ourselves in, we began drunkenly yelling at the police officer through the bars about getting deployed to Iraq as he sped off at a high rate of speed. And it didn't take long to get back. Now I am not sure if he normally drove that fast or if he was just ready to kick our drunk asses out as quickly as possible because we were screaming every time we talked. Either way, it was faster than walking, probably would have taken us at least an hour on foot.

As we pulled up to the front of the cinderblock barracks, a crowd of drunken soldiers in civilian clothes from our unit suspiciously peer through the cop car's window at us sitting in the back, probably thinking "what the fuck did these two idiots do now?" But after the officer opened the rear door of his police cruiser for us as if we were celebrities attending a movie premiere, we jumped out like rock stars and drunkenly screamed, "Wazzzzupppppp, motherfuckers."

The crowd began roaring with cheer and laughing in astonishment at another one of our crazy stunts.

Ah, but the fun is over now.

The fun is over as I am sitting here looking at purple window shades with red rope handles dangling from the front windshield and the side windows of some Kuwaiti bus. The damn handles looking like the Arab bus driver kidnapped the magic carpet character from the cartoon movie *Aladdin* and stretched it across the bus. But this ain't no magic carpet ride my friends.

This is serious shit.

First Sergeant Garcia stands up, barely clearing the seat backs.

"Everyone pull your shades down," he yells. "We are now in a combat zone. Everyone is a threat."

"Hooah," everyone replies.

"Now give me a head count. Start in the back."

"1," I scream.

"2," Robinson yells.

"3" Jameson Screams.

"4,5,6,7,9 … 8…."

"Got dammit," The First Sergeant screams. "You all would fuck this up! Start over."

"1"

"2"

"3,4,5,6,7,8…"

"Good, we got everybody. Squad leaders, check your soldiers for sensitive items… weapons, night vision goggles, ext. Give me the thumbs up when you are done."

Staff Sergeant Jackson comes rushing down the aisle with a purpose.

"Pull out your sensitive items," he says with intense eyes as he towers over our seats. "I need to physically see them."

The Motor Pool squad pulls out our gear and holds up our NVGs, gas masks, and weapons for the 5 billionth time on this deployment. And the yardbird-loving Staff Sergeant touches every single item to ensure they really do exist.

He gives the "okay" and disappears into the front of the bus.

After 10 minutes or so, the First Sergeant stands back up.

"Squad leaders, are we good?"

"Hooah," First Sergeant," they all reply.

"Jackson, are you good?"

"Oh yes, First Sergeant, we good, First Sergeant."

"Ok. Let's move out," the First Sergeant says as he cuts the inside lights out.

We drive for a good while, the sun slipping beneath the Earth as if it doesn't want to witness what's to come. A cool breeze drifts in from Vega's window in front of me. The whistling wind is the only sound on the bus. I can't see anything in the darkness except through the side crack of the window shade where I see tiny glimpses of fires from the massive oil fields burning off in the distance. The sandy city glows like a copper-shaded streetlamp on a dreary night.

I lean my Kevlar helmet on the window and think about home, about my friends, my family, my cat Tiger. I try to think about anything really, except the impending doom that is sure to come.

After being crammed on the bus like sardines in a can for an hour, we finally arrive at some dusty outpost a little after midnight. There are four white Range Rovers parked in front of a giant desert-colored tent surrounded by copper colored light posts at each corner that are just bright enough to illuminate the front edge of the SUVs. Each platoon makes like a line of ants and files in front of each vehicle. One by one, we grab our gear and silently walk up to one of the Range Rovers. All the dark tinted windows are up except for the right rear one. A ball of light glows just bright enough inside the vehicle to where I can make out the silhouette of a female soldier in a US uniform sitting in the back seat with a computer on her lap.

"ID," she says in a low, but stern, tone.

I pull mine out of an old beat-up leather wallet and hand it to her. She puts my info into the database.

"You're good," she says, handing me back my ID card. "Move inside the tent."

Inside, there are 10 long wooden benches that stretch all the way across the tent. I struggle to walk, sinking with every step in what we call "Moon Dust" because the powdery fine sand puffs up in the air and floats for a while after you step on it.

We file into each row by platoons. Maintenance squad, which is probably the most diverse squad in the Army, takes our usual place in the back. Staff Sergeant Jackson sits on the far-right end of our row followed by Sgt. Rodriquez, Sgt. Young, Specialist Sheen, Specialist Arabella, Specialist Lee, Specialist Vega, PFC Robinson, then me.

Specialist Lee looks over at Specialist Arabella and asks, "What is your time in rank?"

"I have been a Specialist for 18 months," she replies.

"Well, I have been a specialist for almost 5 years," he says with an arrogant tone. "I outrank you. You have to switch seats with me."

"It doesn't matter," she replies with a dumbfounded look. "We are both the same rank."

"Yes, it does," he barks back. "Everyone else is sitting in order."

"Whatever!" she says, rolling her eyes as she angrily slides over with all of her gear.

Specialist Lee smiles as he takes his rightful place on his imaginary throne, his short stubby feet dangling back and forth in the air as if he just won $3 on a $2 scratch off ticket.

Robinson leans over to me.

"What's his deal, son?"

"How should I know," I reply, shaking my head. "I am not a child psychologist."

The stupidity is interrupted as a Full Bird colonel with gray hair and silver aviator glasses on top of head walks into the tent. The First Sergeant yells, "Company, A-tten-tion!"

Everyone snaps up out of their seat, standing straight with their feet connected at the heels in a V shape, arms straight down by their sides, each hand clenched in a fist with their thumbs pressed firmly upon the seams of their pants.

"At ease," the Colonel says. "Have a seat. Welcome to Kuwait. I know it's late, so I won't keep you here long, but I have to give you your in-country briefing. As you know by now, the process to remove Saddam Hussein has begun. The Marines and the Army's Third Infantry Division are somewhere around An Nasiriyah. The game is on folks.

"I will cover three sections on this PowerPoint slide. The first I will cover is the threat assessments followed up with Operational Security and then finish up with cultural sensitivity.

"First I begin with the threat assessment."

1) *Scud missiles*

    a) *Take cover in authorized bunkers*

    b) *Keep your protective mask on you at all times*

"We have been taking incoming fire from scud missiles the last few days. Saddam Hussein is desperate. CIA reports state these missiles potentially could be outfitted with chemical warheads. It's imperative that you keep your pro mask with you at all times, even if you go to the latrine or to take a shower. And make sure you have your auto injector syringe in your carry case. It could save your life in the event you are exposed to nerve gas.

"Next slide please.

2) *Unexploded Ordnance*

    a) *Mines*

    b) *Leftover bombs from Gulf War*

    c) *Bombs planted by Saddam forces*

"Stick to the main roads, hooah. Don't go wandering off to take a piss. These bombs are everywhere. Save yourself a trip to the morgue and stay on the fucking road, hooah. Next slide."

3) *T-72 battle tank*

    a) *Armor is not penetrable by light weapons*

    b) *AT-4 anti-tank rocket will disable tank tracks, but will not destroy it*

    c) *Engage rear of tank where the armor is weakest*

    d) *Disengage and call in airstrike*

"Listen folks, if you see a tank, and there are reports that Saddam still has some left over from the first Gulf War, do not attempt to engage it. Live to fight another day. These are heavily armored vehicles with a lot of firepower.

"Next slide."

4) *Enemy Combatants*

    a) *Republican guard*

    b) *Rumored to be about 3,000 spread throughout Iraq*

    c) *Highly trained.*

    d) *Armed with AK-47s, RPGs and RPK light machine guns*

"Next slide."

5) *Fedayeen suicide bombers*

a)   *Wearing white dresses with white hoods that have black writing on the forehead*

b)   *Bombs strapped to their vest.*

c)   *Potential car bombs*

"I am going to be frank with you guys and gals. If you see someone dressed like this and they are coming in your direction, shoot first and ask questions later. The rules of engagement state you are authorized to kill anyone that is deemed a threat. I would rather spend two years in Fort Leavenworth than an eternity of death, but I doubt anyone is going to convict you. This is war folks. Do what you have to, to survive.

"Next Slide."

6)   *Kuwaiti Police*

a)   *When you are driving through the streets of Kuwait, do not pull over for them.*

"We have had several incidents with Kuwaiti Police, one last year who shot two US soldiers. And a couple of months ago, an American contractor was ambushed and killed by an unknown gunman. I personally don't trust any of these bastards here. We have made a deal with the Kuwaiti government that states the police are not to stop any of our soldiers.

"Next slide."

7)   *Stay alert, stay alive*

"Be observant of your surroundings. Be observant of who's in it and what they are doing. Whether it is a local national cleaning up around your base or a fellow soldier who is acting strange, keep your eyes open. Do not hesitate to report it up the chain of command. A few days ago, a US soldier threw four grenades into a tactical operations command tent, killing his commander and shooting another soldier in the back, killing him as well. Reports say he was Muslim and didn't believe in the war. So be alert, there could be terrorists in your own unit.

"Also, when you are out on a convoy mission, be aware of where you are at. Even the lowest ranking soldiers need to be aware of natural and man-made landmarks in case you are ambushed and your superiors are killed. It could fall on you to get the rest of your fellow soldiers out alive. On March 20th, a squad of support soldiers from the Third Infantry Division were ambushed near An Nasiriyah in southern Iraq. Reports state that between 10 and 15 soldiers were killed and others, such as PFC Jessica Lynch, have been taken prisoners. Keep your head on a swivel out there, ladies and gentlemen.

"Next slide."

8) *Snakes*

    a) *Persian Horned Viper*

    b) *Saw Scaled Viper*

    c) *Kurdistan Viper*

    d) *Desert Cobra*

"Peak occurrence for bites: June and July. Mostly at night.

"Next slide."

9) *Scorpions*

   a) *Androctonus Crassicauda (deadly)*

   b) *Leiurus Quinquestriatus (Very deadly)*

   c) *Death Stalker*

I lean over to Robinson and whisper, "Jesus Christ, man, is there anything out there that won't kill us?"

"I know, son," he whispers back. "You better check twice before taking a shit."

The colonel continues.

"If you see any of these creatures, leave them alone and report them to your superiors. Stay alert to your surroundings. Look for trails in the sand. Keep your area clean so it doesn't attract rodents and bugs. Lift up your clothes and shake them before putting them on. Try not to sleep on the ground where many of these animals will take refuge. It gets cold at night. Many of these reptiles will seek warmth, especially that of a US Army sleeping bag with a warm body in it.

"Next Slide."

10) *"Operational security (OPSEC)*

   a) *No divulging your whereabouts or battle plans to family and friends back home*

b)   *No speaking to journalist about tactics and plans*

c)   *Direct journalist to your commander if they ask*

"Listen Folks, this secret information is vital to securing the element of surprise against the enemy. Lives will be lost if it falls into the wrong hands. Just today, we are kicking Fox NEWS Correspondent Geraldo Rivera out of the country because the dumbass gave away the position of the unit he was embedded with on live TV. Be aware of what you are saying and who you are saying it to. I know your families want to know where you are and what you are doing. All you are authorized to tell them is you are somewhere in the Middle East. Do not tell them you are in the middle of the shit. It makes them worry more than they need to. Just tell them you are safe, and you will be home soon. Lessen their stress level, hooah. It will lessen yours."

d)   *Burn all paper transmissions.*

e)   *Destroy all equipment that has to be left behind.*

"Next Slide."

11) *"Cultural Sensitivity*

a)   *Be sensitive to the local culture.*

b)   *Women should not be approached by male soldiers unless deemed a threat.*

c)   *Women should be searched by female soldiers only.*

d)   *No Alcohol. The Middle Eastern culture strictly forbids it.*

e)   *No porn. No porn. No porn. It violates the Islamic religion*

"If you are in possession of any of these items you need to discard them immediately. If you are caught with any of them, you will be subject to an Article-15 which can lead to loss of rank and reduction in pay."

f)   No sexual relationships with locals

"It is also a no-go for soldiers to engage in sexual acts with other soldiers as well. Keep it in your pants."

Robinson leans back to me and whispers "Damn son, the Army just has to take all the fun away, huh?"

"Sounds like it," I reply. "No sex, no booze, no porn, what fresh hell is this?"

He replies, "Right. We out here fighting for freedom and the first thing they want to do is take our freedom away?"

I reply laughing, "sounds about right."

But this shit is no laughing matter. Saddam's chemical weapons aren't filled with laughing gas, my friends.

The colonel's voice comes back into focus.

"Ok, that concludes the in-country briefing," he states. "You will be directed by my major here to your sleeping quarters for the night. Goodnight and Godspeed."

Maintenance squad makes our way out of the dusty tent and into another dusty tent that is lined with Army cots. The AC is blowing so loud it's hard to hear. I make my way over to a cot in the corner and drop all my gear. We all gather up and get a briefing about tomorrow's itinerary from Sergeant Jackson—wake up early, eat chow, go over to the PX on base...etc. Nothing enlightening.

Nothing enlightening ever comes from his mouth.

Afterwards, I pop smoke and head out to the designated smoking area, a giant concrete safety shelter with cement walls and sandbags on top to protect soldiers during a mortar attack that also doubles as the smoking area. The Army frowns upon smokers lighting up the whole base, so they build these safety structures away from all of the flammable canvases. Designing a whole base to keep dumbasses from destroying it is a work of engineering art really. But I am no artist, and I certainly don't want to be painted as an arsonist who burned the whole fucking thing down. When I pull a pack of Camel Lights out of my top right pocket, I light just the one up.

It's quiet, except for the humming sounds of a hundred air conditioners off in the distance. It's nice sometimes to just get away from the craziness of the crowd and enjoy a smoke, to enjoy the peacefulness of the night. It gives me a chance to relax, to reflect, to recharge.

But it's also when those concrete thoughts come creeping in that can weigh a soldier down as they attempt to walk through the fine dusty sand.

What a strange new world I've landed in. And I am not just talking about the environment either. It's a strange new world full of strange new emotions. It's strange how they are turned off and on like a water faucet. One minute it's blazing hot, the next minute the world feels cold and empty. One minute I am riding that high like I am invincible, joking and reliving the good times while standing tall with my chest puffed out, the next I feel myself spiraling down the drain of reality, a reality that's hurling us toward an oh so certain death.

Staring down the barrel of this war makes it hard not to think about home. It makes it hard not to think about all the horrible shit I did that caused my family so much pain. It makes it hard not to think about all the horrible shit I said and did to cause them to drop me off at my grandmother's house when I was 15 and move to Virginia because they were tired of my shit. It's hard not to think about all the horrible things I pulled that cause their marriage so many problems, and eventually caused them to divorce.

Fuck.

I don't know why I did some of the things I've done. All I know is I've been a tortured soul since the day I was born that also happened to be the same day my father's mother died. I have lived with intense emotions that rip me up inside like a category 5 hurricane, spiraling out of control as it barrels its way wherever the hell it wants to go with no rhyme or reason, dragging me along for the ride.

Consuming narcotics and alcohol helped. It helped to keep those demons at bay, it helped to keep them from consuming me. But there is no escaping all of it now. There is no escaping the pain, the remorse, the infinite sadness that now fills my soul, especially since the drugs have been cut off and the booze has run dry, opening the floodgates of emotions.

I try to balance out the cold hard truth with some warm fuzzy memories, thinking about all the good times my family had at our house on Crest Street before it all went to shit, having cookouts with all my aunts and uncles and cousins, and my brother and sister, frying up all the speckled trout we caught off the coast of Florida, smoking up all the deer meat we killed in the Ocala National Forest and the hogs we killed in the Green Swamp Wildlife Management area and my personal favorite, boiling up all the blue crabs we caught in the Hillsborough River and making crab chilau with spaghetti sauce and noodles.

I think about the good times we had fishing the upper Hillsborough River in a Jon boat with my dad and brother, wondering if I will ever get the chance to do it again, to see them smiling while holding up a Freshwater Bass like we held up our Budweiser bottles all those years when someone came cruising by so they could see we were having a damn good time, holding them up high like my dad held up his beer after falling out of the boat, not getting one drop of water in it.

Man, it was great. We didn't give one fuck about anything, except living in the moment out in nature, far away from the all the bullshit of civilization. We were free as every caged animal wished they could be. But as humans, we take those moments for granted. And before you know it, all those good times that seemed to flow straight from the tap, are gone in one twist of the faucet handle.

Fuck.

My mind drifts back to the Colonel's PowerPoint presentation, back to how everything out there is out to kill us; the Republican Guard, suicide bombers, spiders, snakes, you name it. It's a grim outlook splattered across my frontal lobe like his slides splattered across his projector screen, the pressure of this reality pressing down upon my psyche with the pinpoint precision of a psychological thriller. The grim reaper impersonator has taken "Death by PowerPoint" to a whole other level.

Next slide.

The weight of the Colonel's heavy words sends a sinking feeling that drifts deep down into my stomach like a squirming worm descending to the bottom of a freshly filled bottle of tequila, all alone and drowning in uncertainty, gripped by fear, gripped by the thought that everything out there wants to swallow me whole.

Next Slide.

I attempt to wet my dry throat by sucking on my CamelBak's mouthpiece, but nothing flows through. I reach with my left arm around my back and feel the bag. It's empty. Empty as a tequila bottle on Taco Tuesday. And to top it off with a little salt and lime in my wound, the bag is busted. Just my fucking luck. I've never felt so empty in my life. It feels as if the faucet called life is slowly turning that handle closed on me.

Next slide.

I take one last long drag of my Camel Light cigarette and blow the cloud of smoke up into the night. Then I twist the burning end of my midnight cigarette until the cherry falls out onto the ground, squishing it out in the sand below with my desert combat boot and place the dead soldier in my top left pocket.

Next slide.

TWILIGHT ZONE

CAMP ARIFJAN IS AN enormous military base just south of Kuwait City that was built in 1999 by the Kuwaiti government at the urging of the United States in response to the deadly terrorist bombing of Saudi Arabia's Khobar Towers in 1996 that killed 19 U.S. Airmen. The new heavily fortified staging area allows for a safe transition for troops preparing to cross over into Iraq without having to worry about our flesh being ripped to shreds by a bomb while we sleep.

The base is now home to thousands of U.S. military personnel as well as militaries from all over the world who are looking to go fuck up Saddam Hussein and his military for refusing to surrender his weapons of mass destruction. It's our last stop before heading to the big dance.

We arrive down at Camp Arifjan just as the sun begins to creep up over the horizon. A cool breeze drifts in as we get out of the bus that's parked next to a row of giant airplane hangars that are strategically placed in a grid formation and separated by roads. The fighter jets and helicopters are gone now, replaced with a sea of Army cots that stretch from one side to the other. Fans the size of helicopter blades blare loudly as it blows hot air from one side to the other, sending a Cat-5 hurricane of steaming hot body odor spiraling throughout the metal hangar, drowning anyone caught in its path in a pool of perspiration.

The warm stench comes drifting in through my nostrils as I lay out all my equipment onto a cot. The rest of Maintenance squad is doing the same as we are all gathered in the middle of an ocean of people.

Outside the hanger is a concrete bunker with sandbags on top and around the sides. I walk out and sit next to an MP who's about my age that everyone calls "Boston." PFC Robinson comes walking by with a disposable camera in his hands.

"Yo fellows, let me take y'all's picture," he says with a tourist size smile.

"Hold up, bro," I reply back as I pull two Swisher Sweet cigars out of my cargo pocket and hand one to Boston.

"Oh shit, Ruger," Robinson replies. "Now there's some true gangsters right there. Y'all look ready to go fuck some people up."

"You damn right," I reply, as Boston and I throw up a W with our fingers to signify this is war as the cigars hang out of our mouths.

I got the idea for the W after reading a book I picked up at the Post Exchange (PX) back at Fort Stewart called *Charlie Rangers*, which is about the U.S. Army Rangers in Vietnam. Crazy good book, especially reading about how the Rangers would go out and ambush the Viet Cong with claymore mines and machine guns then fly back on helicopters. And if they got a known kill, they would pop a red smoke flare on their way back to base to signify their heroic exploits to all those on the ground.

But the craziest thing about the book was that it listed everyone's name who served in the unit, and damn if my buddy Pat's dad Larry, who I spent many nights snorting blow with and listening to his war stories, was listed in there.

Now, I never wanted to say he was lying, but some of the stories seemed to be straight out of a movie and not based in realism, at least not to a 15-year-old skeeted out on coke. Honestly, I thought maybe he was just a little crazy with all the drugs he was ingesting. I wanted to believe him. It's just hard to read people to figure out if their paragraphs are bullshit or not, especially when the sentences coming out of their mouths are blurred by one too many lines of the nose candy. But it was a surreal moment when I read his name there. It opened my mind to a different view of him, to know that what he went through, the stories he told were real as fuck. It made opening the pages of that book that much more interesting as I felt a personal connection with it, feeling as if I was the one being transported by helicopter into a whole new world, getting dropped off into the middle of the jungle, right in the middle of the shit. I could feel the adrenaline rush. I could hear the bullets whizzing by. I could see the claymore mines shredding the Viet Cong to pieces. I could smell the gunpowder. I could taste the danger—a danger that seems to be a world away from me now as I close that chapter and go back to my cozy little reality in Camp Arifjan.

After our impromptu photo op, Staff Sergeant Jackson comes out of the hangar and tells us to grab our stuff and meet him back here in formation.

"Hooah, Sergeant," we reply.

I hurry inside, but as I cross through the hanger, one of the MPs, a Staff Sgt. who looks like the main villain from the "Grinch Who Stole Christmas," stops me as I walk by. The 40 something year-old former helicopter pilot who lost his ride because of his aging eyes, stands up from his cot wearing a pair of purple panties on his face like it's a superhero mask, bragging to anyone and everyone that will listen to him.

"Hey Ruger, check out what my girlfriend sent me. My wife has never sent me anything this nice. Not even back during Operation Desert Storm. The girls these days know what a man wants. Ah, they smell like sweet wet pussy. It's true, smell them. She said she masturbated in them before sending them to me. Honest to God."

"I'm good Staff Sgt," I reply, laughing while thinking to myself how it feels like I am in the god damn twilight zone sometimes.

Here's this old, strait-laced sergeant running around the hanger with purple panties on his face and giggling like a 14-year-old boy who just got his first pubic hair.

What the fuck, over?

After the unexpected detour down the rabbit hole of insanity, we grab our weapons, gas masks, and NVGs, and form up outside the warehouse.

Staff Sgt. Jackson stands in front of the formation, which consists of all six male mechanics and our two female equipment records parts specialists.

"How's everyone doing so far?" he asks with his usual used car salesman grin.

"Good Ser-geant," the squad replies.

"Glad to be here in this wonderful five-star resort," I reply sarcastically.

Vega chimes in as well, "I am feeling highly motivated, highly motivated to do nothing for the rest of the day,"

Most of the squad burst out laughing.

"You guys need to stop goofing around," Specialist Lee shouts. "It's not funny. You need to start being serious."

I lean over and whisper to Robinson, "Geez, somebody get issued the wrong size underwear? Why's he so uptight?"

"I don't know, man," he whispers back. "I think he may need to put on some boxers and let his ovaries hang free for a while.

Specialist Arabella yells back, "Lighten up Lee, they're just joking."

"Maybe Specialist Too Tight would lighten up if he stopped shoving all those Twinkies down his throat," I reply with my usual shit eating grin.

"Alright, Alright," Jackson says laughing. "Let's go get some chow. Squad, At-ten-tion. Right face. Forward, march.

Left, left, left right left."

We march in a single file for what seems like a good mile and a half, passing a slew of food trailers on our right; Subway, Pizza Inn, and Baskin Robbins, but they are all closed. On our left we pass soldiers coming out of shower trailers in their black shower shoes, desert combat uniform pants, brown t-shirts, towels slung over their shoulders and black shower bags in their hands.

It's dusty. Everyone is wearing sunglasses with their neck gators around their mouths as they force their way through the wind with their backs hunched forward. Sand flows through the air like a light fog as if someone kicked over an enormous ant bed with thousands of pissed off troops marching around everywhere, ready to kill the first thing that tries to stomp on their existence.

Apache helicopters along with Blackhawks, Cobras, Hueys, and Chinooks, which everyone calls "Shithooks," fly across the sky like a flock of fan-tailed ravens.

Every time I hear the sound of their chopper blades spinning in the sky I think of the cadence from basic training, "I hear the choppers hovering, they're hovering overhead, they come to get the wounded, they come to get the dead, shoot the son of, shoot the son of, shoot the son of wooooo, air-borrrr-ne, ranger-ranger, ranger-er-er-er."

As we pass a white picket fence, Specialist Lee yells out, "Hey, is that a pool up there?"

"Yes, but it looks closed," Jackson replies.

Vega looks back at me and smiles, "That would be the first time I've seen him take a bath this whole deployment."

I bust out laughing, as does Arabella and Robinson.

Lee looks back and gives Vega the stink eye.

"Hey there is the PX," Arabella shouts. "I need to get some feminine products."

"Hey, me too," Sgt. Young says, looking directly into Staff Sgt. Jackson's soul.

"Ok, ok, we can stop there after chow," an uncomfortable Staff Sergeant Jackson replies.

After a short march we finally make it to the chow hall as sweat drips down the side of my face. A line of soldiers stretches out of the humongous white circus tent and down the street for about three city blocks.

"Holy shit, Specialist Sheen shouts. "It's going to take at least two hours to get in there."

"That's ok," Jackson replies. "We have nothing but time."

So, we wait.

We painstakingly wait.

Moving inch by inch. Minute by minute. And just when we think we have turned the corner, we are greeted by another long line stretching around another long tent.

We wait some more.

We wait some more underneath the unforgiving ball of fire in the sky that reminds me of the evil sun from the Mario Brothers video game that chases you around, the sweat raining down my forehead, raining down my ribs, raining down the sides of my legs.

I suck on my new CamelBak to stay hydrated, but no matter how much I suck it does little to alleviate the suck.

Holy fuck it's hot.

Roasting in this sun for hours, I start to feel like the writer F. Scott Fitzgerald's wife Zelda trapped on the top floor of a mental hospital as it catches fire, slowly being burned alive.

Fuck, Ruger, how can you roast her like that? Roast her like what? She has already been roasted way worse than my words can ever do. Grab some marshmallows and Hershey Chocolate assholes, the fire is just getting warmed up.

After about an hour and 45 minutes of standing under the sweltering sun, we finally make our way into the tent. A cold blast of AC hits us in the face immediately.

"Goddamn, does it feel good in here," I say, flapping my desert combat uniform top up and down to ventilate the volcano that's brewing underneath. "Can we just fight the war in here, Sergeant Jackson?"

But before he can reply, Sergeant Rodriquez shouts out to everybody, "Dude, it's T-bone steak and lobster day. Here, you Privates go first. NCOs don't eat until their soldiers do."

I poke Vega on the back. "That sucks for you. Are you sure you are still a vegetarian?"

He looks at the ground.

"Yes," he replies, biting his tongue and shaking his head.

I bust out laughing. "You should get an extra plate for me."

"Fuck you," he replies. "I am not getting you shit."

"Ah, come on man, it's already dead," I quip back. "I'll give you my vegetables."

After filling our trays, we make our way to a long wooden table that stretches from one end of the tent to the other with white plastic chairs on both sides.

"Man, this steak is juicy," I say, looking across the table at Vega. "How's the cauliflower?"

"It's surprisingly good," he says with a lying grin. "How's the poor defenseless animal?"

"Oh, it's great. Tastes like freedom. How's the poor defenseless plant? You know I never understood only eating plants. Aren't plants living organisms too? They bleed. They just call it sap. They also breathe. They just call it carbon monoxide. You say poor animal. I say poor plants. At least animals can run away. Plants are truly defenseless."

Vega looks at me and says, "That is the dumbest thing I've ever heard. Plants don't have feelings."

"How do you know?" I reply with an instigating tone. "Just because they can't scream on the outside doesn't mean they don't hurt on the inside."

Vega shakes his head and replies, "You are nuts, Ruger."

"Speaking of nuts," I reply, nudging my eyes toward a soldier sitting a couple tables back. "What is that sitting over there? Is that a guy or a girl?"

Vega takes a quick look out of the corner of his eye and says "That's a transgender person. Let me guess you have a problem with that?"

"Nope," I reply with a grin. "Shit man, people get boob jobs, lip jobs, ass jobs, and hand jobs, who gives a fuck, we are all a bunch of odd jobs at the end of the day. Do whatever the hell you want for all I care. I just want people to be happy with who they are and stop trying to be something they're never going to be able to be. I got a big ass nose. People have made fun of me for it my whole life. I could easily have surgery to make it smaller but fuck it. I don't give a fuck what people say. I ams who I ams. And to quote the great Kurt Cobain, 'I'd rather be hated for who I am, than to be loved for who I am not.' But I am curious though, where do we draw the line when it comes to being trans, like can I ride into work on a pair of roller skates because I consider myself trans-portation? Can I become trans-racial and apply for reparations? Can I become trans-species and have a donkey dick installed because I do in fact identify as an ass? Shit, I think that came out wrong. I feel like what I am trying to say here is getting lost in trans-lation. Ha!"

Vega just shakes his head, "You are certifiable, you know that? If you ever want to get out of this deployment, I am sure you could get a section 8 right out of here."

"Fuck that," I reply, taking a bit bite of my juicy steak. I am not a quitter. Not booze, not cigarettes, not sex, and certainly not this war. I may be crazy, but I ain't no pussy."

Specialist Lee yells down the table at Jackson, "When do you think we will be going to Iraq?"

"I don't know," he replies. "All of our vehicles are still out at sea. Could be a week or two before they get here."

Vega throws in his two cents. "Lee, haven't you learned anything yet? Nobody has a damn clue what is going on. It's one big cluster fuck."

Never being one to stay out of a good debate, I throw my hat into the ring, "Well, they need to hurry up and figure it out. Cotton candy sweet as gold, I'm fucking ready to rock and roll. I didn't come here to sit on the bench. It's time for Saddam and his brutal regime to go."

Vega replies dumbfounded, "That's what you think we are doing here? Ha, we are here for the oil."

"No way," I reply. "We are here to remove that bastard who bombed his own people with mustard gas. We are here to remove him from power before he gives those weapons of mass destruction to his terrorist buddies to use on us."

"Are you kidding me, do you know anything about the Middle East? We've been after their oil for decades."

"I don't know shit about this place other than it's a bunch of goat fuckers whose leader is running around torturing and gassing people to death. The motherfucker needs to go. Besides, what do you know about this place besides some shit you read in some damn book?"

"Well besides studying about this place in college, a place you need to check out some time, I lived in Cairo, which is in Egypt since I am sure you've never seen a globe, you dumb redneck."

"I know where Cairo is, I played 'Where in the World in Carmen Sandiego' there college boy. And fuck that. College is a waste of time. All it teaches you to do is read a book. It doesn't make you smart. It just makes you think you're smarter than everyone else cause you got a piece of paper. Fucking people got a PhD and can tell you everything about anything, but they can't change a flat tire. They don't have applied intelligence, which is what you seriously are lacking. You learn that by getting your hands dirty."

Jackson steps in like a referee, "Ok you two, cut it out."

We both look at Jackson.

"What? We're just joking."

"I know, but that's how fights start off," he says in a stern tone.

Lee asks Jackson, "What're your thoughts about the war?"

"I have no thoughts," he says, as his used car salesman's smile grins from one side of the chow hall to the other." God has a plan for all of us. I just put my faith in the lord and go to bed every night knowing he has me on the path of righteousness."

Vega and I look at each other like "what the fuck, over?" while trying not to laugh.

After chow, we check out the PX, which is like a tax-free Wal-Mart for the military. It has a little bit of everything, but without the low prices. Now, I get the prices on the bases back home in the states, but I can't help but to question why in the hell we are not getting this stuff here for free, seeing how we are getting ready to go to war for our country. You'd think at the very least we could get a little hometown discount.

Nope, apparently not. So it goes, Kurt Vonnegut. So it goes.

I score a Lynyrd Skynyrd greatest hit CD and a 600-unit AT&T phone card. Lee loads up on pork rinds, beef jerky, Mountain Dew, and several DVDs. Robinson grabs rapper Sean Paul's CD.

Arabella and Young load up on tampons, lotions, and wet wipes. Rodriquez gets some writing paper and envelopes. Sheen grabs a carton of Marlboro Red cigarettes. I get a carton of Camel Lights as well. Vega gets a book about philosophy. I look over at Jackson.

"You ain't getting anything?" I ask.

He raises both hands up like they are rising from the dead, "Nope, all I need is what God gave me."

After checking out at the cash register, we march back to the hangar and chill out for the rest of the day. Sheen and I hang outside, smoking and joking on top of the concrete bomb shelter until dark. The boredom begins to lull me to sleep. That's when I make my way back to my cot and check out for the night, drifting away to a world far, far away…

And that's when I see her standing there.

Now, some will say time machines don't exist. But every time I close my eyes at night I am transported back in time, where I can see Katie's beautiful brown eyes staring right at me as if no one else even exists. I can smell her Coolwater perfume, I can taste the Jack Daniels on her lips, I can hear her voice, "I buy, you fly," I can feel what I've never felt with anyone else when I lay there with my arms wrapped around her, her soft touch gently gripping my arm… it all seems so real, it all seems as if I am fully alive… in that space and time… as if we are right back in my front yard in Tampa, standing in the rain looking right into each other's eyes after being broken up for months, my heart pounding like thunder as tears rain down her face.

Fuck.

A waterfall of pressure begins to build. Twisting and turning like a Cat 5 hurricane, thrashing my insides to shreds. I twist and turn, twist and turn until finally a jolt hits me like a bolt of lightning that causes me to pop up in my cot and back into reality. I wipe my eyes and look around the darkness, trying to figure out exactly where I am. It takes a few minutes for me to realize what century this is and what continent I am on.

Fuck.

I have to piss like a pissed off pistol-packing private who's been pounding water in order to pass a piss test.

Fuck.

After getting my bearings straight and figuring out I am back in Kuwait, I grab my Army issue flashlight with the red lens and make way through the darkness, bouncing off everyone's cots like a pinball machine to the grumbles of those still off in a world far, far away.

"Hey, what the fuck dude?"

"Shit man, watch it."

"Yeah, hum uh."

I finally make my way outside and into the night. A few light posts glowing above each bomb shelter help guide me through the base. It's a ghost town except for a few silhouettes off in the distance. A chilly breeze drifts across the road, taking with it a plastic bag down the street as I cross over to a beige trailer. Can't tell you how good it feels to unload my bladder's CamelBak into the urinal, a warm glow flowing through me after barely making it there without getting a little friendly fire flowing down my leg.

After buttoning everything back up, I make my way back, stopping at the bunker for a quick smoke. It's peaceful. It's always peaceful at night here. There's no chaos of a thousand soldiers trampling like a herd of elephants or sergeants screaming like a bunch of baboons.

Nope.

Here it's just me.

I look up at the enormous clear sky and just soak in the sheer magnitude of the moon and the stars shining so close. It reminds me of sitting on top of a mountain in the Shenandoah National Park in Virginia as a kid. It's where my mom is from. Her mom grew up there during the Great Depression, hunting rabbits and going to the bathroom in an outhouse. Her side of the family lived up there until they were forced to move down into the valley when the government turned the land into a national park. It sucks they had to move, but it's a beautiful place and I am glad they preserved it. There is nothing like sitting on top of a mountain there and staring up at the stars, especially during a meteor shower.

Everything seems so close, as if I can actually reach and touch it. I've always enjoyed that closeness with the galaxy. As if we are one. It's the great unknown. A lot of people fear the unknown. But not me. I embrace it. I can't help but think about what's out there in that time and space, asking questions most people don't care to know the answers to.

Where does it all come from?

What does it all mean?

I mean, we are all made of matter

But does any of it really matter?

I take one long drag of my cigarette and blow the smoke up into the night, flicking the cherry out, and putting the dead soldier in my top right jacket pocket. I bounce my way back to my cot, pissing off half the company for 15 minutes trying to find it. It isn't exactly easy to find when everything is fucking camouflaged.

The next day we get up around 0630 hours, wait in line for another eternity to stuff ourselves full of some scrambled eggs, bacon, sausage, waffles, orange juice, and some boxed milk that apparently doesn't need to be refrigerated. After that glorious feast fit for a king, we spend the next few hours getting more anthrax shots to add to the list of Smallpox, Typhoid, Tetanus, Hepatitis A, B, C and every other alphabetical letter that the Army has stored up on the Island of Dr. Moreau. You know something ain't right when they tell you not to have kids for 5 years after getting these shots because they will be born with three legs or one eye.

Great, now if I survive this war, I am going to have to worry about my woman giving birth to a one-eyed-tripod child named cyclops.

But what can you do?

Not a damn thing.

Don't ask, don't tell.

The fourth round of Anthrax leaves me with a headache and a golf ball size knot that painfully throbs inside my arm. After getting every needle in the haystack, we hit up the chow hall for lunch before heading over to a building for a briefing.

A Black Sergeant Major with a thick mustache and flakes of gray hair comes in and stands on a wooden podium in front of our company, which is seated on 4 long wooden benches that stretch from one side to the other. Our unit has front row seats for the show, but Maintenance squad takes our rightful place in the back as usual.

"Welcome my brother and sisters," the Sergeant Major says with a thunderous voice that resembles a lion that's the head of the pride. "The moment is upon us. The time has come to embark on this dangerous journey to liberate Iraq from the devil himself. God is on our side and he will watch over you. But you have to get your mind right. I personally shut down the food trailers because they are poisoning our soldier's thoughts with that junk. It's time to focus on the task at hand."

An MP in front of us whispers to the soldier next to him, "What the fuck is this guy babbling about? Is this a briefing or a goddamn sermon?"

A whisper of laughter spreads around them.

I lean over to Robinson and say, "bro, can't a soldier at least get a cheeseburger and fries before he dies? Maybe a little milkshake."

"Right, son," he replies. "We should at least be able to try all 31 flavors from Baskin Robbins since we are not allowed to try all 31 females in our unit."

Lee looks down the line and angrily whispers, "You guys need to be quiet. Show some respect to who's talking."

The Sergeant Major continues preaching as he paces back and forth from one side of the wooden stage to the other, lulling everyone to sleep except for Sergeant Jackson, who looks on like a groupie looking at the lead singer of her favorite rock band.

The Sergeant Major stops in the middle of the tent.

"Now my brothers and sisters, let's bow our heads and pray that this war will be over soon, and you can safely return home to your loved ones."

As everyone except me and a few others go to lower their heads, a loud siren blares from one side of the base to the other. Everyone looks around with confusion.

"Is this part of the theatrics?" someone asks.

But before anyone can answer, the code for incoming scud missiles with warheads stuffed full of chemical weapons comes blaring across the intercom, "LIGHTNING, LIGHTNING, LIGHTNING."

A shot of adrenaline shoots up my arm and explodes in my chest, sending my heart pounding faster than the Titanic's Morse code machine after it hit the fucking iceberg.

"Holy shit, holy shit, holy shit," I think to myself as my scrambled eggs for a brain, scrambles to reach for my protective mask, ripping the Velcro carrying case open with shaking hands, struggling to grab the mask and strap it around my head like an octopus, covering the canister with my sweaty left hand and sucking in to secure it to my face, getting the proper seal. I struggle to breath as I put on my protective suit and gloves.

After getting everything on, I look out the goggles and see blurry images moving about. As Saddam's military might has unmasked itself, everyone struggles to get their masks on.

Off to my left, I hear two people screaming at each other. I turn to see two black soldiers struggling in a violent tug of war with a gas mask. It's our lazy 38-year-old female supply specialist who didn't bring her mask, fighting one of the cooks for his.

"Come on, Bryant, give me your mask," she says with terror in her eyes. "I ain't trying to die. I have kids at home."

"Fuck you, bitch," he barks back, pulling the mask away from her.

I feel a tap on my right shoulder. As I turn, I see Sgt. Rodriquez there with eyes as big as two pizza pies staring at me from inside his mask. He points and hums something that sounds like get over there. I rush over and sit down with my back against the wall, my eyes staring up at the ceiling while thinking, "holy shit, holy shit, holy *fucking* shit. We're going to die. We are going to die; we are going to *fucking* die."

My rifle rattles back and forth in my right hand like a rattlesnake's rattle as I shake uncontrollably. *Fuck, fuck, oh fuck.* My chest tightens as tight as my asshole as my heart keeps pounding faster than a belt fed machine gun.

Bang, bang, bang, bang, bang, bang.

I look out at soldiers moving in what looks like slow motion while struggling to get all their gear on.

But just as fast as it started, the "All clear," comes over the intercom.

"We just got word that the Scud missile landed 5 miles from here," the strange voice says. "The area is now clear. Carry on."

Still leaning up against the wall, I slowly slide down to the ground, stretching my legs out onto the floor, staring off at a gaggle fuck of soldiers that my life will depend on, their gear strung out across the floor from one side of the building to the other. Some are missing gloves; some are missing their rubber boot covers and some are missing both.

As I pull my mask off, exposing my sweaty dazed face to the rest of the squad, I notice everyone else looks just as pale and in shock as they pull their masks off. No one makes eye contact. We all just sort of look off into the distance like nothing ever happened. But there is no hiding from it. We've all been unmasked now, exposing the dirty truth that maybe we are not as badass as the mythical creatures we make ourselves out to be.

Even the most seasoned soldiers in our company now look like mere mortals.

IN THE AIR TONIGHT

GROWING UP IN FLORIDA, I witnessed a lot of wind related events; tropical storms, waterspouts and, of course, hurricanes. It always amazed me the power of mother nature, how she can take this invisible thing called air that is normally calm and peaceful and spin it with just the right amount force flowing from her lips, creating a very visible tropical cyclone that can be seen from outer space after picking up so much steam that it picks up water and everything else in its path as it smoothly moves across the Earth, shredding everything in its path like a mobile food blender, making smoothies out of mobile homes as if they were as soft as strawberries.

But I ain't never seen no shit like this. As I go to step out of the hangar for a morning smoke, I am greeted by a Category 3 sandstorm blowing through the base like an El Paso car wash, stopping me dead in my tracks.

"What the fuck is this," I say to the line of soldiers standing in awe next to the entrance, completely mesmerized by the blood red sky and the occasional sand tornado passing through.

"Welcome to the sand show," one of them says.

Now I have ridden the Sandstorm ride at the African themed Busch Gardens in Tampa hundreds of times, but I've never given much thought to the origins of the name. Hell, the only time I've even thought about an actual sandstorm was in high school history class when we covered the Great Dust Bowl in Oklahoma during the 1930s.

But here I am now, being thrust into the middle of my own dust bowl, bringing to life those words and images that I read on the pages, giving me a front row seat to experience what all those Okies went through way back when.

And in a strange ironic turn of events, I find myself in the middle of another historic sandstorm, the sequel to Operation Desert Storm, causing me to wonder if one day people will read about us in history class with images of sand flowing through the pages.

Thankfully the shit show begins to die down by noon and is completely cleared out not long after that, giving way to blue skies and a clear path to the chow hall.

After stuffing our filthy faces, Master Sergeant Shortman, a tall upbeat MP with 23 years in service comes walking over to my squad and sits on my cot, his wrinkly tanned skin beating as red as that morning sky.

Staff Sergeant Jackson jumps up,

"What can I do for you, Master Sergeant?"

"Well, we just got word that we are sending an advance party up to Iraq today," he says with a concerned look. "Sergeant Rodriquez and Specialist Vega will be going."

Jackson smiles back, "I will have them ready to go for Master Sergeant."

Shortman replies with a somber tone. "Thank you,"

Hearing their conversation kicks up a F5 sandstorm of anger inside me, causing a few F bombs to drop.

"This is fucking bullshit" I shout. "Vega doesn't even want to fucking kill anybody. I should be the one going."

Jackson turns and shouts with a stern tone, "Hey, cut it out."

He turns to Shortman and asks, "How are they getting up there? Our vehicles haven't arrived yet?"

Shortman then explains "The Commander has secured two deuces, and one Kuwaiti dump truck. They will be leaving in two hours, so they need to pack their bags and be ready to go outside 15 minutes prior. Vega is going because he speaks Arabic. He will be an asset."

Jackson smiles and replies, "They will be ready to go for you, Master Sergeant."

Shortman turns and walks away.

I look at Vega and Rodriquez, their faces as grim as someone who just received news they've been diagnosed with cancer.

Fuck.

I'd give anything to take their place. I didn't come here to sit on the fucking bench. I sat enough while playing little league baseball.

This is fucking bullshit. How come they get called up to the big show while I am still stuck down here in the minors? I should be the one going up. Let Rodriquez stay, hell he has a kid and a wife. He doesn't seem eager to go anyways. Neither does Vega. He'd rather stay here and read his bullshit books in peace.

Fuck.

A couple of hours pass by and maintenance squad lines up outside the hangar to see our fellow mechanics off. They climb in the back of the unarmored deuce-and-a-half with the rest of the unit that is going up. It's going to be one long miserable ride as there must be 20 or so soldiers packed in there like a tube of Pillsbury biscuit dough—their legs, rifles, and machine guns squeezing out of the sides of the truck as they prepare to be shoved into the blazing hot oven called Operation Iraqi Freedom.

"What a sight to be seen," I think to myself. "One goddamn tank round and they're all fucking goners. They are all a bunch of sitting ducks piled on top of each other."

What a shit show. It makes that sandstorm earlier in the day seem like a ride at a theme park. Maybe it is better that I wait until some common sense shows up. In basic training, they always drilled into our heads to keep as much space between each soldier when marching so that in the event a grenade or a mortar lands nearby and rips those unlucky lottery winners to pieces like a fruit blender, you minimize casualties.

Now I am not sure if they teach that in officer candidate school, or West Point, or if our commanding officer, just doesn't give a shit. Of course, this is the same captain who, when we were back at Ft. Stewart during a pre-mobilization formation, looked at our company of reservists and said with a straight face, "fuck your families, I am your family now."

He seems to be in such a hurry to go to war that he forgot his common sense along the way. That's officers for you. They all think they're goddamn General Patton or General Schwarzkopf. They're all out to prove they are among the great war minds; to prove they belong in the history books right alongside the great generals of all time from Alexander to Powel.

But I am not totally convinced that our commander's ambition is that high. I honestly think he's just out to try to prove to the world that he has hair on his balls. Which may be true, but I'd bet it's not much longer than the hair on his bald head.

What the fuck, over?

After a few "good lucks," "be safes," "Godspeeds" and a couple of handshakes, the advanced party advances off down the road and into the unknown.

I storm over to the bunker and light up a smoke to take the edge off. To try to get that sandstorm raging inside me to die down. Master Sergeant Shortman comes over shortly after.

"You got a smoke I can bum?" he asks with a smile.

"Yes, it's a Camel Light though, Master Sergeant," I reply, pulling the pack out of my top left pocket.

"That's fine," he replies, taking the cancer stick and lighting it up. "You really want to go up, don't you?"

"Fuck yeah," I reply, taking a strong drag.

He grins.

"The MPs that are left here will be running convoy escort missions into Iraq until we move up north when our vehicles get here. Would you be interested in being a driver or a gunner?"

"Hells yes," I reply. "I'm qualified on the Mark 19 and the SAW."

"Well, we have a mission leaving here in about an hour," he replies, taking a drag of his cigarette and blows the cloud of smoke up into the sky. "They are escorting some civilian supply trucks up to Basra, which is just across the border. We are borrowing some Humvees from the base motor pool until our trucks get here. We'll be forming up in front of our sleeping quarters. You will need to draw ammo from supply. After you finish your smoke, let Sergeant Jackson know."

"Hooah, Master Sergeant," I reply, hardly able to contain my excitement.

Shortman is a really cool NCO (Non-Commissioned Officer.) Though he's made a career out of the Army, he's not like the rest of the career soldiers who only do what's in the best interest of their careers. He looks out for the younger soldiers like an NCO is supposed to. He's like a father figure. A lot of people look up to him and not just because of his height. He's taken a liking to me like a lot of the other MPs have. I am not sure if it's my willingness to kill or if it's my tattoos that have tipped them off, but that's how I came to become qualified on the Mark 19 and the Squad Automatic Weapon. Back at Fort Stewart, the MP's pulled me out of the motor pool and cross trained me with the heavy weapons. Which was fine by me, because I can't stand being a mechanic.

After finishing my cigarette, I walk over to Jackson who is sitting on a cot next to all of the communication (COMMO) guys. He hangs with them a lot because the whole squad is black. When he's not hovering over us like an attack helicopter, he's over there shooting the shit, like the brothers back home sitting around shuckin' and jivin' on a street corner. The COMMO guys are old school brothers, Marvin Gaye, Otis Redding, rolling dice, 40 ouncers, always quick with a joke to test to see if you're "cool" or not kind of guys. They're way nicer to privates than most of the other NCOs. They're always quick to help you out.

"Hey Sergeant Jackson," I say.

"What's happening, Ruger?" he replies.

"Just wanted to give you a heads up that I am going on a mission up to Basra. Master Sergeant Shortman told me to tell you."

He just laughs, shaking his head.

"Before you go, there are a couple of things I need to go over with you. Our vehicles can arrive at any moment, so don't be getting too comfortable. Once they do, we have to go get them off the ship and get them serviced to be ready to go into Iraq. I also need to brief you on some incidents that have happened. During the scud missile attack the other day, a female Major was raped while showering. A male soldier wearing a gas mask entered the shower trailer and attacked her. There are also reports of someone groping female soldiers while they sleep at night in the hangar.

If you see anything like this happening, alert an NCO as soon as possible. Alright?"

"Hooah, Sergeant."

"OK, let me know when you get back," he says with his signature ivory smile.

I head over to supply and draw 300 rounds of ammo to fill 10 30 round magazines. I put six in my carrying pouch, one in each cargo pocket, one in my pocket for the rifle and one in my backpack. I throw my Vietnam era flak vest on, as well as my load bearing vest, grab my sunglasses, canteen, M-16, Kevlar helmet, and head out to formation with the MPs. The civilian drivers are standing off to the side, their semi-trucks parked over on the main road adjacent to our sleeping quarters.

Master Sergeant Shortman comes over.

"Hey guys, I am going to be giving the safety brief," he says in a stern tone. "Today you will be going on a mission into Iraq. You will be using the Humvees the base has loaned us, so take care of them. The threat assessment from the CIA has stated that every convoy that has gone up has been attacked. There are also reports of tanks and Republican Guard still out there and Fedayeen soldiers have reportedly been coming out of the cities to attack American troops. Stay alert, Stay alive. Sergeant First Class Banks from first platoon will be the NCO-in-charge and Lieutenant Hernandez from third platoon will be the officer-in-charge. They have decided to put a shooter in each truck with the civilians in case the convoy is attacked and their vehicles become immobilized. PFC Ruger from headquarters platoon, Specialist Hicks from first, and PFC

Walker from third will be tasked with riding in the semi-trucks. The civilian drivers are not armed. It is the shooter's responsibility to protect them and get them into a Humvee in the event of an attack. You will put a magazine in your rifle, but you will not load a round into the chamber, Hooah. Be safe out there. Good luck and Godspeed."

I walk over and climb up in the last semi-truck in the convoy. I am greeted by a blast of cool air coming from the truck's AC. It's a welcoming feeling after standing out in the heat for the last couple of hours. A hillbilly with blue jeans, a dirty blond mullet and a blue bullet proof vest greets me with a smile full of chewing tobacco.

"Hey dere, buddy, climb on up in heeer," he says with a thick Louisiana accent. "My name's Billy Ray Thompson. What's yours?"

"PFC Ruger."

"Damn nice to meet ya dere, Ruga," he says as he starts up the truck and shifts it into gear. "Ya' not really gon listen to dem, and load ya gun, right?"

"Hell no," I say, facing the barrel of my rifle to the floorboard, popping a magazine in and racking a round into the chamber."

He smiles as he pushes his foot down on the accelerator. The truck shakes violently as we take off, passing through the main gate of Camp Arifjan and out onto the streets of Kuwait.

The convoy consists of four Hummers and three semi-trucks, looking like one giant serpent slithering down the road. And if any of Saddam's rats even think about crossing our path, well the convoy packs a venomous punch. Black machine guns, shoulder fired anti-tank weapons called AT-4s, and fully automatic grenade launchers are mounted on all of the gun trucks.

The convoy snakes through the streets of Kuwait with aggression like we own the goddamn place; blowing through red lights and cutting off Kuwaitis driving Mercedes and fancy sports cars, the dumbfounded drivers looking up at us like we're aliens from another planet.

Billy Ray turns and asks me, "so where ya from dere, Ruga?"

"I am from Tampa, Florida. What about you?"

"I'm from Lucky, Louisiana. Bone and raised. You a married?"

"Na. I had a good girl once, but she went bad somewhere along the way and ran off with someone else. What about you?"

"Yes sirree," he replies with a big smile, revealing a few missing teeth. "I done been married fur three years now. I met her at da dirt racetrack in town where I raced them sprint cars. She was da trophy girl when I won the final race dat year. We got drunk dat night and the rest was history. Well, dat was until I found out she was my third cousin six months ago. But hell, we'd already had sex all over town and three kids. We gonna stick it out fur now."

"What the fuck, over?" I think, trying not to laugh.

"How did you end up here driving trucks?"

"I droved dem trucks back home fur a living. Then one day dere was dis flyer on the wall at da shop saying dey was paying $150,000 a year tax free to drive trucks into Iraq."

"What company is that?"

"Halliburton/KBR."

"Damn" I think. "Here I am a PFC making $36,000 a year protecting this guy who is making $150,000 a year. I got into the wrong goddamn business."

After shooting the shit for a while, we make our way to the DMZ (Demilitarized Zone) on the border of Iraq. It's a massive hole 30-40 feet deep with sand piled 30-40 feet high on both sides. Concertina wire stretches across the Iraqi side as far as the eye can see. Two Kuwaiti soldiers in plain, dark brown uniforms stand in front of a white security gate that goes up and down. They are smiling and seem very lackadaisical for what is happening just on the other side of the gate. Another Kuwaiti soldier is slouching in a chair, sipping from a tea glass, his AK-47 lying on the ground.

Off to the side of the gate guard is an area with barbed wire encircling a tiny wooden shack and three army fuel tankers. Billy Ray pulls up next to one of the tanker trucks and gets out to top off with fuel. SFC Banks and Lt. Hernandez walk into the tiny beige shack that has two stars above the door, signifying a two-star general owns the goddamn place.

After getting clearance to cross over to the other side, we begin moving across the DMZ as the orange and red sky begins to shrink into the darkness.

Cobra helicopters slither through the sky as enormous green military trucks pulling Bradley Fighting Vehicles and Abrams Battle Tanks on heavy duty trailers line the side of the road. The game is on. The full force of America's military might, is on full display as the race to Baghdad is underway.

The Kuwait soldier, still slouched in his chair, waves us through. My heart shifts into third gear as Billy Ray shifts the semi-truck into gear and presses the gas pedal. I pull my night vision goggles out of my bag and put them on. Gripping my M-16 tight, I scan the green terrain for any movement with my dark brown eyes. Phil Collins' voice comes across my mind's radio waves as we cross into Iraq,

I can feel it, coming in the Iraqi air tonight, oh lord.

And I've been waiting for this moment, for all my military life, oh, lord

Can you feel it, coming in the Iraqi air tonight, oh lord, oh, lord?

THE WAR MACHINE

THE PORT OF KUWAIT

BEING A PRIVATE IN the Army can feel pretty insignificant at times, as if you are a spare tire stored up underneath the military's mighty war machine that keeps rolling along with or without you. Out of sight out of mind, like a ghost, like a ghost who can see everything that's happening, but is powerless to say or do anything. You have no voice. You have no voice when it comes to whose vehicle goes where. You have no voice when it comes to what vehicle goes where. And you certainly have no voice when it comes to why the vehicle goes where it goes. Hell, you don't even have a voice on the vehicle's communication radio when the voice on the other end goes and goes. That is the job of the sergeants. You are voiceless. You just go where you are told to go.

And that is just the way it goes.

I didn't think I could feel any more insignificant than being a private in the United States Army. But that was before I found myself standing in a shipping port on the coast of Kuwait, staring up at a fleet of gray U.S. Navy ships that make the Titanic look like a tugboat. It's mesmerizing to see such massive steel warships towering so high that it creates a lunar eclipse across the land, causing me to shrink down into my thoughts as I begin to question how much my tiny existence truly matters in the grand scheme of things. I imagine it's how a grain of sand feels as it silently sits next to a palm tree in the middle of a deserted desert, questioning its own importance to the universe.

The thought is interrupted by metal clanking coming from a ship's bay doors opening. Vehicles of every make and model in the military's inventory begin pouring out of the belly of the beast and down the ramps. Thousands of tanks, Hummers, ambulances, helicopters, artillery, recovery tanks, recovery trucks, transport vehicles, and troop carriers are unloaded into a sea of heavy machinery parked in perfect little rows as if they were book shelfs at Barns and Nobles.

The mechanized war machine is on full display as Operation Iraqi Freedom is in full effect. Over 300,000 soldiers and their vehicles are flowing into Kuwait and Iraq like mining prospectors flowing into California during the great gold rush. There's money to be made in *dem dere hills Billy Ray.*

Most of maintenance squad is standing over the edge of the concrete barrier looking down below at the vast array of fish that are flowing through the water with the precision of a fighter jet as they dive bomb a school of minnows who are trying to survive their own war, oblivious to what's happening on land.

Staff Sergeant Jackson shouts out from a row of parked vehicles.

"Hey, I found our trucks," he screams, waving us over with his oversized hand. "We have 55 Hummers, 3 deuces with trailers, and one wrecker," he says in a serious tone. "The MPs are going to drive the Humvees, and we are going to take the three deuces and the wrecker. Since Lee is the license wrecker operator, he will take that one.

Lee gets all giddy, smiling as if he gets to go on a first date with his second cousin. The wrecker is a redneck's wet dream. It's his General Lee. He would paint the motherfucker orange with a Confederate Flag on top if they'd let him.

"Sheen, you will ride with Lee," Jackson says.

"Oooh," I whisper over to Robinson. "Sucks to be him."

Everyone tolerates Lee, mostly because it's frowned upon to frag your own people, but make no mistake, no one likes him. I still can't figure out how a poor backwoods bastard from Kentucky can be so obnoxiously full of himself. His wife is the size of Kentucky Lake, and he's uglier than a wild boar that got ran over by a semi-truck. Yet he acts like he is some sort of superior being, like he's the Grand Wizard of the Klueless Klux Klan or something. But he's no wizard, just an idiot running around waving a wooden stick he found in the forest when he got lost as a kid.

Sergeant Jackson continues on, "me, Ruger, and Robinson will be driving the deuces. Sergeant Young will ride with me. Arabella will ride with Ruger. Robinson will be riding with Specialist Malaysia, the finance specialist for our unit who was nice enough to come help us today."

Robinson shakes his head. Specialist Malaysia used to be his main squeeze back at Ft. Stewart during pre-mobilization. I caught him fucking the chubby Asian female one night in the motor pool. It was like the scene from the movie *Titanic* when Leonardo DiCaprio's character was banging Rose in the 1912 Renault Type CB Coupé de Ville, except this was a military deuce-and-a-half, and it was in the motor pool in the middle of the state of Georgia. As I walked by, I could hear her saying "fuck me harder, fuck me harder." Her hands kept smacking up against the foggy window as she tried to reach for something to grab a hold of. I was laughing so hard and looking around for someone to call over when Robinson peeked up, smiled, and then winked at me.

Ah, but the romance is over now as Robinson has moved on to another slice of bread. But here she is still trying to find something to hold on to. She just can't let him go.

I can only imagine how that conversation is going to go.

"Why do you ignore me? Why don't you like me anymore? You get what you wanted and then throw me to the side of road? Is that how it works? I was just a piece of ass to you?"

Goddamn, who needs that kind of drama in the middle of a war zone. Bad enough you have to worry about the enemy killing you, but now you have to worry about some chick nagging you to death. *Fuck.* I'd rather ride with Specialist Lee than have to hear her rattling off like a machine gun.

I lucked out as I get to ride with Arabella. I've had a crush on her since my first day at the reserve unit back in St. Petersburg. I remember she pulled up behind me in the parking lot, her wavy blonde hair touching the tip of her shoulders as she got out of her candy apple red Toyota Supra and put her hair up in a ponytail, her tiny frame barely standing above the door. It was like something straight out of an '80s movie.

"Hey," she says with a soft voice as I climb up into the deuce's driver's seat.

"What's going on?" I reply.

"Ya know, sweating like crazy and my hair is frizzing out of control."

I don't really know what else to say after that. I get nervous as shit and clam up when I am around someone I really like. It's weird. My whole life I've gotten into trouble for not being able to keep my mouth shut and here I am with the perfect opportunity to put my voice to good use, and I can't find a single fucking syllable to say. I am stricken with the fear—fear of rejection, fear of getting into trouble for fraternizing with a female soldier.

Fuck.

Goddamn, when did I start giving a fuck about the rules? Before I joined the Army, I just didn't give one fuck. Now I am a fucking deaf mute that can't so much as make a whistle. Oh, well.

And the Army keeps rolling along.

We drive through Kuwait for what seems like half the day, occasionally screaming over the blasting sound of the deuce-and-a-half's muffler, an engineering marvel of a design, but is obnoxiously placed right next to the windshield on the passenger side.

Thankfully, we make it to Camp Doha before we both become deaf.

Doha is a Kuwaiti industrial base with loads of warehouses that has now become the U.S. Military's supply center for vehicle maintenance and supply issues. We have to take our vehicles there to get inspected before we are allowed to head up to the big dance.

We walk inside one of the buildings. Several Abrams tanks with their gun turrets removed line the maintenance bay with guys in civilian clothes working on them. One of the employees, a male with short blond hair and a thick beard, comes from around the tank tracks in blue coveralls with the sleeves tied around his waist.

"Hey guys, can I help you with something?" he asks with a surfer accent.

"Yes," Staff Sergeant Jackson replies. "We need to have our vehicles inspected and serviced. Our shipping containers with all of our tools haven't come in yet."

You have to love Army logic. If you ship anything together, you can bet your paycheck that it will not show up together… well, that is if your paycheck arrives in time to actually make the wager. I wouldn't bet on it.

"Oh yeah, no problem, Sergeant," the mechanic says. "Just go into that room right behind you and talk to the head foreman. Just you, Sergeant, everyone else has to stay out here."

"Yes, sir," Jackson says.

I head outside and light up a smoke. The blond surfer dude comes running out behind me.

"Hey, man. You can't smoke here. You have to put it out or go 50 yards away. We have way too much fuel and oil in here. You'll blow this place up."

"Oh shit, no problem," I reply, putting the Camel Light out on the bottom of my boot and placing the butt into my right jacket pocket with the rest of the dead soldiers.

"It's all good, dude," surfer guy says. "Are you light wheel mechanics? 63 Bravos?"

"Yes sir," I reply. "What about you? That beard is definitely not within military regulations."

"Ah yeah. No, I am a civilian mechanic now. I used to be a 63 Bravo in the Army, but I got out and got this job. I make $90,000 a year tax free, and my room and board are paid for. I work 7 days straight, then I get three days off. I usually go out into the Persian Gulf to go fishing or jet skiing."

"Let me guess, Halliburton/KBR?" I reply.

"Yeah, how did you know?"

"I met a trucker the other day, said he was making $150,000 tax free to drive trucks into Iraq."

"Yeah man, those guys make a little more, but they are also taking way more risk than me. You should check into civilian contracting when your tour is over. It's easy money."

"Yeah, I am definitely in the wrong business. I am only making $36,000 a year."

Jackson comes out of the warehouse.

"Ok, here's the deal," he says, wiping the sweat off his forehead with his desert colored boonie hat. "We are going to spend the night here. We will inspect all our vehicles tonight for anything that dead-lines a vehicle, especially class three leaks. Any oil or transmission pans that continuously leak, will be fixed by the civilian mechanics beginning at 0800."

"What about class 1 and 2 leaks where you can see oil on the pan, but it's not dripping down?" I ask.

"Those are okay," he replies. "Just check the dip sticks to make sure there is enough fluid in the reservoir. Once our tools arrive off the ship, we will address the minor stuff. Right now, we just need to do what we can to get them to pass inspection and on the road."

For the rest of the day in the motor pool, we open up the hoods of 45 Hummers, 3 deuces, and one wrecker. We crawl under every vehicle looking for leaks, broken tie rods, and anything that doesn't look right. We spend hours going over every vehicle searching for flat tires, missing lug nuts, doors that don't open correctly, gun turrets that don't spin, low oil, and too much transmission fluid.

We work deep into the night, smoking cigarettes and chewing coffee grinds from our MREs as if it was chewing tobacco to help get us through it. The total count for vehicles that are dead-lined is seven. Five have class three fluid leaks, one has brake issues, and one has a gun turret that won't spin. Apparently, some dumbass MPs got the bright idea back at Ft. Stewart to spray thick foam insulation inside the gun turret in order to stop the rain from leaking in. It stopped the rain, but it also completely stopped the turret from spinning. Ah, the things that make a mechanic's head spin.

What the fuck, over?

PACKING UP, GETTING READY TO GO

BEFORE I JOINED THE Army, I was never much of a neat packer. Not because I was a slob or anything, but mostly because I didn't exactly go anywhere that needed that level of fine detail due to lack of travel space. We were too poor to go jet setting around the world, that's why I never picked up that skill set. When we did go off hunting or fishing, we'd just throw it all in the back of the truck next to the cooler full of Bud Light. That's just how we rolled.

And that's why it was eye opening when I went through basic training. It blew my mind how much stuff you could fit into such a tiny space, like trying to fit my dick into my virgin ex- girlfriend's pussy. It's hard at first, but with the right angle and a touch of force, you can get it in there. Socks and underwear and shirts and uniforms are no different. Fold them at the correct angle and with a touch of force, you can roll them super tight, much like rolling a fat joint. Puff, puff pass motherfuckers. And before you know it, you have perfect little rows of clothes that allow you to fit a whole wardrobe inside a tiny desk drawer inside a footlocker.

This skill set comes in handy in the Army as soldiers are constantly packing their bags and moving from one place to another. You become highly proficient at moving on a minute's notice. After basic training, I had to pack my duffle bags and march down the road to mechanic school. After that I had to pack up my whole life and report to my reserve unit in St. Petersburg, Florida within three days for our deployment where we had to pack up all of the tools, parts, weapons, night vision goggles, and everything else at the unit, and move it all to Fort Stewart, Georgia within a week. We also had to pack up all our vehicles and put them on a train destined for a Navy Port in Texas. And my personal favorite moment of insanity of the deployment, we had to dump all of our shit out of our duffle bags and pack it back up five different times because some dipshit butter bar lieutenant kept changing the goddamn packing list before a sergeant finally stepped in to bring some sanity to the situation so we could ship ourselves to Kuwait before the war was over.

And now here we are again, all packed up and ready to go, staged next to our warehouse in the early morning hours. All of our duffle bags are packed up in the back of the deuces. The rest of our shit, Meals Ready to Eat, water jugs, ammo cans full of ammo, cans of chewing tobacco, packs of cigarettes, and chemical weapons suits, are packed into desert-colored unarmored Humvees—called M998s—and two green medical Hummers with a giant red and white cross painted on the canvas doors. All of the gun trucks have someone sitting in the military's version of a sunroof. Every vehicle is heavily armed. Some have M249 machine guns mounted on the gun turret while others have Mark 19 fully automatic grenade launchers. All have AT-4 (Anti-Tank) rocket launchers.

Sergeants walk up and down the lane, poking their heads in one window before going to another to do a sensitive item check, but to also check on those sensitive soldiers sitting there scared as shit. Not everyone is as excited as I am to be heading into the shit.

Several Army semi-trucks with our shipping containers that finally came in, are staggered throughout the convoy. I am the gunner in the last Humvee, a Mark 19 at my fingertips, the 30-round belt of 40 mm grenades sitting in an ammo can next to it, ready to be locked and *fucking* loaded. I also have an M-16 and an AT-4.

The category 5 hurricane is upon us now as we get ready to head straight into the motherfucker—a whirlwind of emotions swirling throughout the convoy. The mood is intense, the adrenaline pumping as high as the volume on my headphones as Metallica's *Ride the Lightning* CD gets me jacked up even higher. I pull out a pack of Camel Lights and light one up.

"You need one Robinson," I shout down into the driver seat.

"Hells yeah, son," he replies.

"What about you Arabella?" I shout over to the passenger seat.

"I am good," she replies. "Those things will kill you,"

"Suit yourself," I reply laughing. "This war will kill you a lot faster. A smoke is the least of my worries with so many Iraqi tanks out there looking to smoke the shit out of us."

We shoot the shit for a few hours while sitting in our staged formation, just sitting there in the heat, the sun bearing down on us with the pin-point precision of a stove top oven, cooking our little saucepan in perfect uniformity. *Hurry up and wait, right?* Who knows what the actual fucking hold up is? But we hold fast. Which drives some soldiers nuts, such as maintenance squad's Specialist Lee. The pack rat constantly gets in and out of his wrecker, pacing back and forth, the anticipation clearly wrecking his clouded mind. I honestly don't know how he can think with all the crap he has packed up in his truck anyways. Gives me claustrophobia just looking at it. I clear that thought out real fast though with a strong drag from my cigarette and blow that cloud of smoke high up into the clouds.

After roasting to a crisp underneath this unforgiving sky like a Buddhist monk protesting the Vietnam war by dousing himself with gasoline and lighting it on fire, we finally get the go-ahead and make our way out of Camp Arifjan. The convoy aggressively snakes its way through the streets of Kuwait, cutting off every car and blowing through red lights as if we own the goddamn place. An overwhelming feeling of power comes over me as I point my Mark 19 at the Merzedes Benzes behind us, the *oh fuck look* on the rich Kuwaiti's faces brings a big smile to my face. There is just something empowering about riding in the gun turret, knowing that with one push of the trigger you can send out a burst of grenades that can wipe the grin off even the biggest baddest asshole's face forever.

We travel along like this for a while before making it to the last check station before crossing through the demilitarized zone. We fill up with gas while the commander and his lieutenants go into the metal, air-conditioned shack to check in with the general. They come back out a few minutes later and a voice comes across the radio.

"All soldiers must put their DCU tops back on, over."

I look down from the turret at Robinson.

"Are they fucking serious? It's like 180 got damn degrees out here. You telling me some fucking general sitting in an air-conditioned shack is going to tell us to put more clothes on? What the fuck, over?"

"I don't know, son," Robinson replies. "Just put it on until we get out of here."

I angrily put my DCU top back on, and we head out again. The Kuwaiti soldiers manning the gate at the DMZ actually seem attentive and alert this time, like there is actually a war going on. One of them waves us through. As we pull through the gate and enter Iraq, I slink down into the truck and take off my flak vest, ditching the DCU top and putting body armor back on as I stand back up in the gun turret, peering out at the strange new ecosystem laid out before us.

On the other side of the divided desert, we make our way through a tiny village that looks like it's been abandoned, not a soul in sight. Even the animals must sense danger because there are no camels or goats or sheep; nothing but a blinding sun and sand for as far as the binoculars can see. At the edge of the town, we make a left and head out onto a main highway where we do a loop and head north onto another highway. We pass village after village but still no sign of any Iraqis, just blown-up T-72 tanks that line the side of the road. It reminds me of all those end-of-the-world apocalyptic movies. But this isn't a fucking movie. This is the real deal. What a spooky fucking feeling as we go through ghost town after ghost town. It's a strange sight to see such emptiness spread throughout such a vast landscape as the desolate desert full of nothingness gives me a feeling of being… powerless.

The only people we do see are our fellow Soldiers and Marines, whose giant green semi-trucks are pulling everything from tanks to shipping containers in the lanes next to us. Some are even traveling in the lanes usually reserved for traffic going in the opposite direction. Everything is heading North. Special Forces soldiers go blasting by in stripped-down Humvees called Dumvees because they have no armor. At least our trucks have windshields and Kevlar doors. Their vehicles are bare bones. But they are fast and heavily armed with machine guns mounted everywhere, even where the front passenger windshield used to be.

Apache and Cobra helicopters periodically fly overhead. The chopper blades make a welcoming sound. It's a comforting feeling to know that there are angels above with Hellfire missiles watching over us.

We continue to travel along, the heat of the day becoming so hot in the turret that the smile on my face starts to feel like it's melting, it's melting as if the Wicked Witch of the West is standing there with a supercharged blow dryer an inch away from my face. I lower my head to where only my helmet and goggles are exposed. We turn off onto another road. This time, our convoy is the only one in sight as we make our way down a lonely stretch of highway.

There's not much going on. It's nothing but more desert and more small clay huts off in the distance. We travel along for about another hour, sweat drenching my brown T-Shirt and brown underwear.

I reach down by my foot and grab a water bottle. As I go to take a sip, I instantly spit it back out.

"Holy fuck that's hot!" I scream. "I just burned my got damn lip."

I look at the bottle of water. Tiny bubbles shoot to the top as if it's carbonated water. I yell down into the Humvee.

"Are there any waters down there that aren't boiling fucking hot?"

"No," Arabella shouts back up. "That's all we have."

I begin to stew from the lack of AC and cold water—and hydration for that matter. It amazes me that we can build billion-dollar stealth bombers that can fly around the world, but we can't get a vehicle outfitted with AC in order to go fight in the sandbox? *WTF?*

I pull a sock out of my bag and wrap it around the water bottle, pour water on it from another water bottle and set it in the wind next to the Mark 19.

As I go to look out in the vast desert of nothingness, a loud explosion rocks the left side of the truck.

I scream down, "What the fuck was that?"

"Yo, I think we got a flat tire," Robinson yells back.

The Humvee comes to a stop on the side of the road. Arabella frantically tries to get a radio message out.

"Mayday, Mayday, we have a flat tire, over."

No one answers back.

"*Fuck*, I can't get anyone on the radio," she screams. "It's not working."

"Try flashing your lights," I yell down to Robinson.

He clicks the lights off and on as I try yelling at the gunner in the Humvee in front of us, but they aren't paying us any attention. We try everything. I even throw a hot ass water bottle at them. But the convoy just slithers on without us.

"What are we going to do now?" Arabella asks with a worrying tone.

I yell back down, "we have to cut the tire off. It has that rubber doughnut, run-flat thing inside of it."

Robinson jumps out and begins hacking away at the blown-out tire with a Gerber knife as I rotate the turret 360 degrees looking for any possible enemy activity.

"I got it cut off," he says. "Let's go."

After we drive about two miles, sparks begin to fly and a metal clanking sound radiates from underneath the Humvee. The vehicle suddenly whips off to the side of the road.

"Why are we stopped?" I yell.

Robinson replies, "the run flat is gone. We are riding on the rim" The asphalt is too hot. It melted the rubber doughnut away.

Fuck. Won't be hard for the enemy to find us now. All the Republican Guard would have to do is follow the long black line stretching down the highway.

"I can't believe they just left us," Arabella shouts out in anger.

We form a defensive perimeter with Arabella and Robinson pointing their weapons out the window in the 9 and 3 o'clock position while I face the rear. We wait. And we wait. Nothing. Just sand trickling across the highway by a light wind. But in my mind, all I can think of is the fact that we aren't too far from where Jessica Lynch and her convoy were ambushed and taken prisoner.

The thought of being a POW is a scary thought for soldiers. It's an even scarier thought for female soldiers such as Arabella. The enemy will just beat the shit of us men, probably kill us quickly. But females on the other hand, have to worry about being raped and sold off as sex slaves to some old crusty farmer who got tired of fucking his goats. Rumor has it that was what happened to Jessica Lynch.

Fuck. What the hell are we doing here? Our reserve unit has no business being here alongside the Marines, Special Forces, and the Army's 3rd Infantry Division. Our vehicles are pieces of shit. Our radios are pieces of shit. Our training back at Ft. Steward was shit. Welcome to the Army Reserves—hooah.

What seems like an eternity later, the convoy comes heading back down the road.

Staff Sergeant Jackson jumps out of the truck.

"What happened with you guys?"

"We got a flat and our radio comms went out," Specialist Arabella explains.

Lee pulls up with the wrecker and Jackson grabs a spare tire out of the rear. Robinson jacks the truck up, removes the lug nuts, pulls the tire off and places the new one on. After a few minutes of making sure the lug nuts are good and tight, we are back on our way. But this time we are second to last in the formation.

The convoy slithers through a few more abandoned towns before we finally make it to Tallil Air Base. The sun is on its way down as we pass a large brick pyramid with a flat top off to our right. We make our way up to the gate. It's our guys from the advance party pulling security. They quickly wave us all through. We curve right, and head down a long hard road to a desert-colored brick building that looks like a military barracks.

Clothes lines with military uniforms on them line the front of the building. A wooden shitter is off to the right. We park off to the left. A few male soldiers sitting on a wooden bench in front of the building look on as the rest of the circus has come marching into town. Someone shouts from the second story window.

"Hey Robinson, Ruger. Up here."

"Yo, Vega, what's good, son?" Robinson yells back.

Vega and Rodriquez come rushing down.

"Yo, what is this place?" I ask Vega.

"It's an old Iraqi Air force barracks," he replies with his hands in his pockets. "But they abandoned it before we got here. They took a shit in each room before they left. It was pretty nasty. That big building over there was the airplane hangar. The MPs have been using it to hold EPWs. The Air Force has a tiny base within our base over there. They have a bunch of A-10 Warthogs. Our company guards half the outer perimeter and the Florida National Guard's 53rd Infantry Brigade secures the other half. These dumbasses freaked out the other night. They had a trip wire connected to a flare to detect anyone trying to sneak through. I guess a goat or a chicken set it off and they were running after nothing. It was quite funny."

I look over at him, "What the fuck is that pyramid thing out there by the entrance?"

"Oh, that's the Ziggurat," he explains. "It goes way back to biblical times. The ancient city of Ur is right across there. It dates back to Mesopotamia. Abraham's house is right there. We went over and checked it out the other day."

I turn and ask him, "So what the hell else y'all been doing besides jerking off?

Vega laughs and replies, "More than you. I've been doing missions down to Nasiriyah as an interpreter to build relationships with the locals there. What have you been doing besides sitting on your ass and enjoying all the nice amenities at Arifjan?"

Staff Sergeant Jackson comes over to the squad.

"Ok guys. The honeymoon is over. We have a lot of work to do. Go put your stuff in your rooms and then come back down with your weapons and some water. We have to unpack our shipping container and set up our maintenance tent, hooah?"

"Hooah," we all grudgingly reply.

Robinson and I follow Vega through the doorless entrance in the center of the building and head up a set of concrete stairs that curve 180 degrees to the second floor.

We struggle with our two green duffle bags, backpacks, weapons, sleeping cots, gas masks and everything else. Vega turns left and leads us down a hallway with windowless windows on the right and doorless rooms on the left.

"Oh god, what is the wretched smell," I say out loud after passing the first door, pinching my nose while trying to prevent myself from throwing up at the same time.

Vega replies with a laugh, "That's the female's room. Apparently, they all get their periods at the same time. You get used to the shit after a while," he says with a grin.

We finally make it to the last room.

Sergeant Rodriguez comes walking up to us.

"You guys will be bunking in here with us," he says, looking at Lee, Robinson, Sheen and me.

"All six of us in this tiny ass room?" I reply with a confused look on my face.

"Yep," he replies laughing.

"This wasn't in my recruiter's brochure," I reply sarcastically. "I was promised 5-star accommodations."

Rodriguez chuckles. "I think they must have given you an Airforce brochure."

"I joined the wrong branch," I say laughing.

"I think we all did," Rodriquez quips back.

We dump our gear and make it back downstairs to meet Staff Sergeant Jackson over by our shipping containers and vehicles. A wrapped-up green maintenance tent with U.S. Army spray-painted black on the side of it is sitting halfway out of the faded red Conex.

"Ok boys, we are going to lift this up and carry it over to the other side of the building and set it up," Jackson says in a stern supervisory tone as he bends down toward the tent.

'Warning: Injury may occur if not properly lifted: 600 pounds: Eight Man Lift,'" I say, pointing down at the tent. "We only have 7 people."

"That's ok, hard work will teach you character," Jackson says smiling.

I rely back, "why don't we wrap some straps or chains around it and use the hydraulic boom from the wrecker to lift it up and drive it over there?"

"That's actually a good idea, Ruger," Vega says with his left arm across his stomach and his right hand holding up his chin."

"No, we are going to do it my way and that's it," Staff Sergeant Jackson says with his eyebrows down low and his eyes straight at me. "Now three people get on each side."

Thinking outside of the box might be ok for Special Forces, but it's frowned upon here in the traditional Army. Especially any kind of rational thinking that makes a soldier's life easy. If you're not miserable then you're not working hard enough. And if you're not working hard enough then they will find something hard enough for you to do. That's the fucking Army for you. A bunch of goddamn old men stuck in their old goddamn ways of thinking. You got to be a man. You got to show everyone what kind of man you are, what you're made of. Let me see your work face... *Ahhhh.*

We lift the mammoth tent and slowly carry the goddamn thing though the powdery sand. I struggle to hold up my end of the bargain, sinking under the pressure. I can feel every disc in my spine throbbing under the crushing weight. The only thing heavier is the weight of already having one hernia surgery weighing heavily on my mind. I imagine it's how all the slave laborers felt spending years building that Ziggurat thing, struggling under the weight of such oppression, with some asshole cracking the whip at you every time you try to make things easy.

The beatings will continue until morale improves!

One hundred yards and 6 drops later, we finally make it to our final resting place. We stand around for a while trying to figure out how in the hell we are going to put the fucking thing up. It takes Jackson two hours to realize that all of us, all 7 of us, are not enough to lift up the two side beams together while two geniuses attempt to connect them. Not even with God helping us, is seven people ever going to be enough.

After Jackson begrudgingly convinces some of the MPs to give us a hand, we get to building the circus tent, connecting one pole at a time using just the right amount of angle and a touch of force. And it doesn't take long to get it erected and covered like a condom with a giant green canvas that sticks out in this desert environment like a sore penis in an all-girls college. The motor pool tent is almost as big as the Ziggurat. And it can be seen by the enemy from miles away. But whatever the fuck, the mechanic shop is now officially open for business.

And our lives as mechanics... are officially fucked.

MOTORHEAD

THE ONLY THING LOWER than a private in the U.S. Army is a private whose MOS (military occupational specialty) is mechanic. We are not real soldiers in the eyes of the infantry. They call us POGs or positions other than grunts. Even the combat MPs look down upon us because we are not a "combat" MOS. We are at the bottom of the food chain. We are at the bottom of the barrel. We are at the bottom of the totem pole. We aren't anyone special. We aren't special forces. We aren't special operations. We aren't in the cool kids crowd. We are outsiders. We are low lifes. We are the lowest of the low. We are nobody important. We are... light wheeled vehicle mechanics.

And that's just fine with me.

Our daily life as Army mechanics is like a game of limbo, how low can you go. And just when you think you can't get any lower than having to deal with all the shit as a private that rolls downhill from the chain of command, piling up on your young shoulders, you get the pleasure of getting down on your back and crawling up under a Humvee as oil, transmission fluid, radiator fluid, battery acid, dirt, sand, gunk, and whatever the hell else is in there comes rolling down on top of your face, arms, stomach, legs, and shoulders, piling up on your uniform as you try to fix all the things that constantly get fucked up from other soldiers who treat their vehicles more like a rental car than something that their life depends on. It's a shitty job for sure.

But I take pride in being a mechanic—a grease monkey, a wrench turner, a ratchet jockey, a carburetor cowboy. There is just something empowering about knowing that I have the ability to repair what is broken, the ability to pick up the pieces and make things whole again, to not have to depend on others in order to keep rolling along.

It's something that I learned from my blue-collared father. He isn't anything special in the eyes of our judgmental society. He isn't rich. He isn't famous. He is the lowest of the low who the intellectual elite thumb their noses high up in the air at because he isn't a movie star or a professional athlete or a lawyer or a doctor or have a fancy PhD. on the wall or a cabinet full of fancy China to show off to all his aristocrat friends. He is just a redneck factory worker who puts in his 40 + hours in order to put food on the table for his family, just like the rest of the working-class peasants in America—the truck drivers, the mechanics, the plumbers, the cooks, the construction workers, the miners, and everyone else who bust their ass for a living so the wine and cheese crowd, who considers people like us to be "low skilled, low class," can live a comfortable life of luxury off the backs of our hard work.

Now, my father may be a factory worker, but he is far from being low skilled. Damn if he doesn't know how to fix all kinds of shit. He can rebuild a carburetor. He can change his own brakes. He can change his own oil. He can fix wobbly cabinet doors; he can fix a leaking sink. Hell, he can fix just about anything but a broken marriage. He may not be important to the latte-drinking intellectuals, but he is important to me.

"People have a college education but can't change a tire," he always says.

That's why I embrace being an Army mechanic just like I embraced being a loser in high school. I wasn't a jock or a homecoming king or a teacher's pet. I was a back of the bus kind of guy. I was a back of the class kind of student. I was a class clown. I was a misfit, an outsider, a habitual truant who spent more time being suspended from school than actually being in school. "School sucks, so skip" was my motto. As was "Sex, drugs and rock and roll, speed, weed and birth control, life's a bitch, then you die, fuck the world, let's get high."

School was overrated anyways. All it taught you was how to read a book and pass the SATs and be obedient. It didn't teach you critical thinking skills. It didn't teach you how to adapt and overcome hardship. It didn't teach any real-life skills at all. That's what the streets teach you. You learn real quick too because you either adapt or die, just like out in nature where I got my other education from while hunting and fishing. School teaches students this fantasy world bullshit. The streets and nature teach you real shit. And you learn to work together with people to achieve similar goals. I got your back, you got mine.

In school, everyone was always posturing to be on top of some imaginary throne, to rise to the top of the food chain, competing with everyone else to achieve some meaningless medal in order to stand up on some podium looking down at everyone standing below their feet just so they can feel important. I was never into any of that. I was just a cook at ABC Pizza who busted his ass slaving over a boiling hot spaghetti table. I was never anybody important. I never wanted to be anybody important. I never understood wanting to impress a bunch of people that I don't even know who don't give a fuck about me at the end of the day. That's why I only cared about my real friends and my real family. They're the only ones that I want to impress. That's it.

I've never wanted to be like any of those other people, the in-crowd, the cool kids, the popular class who shit all over the peasants crawling on the ground beneath their gold studded shoes begging to be accepted, the ones who all look the same and act the same. The ones with no soul. That's why I enjoy being nobody important. I enjoy being myself. I enjoy my individuality. I enjoy not acting and looking like a school of fish that all look and act the same, blindly following the crowd that mindlessly wanders from the latest hip cool thing to the next.

The only thing I follow is my heart and I wear it on my sleeve like a tattoo. That's why I wear who I am like a badge of fucking honor. When most people run away from hard work and anything that makes them feel uncomfortable for that matter, I thrive on it. When they are quick to give up, I keep pushing through, I keep pushing through the busted knuckles, the sliced fingers, the burnt hands, the scraped-up forearms while fixing all the mechanical fuckups.

Never surrender, never fucking quit.

Now the mechanic life isn't for everyone though. Certainly not for beauty queens who are afraid to get their hands and clothes dirty. It's a hard job no doubt. But we are the ones that keep the

Army rolling along just like the working class keeps America going, keeping the gears greased and the lug nuts locked tight, preventing the wheels from fucking falling off the rails.

Maintenance squad's day starts at 0600 hours and ends at 2100. Most of the time I am so tired at the end of the shift that I don't even bother to take my boots off, let alone take a shower with a bottle of water and some Gojo hand cleaner in a futile attempt to wipe away all the oil and dirt from my hands and forearms. What's the point when you are just going to get up a few hours later and get dirty all over again? The work is grueling at times, turning wrenches so long that your forearms seize up, turning wrenches so long that your fingers lock in place. We have no power tools thanks to Staff Sergeant Jackson, who left them back at the unit in St. Pete, because he wants to "teach us some character." We have no days off because he is one of those people who believes in working too much and thinking too little. We have no amenities such as air conditioning or electricity or vehicle lifts. We have nothing but our tools and hands that we bleed and sweat with day in and day out to complete the task at hand. We have no cheerleaders to help get us through the day. We have no pep rallies to help motivate us. All we have is each other.

We are a motley crew of mechanics. We are low down dirty motherfuckers who work hard and play even harder. We can empty a bottle of Jack Daniels faster than a bottle of oil into an engine, without spilling a goddamn drip. Hell, we can drink enough whiskey to float the whole goddamn military around.

"In the rear with the beer and the gear," that's our motto.

Out of the squad, me, Specialist Vega, and PFC Robinson are the tightest, despite our vast differences. We are around the same age and the same rank, but that's about the only thing we have in common. Vega is a Hispanic college kid who comes from a wealthy family and likes to read books in his down time. Robinson is a black dude from the Bronx and loves listening to Bob Marley and Sean Paul. He likes to chase women whether it's his down time or not. I am a white redneck from the hood who likes listening to rock music and watching shows such as the *Sopranos* and movies such as *We Were Soldiers* and *Full Metal Jacket* when I am not slaving away in Jackson's internment camp.

Though we may come from different backgrounds, listen to different music, and have polar opposite personalities and political views, that doesn't stop us from getting along. We are constantly talking shit to each other, but no one gets offended because we aren't a bunch of bitch ass fairies. We give it as good as we take it; unlike a certain someone in our squad, who will remain nameless so I don't get sued, who gets upset about everything. Hell, the guy even gets upset while watching the sun go down.

But Vega, Robinson and I are as thick as thieves. The running joke between us is a white guy, a black guy and a Hispanic guy walk into a motor pool, who's the better mechanic?

Robinson and I are pretty close as far as being good mechanics. Sergeant Rodriquez is the best out of the squad. He's been in the Army for ten years and really knows his stuff. It still amazes me how he can fix all kinds of mechanical issues and not get one spec of dirt or oil or radiator fluid on his perfectly pressed uniform.

Our wrecker operator, Specialist Lee, is also a great mechanic and an expert at vehicle recovery but differs from Sergeant Rodriquez in the fact that he could take a shower and still come out dirty. Grease and oil seem to be attracted to him like a tornado is to a trailer park. He is a better mechanic than me for sure. There is no doubt about it. He really knows his shit. But I will never say that to his filthy face. If the guy's ego gets inflated anymore his skull will probably blow a head gasket like an overheated engine, sending steaming hot radiator fluid spewing out both ears.

But as good of a mechanic as he is, when it comes to working on himself, well he lacks the skill to fix the glaring hole in his people skills. Now that doesn't make him a bad guy. It's just my opinion of him looking through the lens of my eyes. Others' mileage may vary. But I can only deal with the guy for so long.

Like earlier today, I asked to borrow a knife to cut open a cardboard box full of transmission fluid. He pulled his blade out from his desert-colored belt that has all kinds of attachments dangling off it, which is reminiscent of something Batman would have. He unfolded the knife and handed it to me. I used it to cut open the box, closed the blade, and handed it back to him like a normal person. I thought that would be the end of it. I was wrong.

"That's not how I handed it to you," he snidely remarked.

"Dude, I always close the knife when I hand it back to someone," I replied with a confused look. "It's a safety thing."

"I don't care, that's not how I handed it to you," he said, stomping and whining like a spoiled child. "When I hand you something, I expect it back the same way I gave it to you."

I stood there for a few seconds, looking into his obnoxious face, thinking about how good it would feel to open the blade and shove it into his neck. But I waved the white flag and gave him his flipping knife back the same way he gave it to me. He smiled and walked away, shaking his tail like a dog that just got a treat.

I try to avoid working with him at all costs. I much rather work with old college boy Vega. At least he has a sense of humor. Staff Sergeant Jackson always tries to keep us apart though, because when we work together, we cause all kinds of mischief. One of our favorite pastimes is fucking with Lee by hiding his tools and drawing funny faces of him on cardboard boxes with quotes such as *"waa, waa, waa,* I want my milk and cookies," which pisses him off more than a West Virginia trailer park having to watch a Black NASCAR driver race on Sunday.

The motor pool is constantly cracking jokes and pulling pranks on one another. That's why the female soldiers from other squads, from cooks to MPs to finance soldiers gravitate to the maintenance tent, or, as I call it, the circus tent. That and I think they are also there to check out Robinson, who attracts them like Lee attracts dirt. They are constantly hanging around to watch the show and laugh at all the motor pool madness. It helps to break up the mundane life at Tallil Air Base.

Our other game Vega and I like to play with Lee and Jackson is the old switcheroo. Lee is like an electron that attaches to the nucleus of your atom when he's talking to you. And if you attempt to walk away, he mirrors your every step as if you're two-step partners at a country music club. It almost feels like there is this electromagnetic field you just can't break away from. The only way to ditch the stubby subatomic particle is to circle around another atom.

That is where Staff Sergeant Jackson comes in. In order to shake Lee off of us, we will orbit around Jackson like the space shuttle orbiting around the moon as we "look" for random space junk floating around the maintenance tent. Once Lee docks to Jackson's space station, we break contact and sling shot ourselves back down to Earth. But Lee is short and has a good center of gravity and sometimes we have to take a more direct approach.

Either Vega or I will walk up to Jackson with a question we already know is wrong, asking him some sort of automotive debate question we know Lee will angrily object to, like the wrecker's max towing capacity being only 5,000 pounds. You see, Lee is one of those people who has to be right about everything and will argue to death about it to prove his point. After getting Jackson involved, the heated debate kicks off. And after a few seconds of verbal jousting, we will say "I need to go to the bathroom," or "I forgot something over there," or Vega will ask me for help with something.

And just like that, we pop smoke and break contact, waving at Jackson as he is stuck there staring at us like the enemy fading into the civilian population. Though, he usually finds us later in the day and gives us his usual speech of "hey you two, cut it out. I know what you are up to." And we always reply with our customary, "What? I don't know what you are talking about." He hates it when we do that to him more than the city of Compton hates having to watch a white basketball player from Boston win the NBA Finals.

The only downside to working with Vega is that he is probably the worst mechanic in the squad. The guy is intelligent as hell. He is smart as shit when it comes to talking about philosophical stuff. He can tell me all about how the Humvee works, from the electrical system to the mechanics of the diesel engine. But when it comes to translating that information into actual physical work, well, he gets lost in translation.

The book worm lacks what I call applied intelligence, as in, *here is your red toolbox now go fix some shit.* That's when he seems more lost than a virgin in a whorehouse. It takes the guy over an hour to change one glow plug.

But his lack of mechanical skills isn't the only thing quirky about him. He is a little odd sometimes too, which brings unnecessary attention our way, like when we caught him rescuing flies out of a pan full of bright green radiator fluid the other day. I looked over at PFC Robinson.

"What the fuck is he doing?" I asked, pointing my finger toward him.

"I don't know, son," Robinson replied, shaking his head as he pulled a tire off the truck. "He thinks he's Dr. Doolittle or something."

I yelled over at Vega. "Hey what are you doing? You like a little lubrication on your asshole when you take a shit? That thing is going to be all up in your business later."

"No" he responded in a Zen-like state. "I am a Buddhist. It's my job to help all creatures live. It's called good Karma."

I yell back, "speaking of good Karma, how about you come help the creatures over here doing your job? Man, you think too much and work too little. Need to get some dirt on them clean hands of yours."

You can tell a lot about a person from their hands, whether they work too much or work too little. The key is to find the right balance. Vega's hands are tilted too far on the soft side. Mine, on the other hand, are a little worn from years of flipping burgers and working over a hot oven at ABC Pizza. I've never been afraid to get my hands dirty, whether it's skinning a deer or changing out spark plugs on my truck or working in the restaurant industry. I am nowhere near as book smart as Vega. I can barely tell you the difference between direct current and alternating current, let alone what some 15th century philosopher or poet said, but I have enough common sense and practical knowledge I learned from my father to figure shit out. My dad taught me how to work on my gray Ford Ranger 4x4, changing the oil, brakes, and tires. He always taught me the best way to learn how to do anything is to actually do it. It helps build your confidence. That's why I enjoy learning how to do things with my bare hands, it helps keep me off the stripper pole, helps keep me from having to bare it all on the main stage for some dollar bills in order to get by. My only problem though, is I don't have an oil filter on my mouth to help stop my vocabulary of dirty words from getting on everyone's sparkling clean frontal lobes. Vega is the same way. I think that's why we've become tight. We both subscribe to the same brand of sarcasm. And that's why we usually have to be separated because once one of us starts in, the other is quick to follow.

"Why do we have to work 15-hour days without a day off? Yeah, I am sure that breaks some kind of labor law. I want a lawyer.

Let's start a union, Ruger. We are going on strike. We demand better wages and less hours. I want a promotion too."

But as odd of a crew as we are, we work hard together to keep the MP's vehicles on the road. We spend our 15-hour days on Staff Sergeant Jackson's automotive plantation meticulously examining the vehicles for damaged parts, checking for low air in the tires, loose lug nuts, low radiator fluid, cracked windows and windshields in what the Army calls PMCS—Preventive Maintenance Checks and Services.

We lay a piece of cardboard down underneath the truck because our creepers don't roll very well in the sand, and slide up underneath, checking for worn brake pads, class 1, 2, and 3 leaks, busted tie-rods, half shafts, drive shafts, suspensions, and anything that just looks out of place.

We go around and open each door to ensure that they open properly and that the windows go up and down. We check to make sure that the seat belts are operating properly. As much as the MPs take us for granted, it's our job to ensure their safety. If something happens to them, it is our responsibility. We follow our maintenance manuals closely.

We pop open the hoods and inspect the fan and alternator belts. We check the radiators and power steering for damage to the fins that would prevent air from flowing through them, causing the vehicles to overheat. We reach over the engines and pull the oil dipsticks out to see if it might be low or overfilled. If it's in the correct zone we check it off as a go. We start up the engines and check the transmission fluid dipstick.

If it's a little low, we either grab a bottle we have lying around or we walk over to where our shipping container full of parts is. That's where Staff Sergeant Jackson and the female clerks spend most of their days going over inventory and ordering any new parts we may need. I always try to get a quick smile from Specialist Arabella while I am over there getting a box of transmission fluid or oil or whatever excuse I can find to go see her. One glance of that smile will fill a mechanic full of the highest-octane fuel available, helping him push farther and faster into the night.

Once we do find something wrong with a vehicle, we go see Arabella to sign out what parts we need. We spend hours grinding away in the heat—sweating, grunting, and turning every rusted bolt, every rusted screw and every rusted clamp by hand. It's brutal. The worst though, is replacing a flat tire. The Humvee rim has eight lug nuts that connect it to the truck. Then the rim has 24 outer nuts that keep the tire and rim together. So, once we get all 32 lug nuts undone by hand, we cut the old tire off and use a giant flat head screwdriver, tire iron, and a whole lot of muscle to get the new one on.

Then once we get all 24 of the outer nuts back on, we pray, throw rice, and yell a couple of Hail Mary's that the fucking thing sealed correctly as we fill it with air then pour soapy water along the outer edge of the rim. Any air that tries to escape like an Iraq prisoner will be seen bubbling up along the edge of the rim's perimeter. That lets us know that the tire didn't seal properly, and the whole thing will have to be taken apart again. I get that same sinking feeling that I imagine an MP gets every time there is a prisoner escape. There is nothing that will drive a mechanic more insane than when that same bullshit keeps bubbling up in their faces every time after all their hard work to keep things secure.

It's man vs machine in the maintenance tent. Today it's me versus a tire. Today it's me being defeated by a rubber fucking circle that was invented thousands of years ago. It's maddening. It drives me nuts, twisting and turning lug nut after lug nut after lug nut—the pain radiating from my forearms to my head like a thermometer stuck out in this unforgiving sun, the pressure shooting and squeezing until I turn red.

"What the fuck am I doing wrong? Why is this shit not fucking working? *Fuck!!!!!!!!* Am I just a goddamn dumb ignorant retard who can't change a fucking tire!!!! Let me see your war face... *Ahhhhhhh!!!!!*"

A when you think matters can't get any worse, just when you think you can't feel any lower, Specialist Lee, that fucking little fly Lee, will come over and get it on his first try.

Fuck!

Welcome to maintenance squad.

ON THE ROAD AGAIN

WHEN I AM NOT slaving away in Jackson's Soviet Siberian labor camp, I am going on missions as a driver, a gunner, or as "mechanical support." I come up with any good reason to go outside the wire. I have a love hate relationship with being a mechanic. As much as I enjoy a hard day's work, I need a break from it. Working 7 days a week for God knows how long without a day off has gotten old real fast. Working hard is good for the mind, no doubt, but getting out and seeing the world is good for the soul.

That's why I enjoy going on these missions. It reminds me a lot of back home, when I would go out on adventures with my brother, uncles, and dad. They would bust their ass all week at their blue-collar jobs in the paper factory or running up telephone poles for the phone company, but as soon as the weekend came, we'd blast off to the Ocala National Forest and get drunk and go four wheeling down Forest Service fire trails out into the middle of nowhere. We'd take the Jon boat and go gig frogs at night and have fried frog legs for breakfast. We'd go off hog hunting in the swamps or bass fishing in Lake Tarpon and the upper Hillsborough River. We'd take the boat out to go trout fishing in the flats off the Coast of Clearwater, having to brave the elements of Florida weather that can change as fast as a flip of the wrist, sometimes getting caught in six-foot whitecaps while riding in a ten-foot Jon boat as lightning was striking all around. We'd take the boat to Rainbow River and Silver Springs where we'd tie a rope from a tree and swing out into the clear blue and green water as alligators swam by. We'd go camping in Anastasia State Park in St. Augustine, surfing in shark infested waters during the day and having s'mores around a campfire at night. Those were the best times of my life. We were like the Lewis and Clark Expedition exploring the wilds of Florida. I learned more about life out there than I ever did in a classroom. Even when my inner-city elementary school was sent out to Nature's Classroom, I already knew more about the animals than all the teacher's pets combined.

That's why going out on missions is second nature to me. I'm used to braving the elements, braving the dangers that lurk in the murky waters below. Most people hide from this danger. They'd rather be in the rear with the beer and the gear. They hide from it. They hide in their cubicles. They hide in their gated communities. They hide from the inevitable. They hide because they are afraid to die. They sacrifice freedom for security. But that sacrifice comes at a cost, the cost of never truly feeling alive, wasting away in some mediocre existence. I'm afraid to die too. It's a natural thing to be afraid of. It's a natural thing that all mammals feel because it's woven into our DNA. We don't call it fear though. We call it our fight or flight response. But I'd rather fight to be free than live in a cage where you never get to take flight. I'm more afraid of being trapped inside the confines of a walled-off existence, slowly rotting away into nothingness. I'd rather die living life out in the wild than die wasting away inside some box built for me by some big box store, so they can bilk workers out of their short time on this Earth in order to make billions of dollars off the backs of their hard work.

Going on missions can be difficult for some, the fear of the ever-present danger can be hard to overcome. But the hardest part of it all for me is convincing Staff Sergeant Jackson to let me out of the prison walls of his maintenance tent to even go on missions. But thankfully, the higher-ranking MPs have taken a liking to me. And not just Master Sergeant Shortman either. Even the First Sergeant has taken notice. His right-hand man, Master Sergeant Bragg has as well.

It's just after breakfast when Bragg comes walking into the maintenance tent. Staff Sergeant Jackson rushes over.

"What can I do for you Master Sergeant.?" he says, pulling a drag from his Marlborough Light.

"I need to borrow Ruger for a mission," Bragg replies, pulling a drag from his Marlboro Red.

Jackson yells over at me. "Hey, Ruger, come here for a minute."

I put down my ratchet and rush over and stand with my black greasy hands locked together behind my back in what the Army calls "Parade Rest." Master Sergeant Bragg stares down at me.

"We are going on a mission to deliver some supplies to a Marine unit in downtown Nasiriya. I need a gunner for my Humvee. I heard you are just the person for the job. Are you ok with that?"

"Hells yeah," I reply, smiling over at Staff Sergeant Jackson.

"Good," Master Sergeant Bragg replies with a smirk. "Are you ok with me borrowing him for a few, Jackson?"

"Yes, Master Sergeant," he replies as if he actually has a choice. "I don't mind at all."

Master Sergeant Bragg looks back at me, "Okay, Ruger, go get washed up and grab all your gear and meet me over in the parking lot."

After picking up my tools and putting them in a red steel toolbox, I head upstairs and throw my flak vest on and sling my load bearing vest with six magazines full of 62 grain 5.56 mm green tip penetrator rounds around my shoulders and lock it all into place. Grabbing my Kevlar helmet, M16, and desert colored backpack with water, a first aid kit, a two-day supply of Meals Ready To Eat (MREs,) I make it out the door.

As I hurry down the hallway, I am stopped by PFC Boston.

"Hey Ruger," he says, poking his head out of the room next to mine. "You know how to make a baby float?"

"No," I reply, confused by the question.

"You put it in a blender with vanilla ice cream and root beer," he says laughing.

"That's fucked up, bro," I reply.

"What's your fucking deal?" he quips back, "If you can't handle dead baby jokes, then how the fuck are you going to handle seeing real dead babies?"

"I can't argue with that twisted logic," I reply, shaking my head, laughing as I make my way down to the convoy.

I walk up to a crowd of MPs standing semi-circle around a Humvee with a gunner standing on top of it looking down at Master Sergeant Bragg as he shoots the shit with the other soldiers. The MPs all kind of look at me funny as if I am a third string junior-varsity football player stepping into an All-Star Varsity's huddle. Bragg makes eye contact with me and nods his head.

"Ok, now that we have everyone here, I can begin the safety brief," he says in a serious tone. "Today, we are going to be going down into downtown Nasiriya to deliver supplies to Staff Sergeant Smith's brother, who is stationed down there with the Marines. The threat assessment is moderate. Marines have driven the Republican Guard out of the city. But they have found uniforms that have been deserted. The enemy may be attempting to blend in with the civilian population. Stay alert, Stay alive. There is only one road down there and one road back. In the event of an ambush, we will fight through it to get back here. This is where Jessica Lynch was ambushed and taken prisoner. Keep your head on a swivel. The rules of engagement for this mission are shoot to kill. Anyone that you deem a threat is fair game. If they point a weapon at you, you put a bullet in their head, hooah."

"Hooah," the crowd roars back.

"Let's load up."

I climb up in the turret of Bragg's Humvee and stand behind a SAW (squad automatic machine gun) with a 200-round belt of 5.56mm ammunition lying to the left of it. The gunner in front of me cranks up Metallica's "For Whom the Bell Tolls" from a CD player he has connected to some box speakers. The music gets me pumped. My jaw and hands clinch tight as my head bobs up and down to the music, the adrenaline shooting a warming glow though my veins.

The Humvees' engines fire up, and the eight-vehicle convoy of gun trucks snakes its way through Tallil Air Base and out the front gate that's being manned by the Air Force's Security Forces that are decked out in all the latest and greatest gear money can buy.

Here we are going out into the shit with green Vietnam era flak vests, no headphone communications, and a Humvee that has no heavy armor, meanwhile these fucking assholes are dressed like god-damn Delta Force.

As we make it through the wire, the convoy is bombarded by Iraqi men in white man-dresses, crusty brown sandals and red head wraps, waving bottles of dark brown liquor in one hand and porn DVDs in the other.

"Mistah, mistah, five dinar," one of them says in an aggressive tone.

I lean my head down into the cab of the Humvee and yell at Master Sgt. Bragg, "Hey, I thought that shit was against their religion?"

"Are you kidding me?" another MP riding in the back seat says. "Don't believe all that politically correct bullshit that colonel told us in Kuwait. These motherfuckers are notoriously drunk horny bastards; a bunch of got damn goat fuckers. They just use all that religious bullshit to control people, to get them to blow themselves up in the name of Allah."

"Holy shit," I think. "Kind of feels like finding out Santa Claus isn't real. Lies. All lies."

We make it past the rated R flea market and travel down a dusty stretch of highway. More Iraqis seem to be venturing outside their clay huts to see what is happening now that the fighting has settled down in this area. Old women with cracked tanned faces that resemble a sun-dried lake walk by dressed in black from head to camel toe while carrying a metal pot on their head with a balloon size bowl of vegetation that I assume is some sort of wheat stuffed on top.

You can see the fear and despair in their eyes, the byproduct of nightly firefights and bombing runs from Apache and Cobra helicopters. It's the saddest place I've ever seen, even sadder than the projects back home in Tampa. It must be crazy for the civilians to be caught up in all this shit. One day they're going about their lives, then the next thing they know, it's raining fucking bombs—the thunderous blast shaking the sand right out of their hour glasses.

As we approach the city, a voice comes over the radio, "Keep your eyes out. The enemy could be anywhere."

I grab the pistol grip on the M249 machine gun and point the barrel up at the rooftops of the desert-colored building as the convoy swerves around broken-down cars, donkeys, and people walking along the highway. Trash litters the streets. A bunch of the buildings are bombed out, its beige bricks spread across the street. We pass a rusty playground with tall shrubbery, but no kids are playing in it.

Women gaze out at us from doorways and windows and hijabs. A bunch of men in white man dresses and red head wraps stand on the side of the road, some staring, some cheering, but most just wave as we go by, happy to see us. Happy that we will finally end their pain and suffering from the hands of Saddam Hussein and the Republican Guard who terrorized these poor citizens.

Rumor has it that one of Saddam's sons used to drive around the schools and kidnap girls, rape them, then drop them off at their parent's house, which is fucked up because the family will shun their own daughter for being raped. It's a brutal place out here. We ain't in Disney World anymore, Toto. This is the wild, wild west of the Middle East.

We turn down a few more streets when the convoy stops in front of a group of Iraqis who are standing in front of a line of concertina wire that stretches across the street. Several Marines in digital camouflage uniforms clear the civilians out of the way while one of the jar heads pulls the wire back so our convoy can pull through to the end of the dead-end road.

A machine gun with sandbags packed around it hangs out the second-floor window. Marines with M16s line the rooftops. Several jarheads come walking out of the building and help the MPs grab stacks of water bottles and MREs out of the back of the Humvees and take them inside.

A towering lance corporal, who's built like a tank comes rumbling over to our Humvee and sticks his head into the window.

"Hey, thanks again Master Sergeant," he says, shaking Bragg's hand. "We were rationing down to one bottle of water and one MRE a day."

"No problem," Bragg replies.

"Poor bastards," I think. "Here we thought we had it bad in the Army."

The Marines really get fucked. The Navy treats them like stepchildren they don't want. While the seamen get billions of dollars for warships and fighter jets and nuclear submarines, very little of Ronald Reagan's Soviet era trickledown economics trickles down into the hands of the Jarheads. You have to be blown up in Beirut to get any financial love.

When I joined the military, I thought it was one big club with different chapters. I never realized the class disparity between the branches. The Marines are like lower class citizens that do all the dirty work that no one else wants to do. They're the Mexicans of the military. The Army on the other hand is the backbone, the hard-working middle class that does all the heavy lifting. And then there is the Chair Force, which is the upper class with their hip cool expensive aviator glasses, getting most of the Pentagon's budget while having one of the fewest numbers of personnel of any branch and whose troops rarely ever get their hands dirty. The Navy might as well change its name to the department of transportation. That's what Marines stand for anyways. My Ass Rides in Naval Equipment. The Navy is like those rich people who vacation at fancy resorts with big pools and big lakes. And then there is the Coast Guard, which is technically a branch, but is more of a glorified lifeguard outfit that reminds me of the lifeguards at those fancy pool resorts, having to deal with assholes in boat shoes complaining about the Coasties' boots scuffing up their bows on their fancy catamaran boats.

We hang around for a while so Staff Sergeant Smith can spend time with his brother. But as time goes on, the crowd of angry Iraqis grow more and more agitated. I rotate my Squad Automatic Weapon toward the unruly citizens and watch for any sign of a weapon. Master Sergeant Bragg gets on the radio and tells everyone to mount up. We make our way out the wire and back to our base uneventfully. I hop out of the truck, drop the magazine out of my M16 and place the end of the rifle into a makeshift clearing barrel full of sand with a notch cut out the top to stick your weapon in and safely eject a round out of the rifle.

As I make my way into the building I hear a *pop, pop, pop, pop*. I immediately hit the deck with everyone else in the area, looking around with confusion as to where the incoming fire was coming from.

When the smoked cleared, I look over at the clearing barrel and see one of PFC Robinson's old squeezes, yelling "SORRY!" while holding up her right hand. Apparently while clearing her Squad Automatic Weapon, she squeezed off a few rounds. Who the fuck knows how? Maybe it was a gun malfunction. Maybe she was still mad at her Jamaican lover for blowing her off and decided to blast off a few rounds in an attempt to blow off some steam or his head (off with his head!) in order to make it look like an accident. Or my guess is that maybe she is just a fucking idiot who has no business handling a fully automatic machine gun.

But what do I know?

I am just a private that does what he is told. Don't question anything, soldier. Stay in your lane.

I get up and dust the sand off my rifle and think to myself, "Jesus Christ. It's bad enough I have to worry about getting killed by the enemy, but now I have to worry about some dumb fuck in my own unit accidently shooting me in the back. What the fuck, over?"

I make my way up upstairs and flop down on my cot, staring up at the ceiling, my heart still racing from the near-death experience. My thoughts begin to drift back home, thinking about all my family and friends and all the good times we had, hoping like hell I will be able to survive this bullshit to make it back so we can make some more fun memories.

The pleasant thought is interrupted by footsteps trucking down the hallway, stopping right in front of my bunk.

"Hey Ruger," Staff Sergeant Jackson says in a stern tone. "You just get back?"

"Yes Sergeant," I reply sitting up in the cot.

"Well good," he replies with his signature wide smile. "Time to go back to work in the motor pool."

Fuck.

KILLIN' TIME

SOUTHERN IRAQ

IT'S LUNCH TIME AT Tallil Air Base. Vega, Lee, Robinson, and I are sitting around the room eating MRE's while waiting for Sgt. Rodriguez to come get us to finish another miserable day turning wrenches inside Staff Sergeant Jackson's reeducation tent. The stench of sweaty feet and sweaty socks and sweaty balls and sweaty assholes circulates throughout the four corners of our 100-square-foot hellhole. We stink so bad I'd bet the enemy can probably smell us all the way over by the Syrian border. But the only combatants we've seen so far are these goddamn flies. And they are one hell of a determined enemy; so much so that we have had to dig in with multiple fighting positions.

Yellow fly traps now dangle throughout the room. Two of them hang above Robinson's and Rodriquez's cots, and there are six above Lee's, who has them circling around his bunk like a shower curtain. Vega doesn't have any because he still doesn't believe in killing, not even these nasty ass flies. I just have one fly trap that spirals down from the ceiling and stops an arm's length away from my head. I count around 30 dead flies stuck to it. The damn things are drawn to it like young men are drawn to war. The shiny glue-like substance shines as bright as the Silver Star and Medal of Honor. And young soldiers seem like they will do anything to get awarded those 30 cent pieces of metal, even if it means dying for it. Several more flies buzz around the yellow strips, but they seem like they haven't worked up the courage to storm the beaches of Normandy yet. They are probably gripped by fear; gripped by the images of their bloody dead comrades lying in front of them.

Clusters of those tiny black bastards line the wall next to my bunk like a battalion of reinforcements, making the tan paint look more like a spotted leopard. I set my M-16 aside and grab my main battle rifle—the fly swatter. I begin taking them out with sniper-like precision. I hear Drill Sergeant Safewright singing in my head as I do it. "A little bird, with a little bill, was perched upon my windowsill. So, I lured him in, with a piece of bread, then I smashed, his fucking head."

The My Lai Massacre goes on for a while, but when I look up from the killing fields, it occurs to me that the mission is a pointless one. These flies are like the Chinese during the Korean War. No matter how many I kill, they just keep coming in waves after waves. Fuck it, though. It helps to kill time, like listening to Clint's Black's song, "Killin' Time." So, I continue smashing their little heads and splattering their squishy guts across the wall.

"You feel better about yourself Ruger?" Vega asks. "What did those flies ever do to you?"

"Yes, I do," I reply, swatting another one. "That's one less fly licking my lips at night. Besides, you don't think that fly would kill you if it had the chance? You don't think if it was 10 times your size it wouldn't rip your head off and suck your blood dry? It's a kill or be killed world. It's eat or be eaten. I didn't make the rules. If you have a problem with it, then take it up with the gods."

Vega shakes his head and retreats to his book.

"Thirty-eight confirmed kills," I say out loud. "Today was a good day; I didn't even have to use my Iraqi AK.

THE MAN IN THE BOX

TALLIL AIRBASE, SOUTHERN IRAQ

WE'VE BEEN BAKING IN the sun for weeks now with the war's end nowhere in sight. Our thermometer has been pushed to its 120-degree limit. If it's pushed any farther, it might explode like a suicide bomber. The Iraqi heat out here is unforgiving. And with no air conditioning or ice cubes I feel like Sylvia Plath with her head stuck in an oven, dripping sweat all over my toasty little vagina.

It's mind blowing how people actually live in this shithole. But I guess like anything you do that's physically challenging; you sort of get used to the suck after a while. Just like 18-year-old civilian recruits going through Army Basic Training get used to waking up at 0600 without their mommies and running five miles. They adapt and overcome. They become as tough and hard as their environment. The Iraqis are no different. They've become just as tough and bitter and unforgiving as their environment. They've become just as brutal as this suffocating heat.

Women are beaten, raped, and sold like soda cans. Goats are strung up in the middle of the city with their throats slit, dripping bright, red blood all over the sandy sidewalk as women and children walk by. The Fedayeen blow themselves up in the name of some imaginary God because the thought of a better after life is still better than the thought of having to live another day in this God Forsaken Land.

This isn't a place for the weak minded. This isn't a place for sensitivity or feelings or political correctness. This isn't some hippy fantasy land where we get to roll around in a field full of flowers and live like the world is all goddamn rainbows and unicorns.

This is war.

Welcome to the shit.

Welcome to our life at Tallil Airbase. Though it is a relatively safe area, the living conditions are primitive, disgusting, and quite hazardous to our health. There's no running water. No showers. No electricity. No chow hall. No malls. No TVs. No hospitals. No 9-1-1.

Our nicest luxury is a top of the line, handmade, three-stall-wooden shitter that was built by the British engineers in exchange for six Gerber multi-tools, a few Army jackets, and a handful of cash. It sits on three steel beams that lay flat across a 60-foot hole. It's a lot nicer than grabbing a shovel and crapping like a cat in this giant kitty litter of a country.

But the shitty thing is, it doesn't take long for the shit to stack up, especially with 180 soldiers pressing their sweaty butt cheeks on it every morning. Just about every two days we have to slide the thing off the rails and burn all the turds, toilet paper, porno magazines, and sometimes underwear that went on an impromptu mission to the shitter while taking some friendly fire along the way, dripping liquid shit down someone's leg. Those clothing items end up resting peacefully on top of the pile of poop that's been out here stewing in the 130-degree heat. I always snap to attention and give the fallen brown soldiers one final salute before dowsing the trousers in diesel fuel and cremating the remains.

It's definitely not a job for those with weak stomachs. Of course, it's always me and my fellow mechanics who get stuck doing it every time, like we have nothing else better to do. Unfortunately, there is nothing we can do about it. We are just low-ranking soldiers stuck in this shit hole. I can hear Lane Staley's voice from the band Alice in Chains singing every time, "I am the soldier in the sand box, buried in this shit, won't someone come and MEDEVAC me? MEDEVAC me?"

The key to burning shit though is to feel out the wind first and then stand where it's blowing the opposite way. Nothing will ruin a soldier's day faster than getting a big whiff of burning manure right through the nostrils and down into the throat. It tastes like shit, literally.

Once the pot gets boiling at around 350 degrees, one lucky soldier always gets the job of stirring the chocolate pudding with a long metal pole. Since my odds are always better at winning because of my rank of Private First Class, I usually draw the short stick, or in this case, the long one, to stir the pot. As much as I love stirring shit up, this is not what I have in mind.

But the shittiest shitter to burn is the females, which is just one wooden stall with a giant frying pan underneath it. I had the pleasure of pulling it out yesterday. It looked nothing like the rainbows and strawberries that all my ex-girlfriends promised me it did. It looked more like an Iraqi silenced a lamb with one swipe to the throat using a butcher knife.

It sucked burning all the bloody shit and bloody tampons and bloody cigarette butts and bloody blood everything. It sizzled like bacon when I set it on fire. There was a snap, a crackle, and then something popped out and smacked me in the face. I guess that's what I get for talking shit about the female shitter.

But that's not even the shittiest thing that's happened to me out here. No, that award might have to go to dropping a deuce with all the flies that have taken up residence like thousands of bug-eyed bats in a cave full of crap. I can feel every one of their tiny little tentacle-like toes tickling my asshole every time I drop my trousers in that wooden prison cell.

"Good god, man," I think every time I enter that mental ward. "What the hell have I gotten myself into? This wasn't in my recruiter's brochure.

This wasn't in the movie *Black Hawk Down* or the book *A Farewell to Arms* or the video game, *Medal of Honor: Frontline.* They never showed me this side of war on CNN or Fox News.

What the fuck, over?"

Though it was traumatizing at first, I am slowly starting to get accustomed to it. Crazy, the mental shit you can get used to out here. We adapt and overcome in order to survive. And I've become a master of the drive-by-shit.

I start by jogging to the crapper, shaking up everything really good. Then I do a preemptive strike by squatting really fast, hovering like a helicopter two inches above the wooded cut out and dropping my payload before those pesky little bastards even know I am in there. Then I jump in the shadowy corner, watching as a few reconnaissance flies come up from below and circle the hole, searching for any sign of anal activity. I remain motionless.

The older fat flies never seem too interested and they usually glide back down into the abyss pretty quickly, but the younger muscular fly boys always go off in search of something to attack. It's usually the poor bastard in the stall next to me, especially if he is moaning from the Iraqi stomach bug and squirting it out like a shaken can of Coca Cola.

Once the coast is clear, I fly in on another stealth bombing mission, dropping several heavy payloads. I repeat the process until I am out of ammunition, or I show up on their radars. It's an effective means of taking a crap without getting an egg sack full of fly larva stuck in my colon; growing, breeding, bleeding.

And just when it seems like life can't get any shittier after I leave that wooden mental institution, one of those flies that was just eating someone's asshole out like it was a Greek salad will fly over and land right on my lip and tickle my tongue as I take a big bite of my beef vegetable soup.

But the horror movie doesn't end when I swat the fly away and spit out my food. Oh no, it continues the next day when I wake up with the Iraqi stomach bug myself, which is a nauseating and painful punch to the gut that has already caused several soldiers to spew puke out of their windows while shitting their pants.

The environment here is fucking brutal. It will kill a soldier faster than an Iraqi with an AK-47, or at the very least it will make us wish we could borrow Ernest Hemingway's shotgun and bid a final farewell to our brothers in arms. At least then it would be a quick and painless death, and we wouldn't have to suffer out here anymore in this God Forsaken Land.

Jesus Christ, Allah. What the hell is happening to me? I am starting to sound just like the Goddamned Iraqis.

Shit.

Get it together, soldier.

America's freedom depends on you.

EVE OF DESTRUCTION

THURSDAY, MAY 1, 2003, POSTED: 9:48 PM EDT (0148 GMT)

ABOARD THE USS ABRAHAM LINCOLN (CNN) — The following is an unedited transcript of President Bush's historic speech from the flight deck of the USS LINCOLN, during which he declared an end to major combat in Iraq:

"Thank you. Thank you all very much.

"Admiral Kelly, Captain Card, officers and sailors of the USS Abraham Lincoln, my fellow Americans, major combat operations in Iraq have ended. In the battle of Iraq, the United States and our allies have prevailed.

"And now our coalition is engaged in securing and reconstructing that country.

"In this battle, we have fought for the cause of liberty and for the peace of the world. Our nation and our coalition are proud of this accomplishment, yet it is you, the members of the United States military, who achieved it. Your courage, your willingness to face danger for your country and for each other made this day possible.

"Because of you our nation is more secure. Because of you the tyrant has fallen, and Iraq is free.

Tuesday, 24 June 2003, 20:55 GMT 21:55 UK

Battle of Majar Al-Kabir

British military police killed in Iraq

BBC—Six British military police officers have been killed and eight other servicemen wounded in two separate incidents in south-eastern Iraq.

Both incidents happened at the edge of the British area of operations within the country, in the region of the town of Amarah.

They mark the heaviest losses to enemy action suffered in a single day by US-led coalition forces since the war in Iraq was declared largely over on 1 May, after the toppling of Saddam Hussein's regime.

It is also the heaviest loss of British life in a single hostile incident since UK forces entered Iraq at the start of the war in late March.

About 20 US troops have been killed in attacks in the capital Baghdad and surrounding cities and towns since President George W Bush declared that large-scale combat operations had ended.

WELCOME TO THE CIRCUS

THE CIRCUS IS FUN when you are a fan in the stands eating cotton candy with your bare hands. The shit show, however, is not as bearable when you're the circus bear being beaten on stage as you're forced to jump through burning rings of fire. It's not as fun when you are a caged animal that gets cracked with a whip when you don't do what you're told by the ringmaster. But that's how it feels to be a Private in the Army. And it's how it feels being a mechanic in maintenance squad. It's how it feels slaving away for days on end without a day off. We go from our room where we sleep to the circus tent where we work and then back to our cage when we're done. And if we get out of line, well, our ringmaster Staff Sergeant Jackson will make us work until our arms fall off.

At the end of the day, however, he's just a circus animal too, doing whatever his higher-ranking handlers tell him to do. And if he gets out of line, well the Platoon Sergeant and First Sergeant, with the blessing from our Captain will crack the whip on him, forcing him to jump through hoops. It must be nice to be at the top of the unit because there is no one to crack the whip on them because we are out in the middle of fucking nowhere and they are at the top of the food chain out here. They are the big top. They do whatever the hell they want.

But that is all about to change as the rest of the circus has finally caught up to our shit show. A battalion level of MPs has moved in next door, with a lieutenant colonel now sitting in the ringmaster's chair. It's funny how all the high-ranking soldiers in my unit started to act when he came for a visit. You should have seen them all freaking the fuck out, putting on a trapeze act to woo him. The old dog and pony show was on full display. They acted like magicians, trying to make some things disappear while making other things appear to be something they aren't.

"Tuck in your boots," and "shave your face," and "stand up straight" and "make it look like you're doing something," they screamed at everyone they came into contact with.

What a show to be seen. I find that the higher up in rank you go the bigger the pool you get to swim in. It allows you more space and freedom, but the bigger the pool, the bigger the splash you have to make in order to justify you being allowed to swim in it. So that's why the higher ups always do a cannonball when their higher-ranking ringmasters come strolling poolside. But most of the time they just belly flop because it doesn't take an art appraiser to spot who is genuine and who is fake as fuck.

The good news is, we mechanics don't have to fake doing anything. The grease on our hands and face says it all. But the colonel never made it out to our circus tent to see all of our hard work. Hell, I bet our commander didn't even tell him we even existed. No one wants to show the world the reality of circus animals who have been worked into the ground. No one wants to show the world the reality of circus animal's lives when they aren't all dolled up on stage. They keep us grease monkeys locked away in our cage out back, far from prying eyes. Out of sight, out of mind. The big top only wants to show the world their show quality animals that prance around on stage. They don't want to show the audience the dark side of the moon. And I am not so sure the fans in the stands care to know about it anyways. They don't want to know how their steak got onto their plate. They just want to be spoon fed. And they don't care how it's done.

What a circus. And it's not just the dog and pony show full of acrobats bending over backwards to please the masses that are a part of the show, there are also plenty of clowns to go around. We had one MP go home on leave only to be arrested. Apparently, he was married to three different women in three different states. And when our higher ups started looking into the Sgt.'s file, they found out he doctored his paperwork when he transferred to our unit from Oklahoma. They discovered he was actually a private. And it also turns out he was never a sniper as he claimed.

But he isn't the only clown in town. A sergeant first class MP from first platoon was busted for sending Iraqi pistol parts home through the mail. But he never got busted down in rank for it. Apparently, it takes an act of Congress to demote him. But I doubt it ever even made it up that that far in the chain of command. I bet it just got swept under the Persian rug lying underneath the cot of all those in charge just like everything else. War pigs, they have all the power. And they love to brag about it too, "A military policeman with the rank of private can tell a general what to do. We are that powerful. We are special forces and beyond." Which is funny because their inflated egos lead them to believe they are above the law themselves, which is reinforced by the fact they get away with all kinds of shit because they look after their own.

Then there are the clowns I've been on missions with like this tall white Staff Sergeant who carries around a sling shot and shoots at Iraqi's roadside stands with soda's stacked high while yelling "Fucking rag heads!"

But if you think it's just the white soldiers who are racist, then you are as big a clown as them. I've been on missions with Blacks and Hispanics who call the Iraqi's "Sand niggers" and "rag heads" as well. Clowns for days.

One of my favorite story lines of this little tragicomedy of a deployment is the female medic who ended up pregnant but doesn't know who the father is because she has slept with over 30 soldiers. There's a pool going around the motor pool with odds on who the father is. My money is on several different soldiers, but it's really a crapshoot at this point.

Now you would think you could just chalk it up to all of their animal behaviors to the individual, but then a whole squad of MPs, a rolling band of thieves who would steal from their own mother decided to steal some Air Force generators from a base in Baghdad. The craziness is contagious. The funniest thing about it though was that the dumbass clowns didn't realize that their squad and unit number is spray painted on the side of their desert-colored truck in big black letters. By the time they made it back to Tallil Air Base, the commander had already been contacted. Let's just say the MPs had to travel all the way back there and put them right back where they found them. And of course, nothing happened to them either. They just got the usual "don't do that again" along with a wink and a pat on the back for taking initiative. Generators are a hot commodity over here. Those bastards have been trying to steal the mechanics generators since we got here. As the saying goes—*Soldiers, trust them with your life, but not your money or your wife.*

And just when you think the circus show couldn't get any more entertaining, several of these Military Police clowns started faking heart attacks in order to get out of the deployment. There was also an MP who fell out of his guard tower "on accident" and busted up his leg enough to get sent home. He tried to commit suicide while in the hospital, so they say. But you can't believe these clowns. They don't have a leg to stand on. There were also several MP's who got busted drinking the Iraqi whiskey. They busted the privates and specialists down in rank to send a message, but not the Staff Sergeant. While the higher ups look down upon privates for breaking the rules because they are not in the big NCO club yet, they look out for their NCO's.

So it goes, Kurt Vonnegut, *so it goes.*

Maintenance squad hasn't been immune from the circus show either. Specialist Sheen, who is technically a part of our squad, but who's spent more time with the medics, went home on leave and never came back. Not even a letter or a phone call to let us know where he is. He's AWOL out there somewhere.

Then there was Sgt. Young, the head of the mechanics parts department, who came back from leave pregnant, and now is getting out of the deployment. And there is also a pool going around the motor pool on who the father really is. Everyone's money is on Staff Sergeant Jackson as they seemed to be really cozy together before she left and were always hanging out in the shipping container full of automotive parts.

And last, but not least, just when you think it can't get any hotter out here, whether it's the unforgiving sun or having to jump through rings of fire by the chain of command, Vega goes and puts in for his consciousness objector status because he refuses to kill anyone based on his Buddhist faith, pushing it up the chain of command.

All of it is fitting because there is no bigger circus in town than under the maintenance tent. And I fit right in because I've always been a class clown. And a class clown always needs an audience to entertain, they need a platform to perform. That is why this circus is the perfect venue to perform my high wire act, to push the limits of reality, to push the limits of sanity. And this show just keeps on getting crazier and crazier. I was in the middle of fixing a flat tire when an MP with Sgt. rank on his collar came up to me.

"Hey private," he says in a stern tone. "You have to go over to the mess tent and pull KP."

I give him the what the fuck look and reply, "so you want me to stop doing my job to go do the cook's job?"

"Yes," he replies back with an agitated tone. "You need to go right now."

I chuckle and reply, "are the cooks going to come clean up my workstation and put away all my tools since I have to go clean their dishes?"

"This isn't up for debate, Private," he screams. "You need to go now."

"Well, that is fucking bullshit," I scream back, throwing my ratchet at the Humvee full force then storming right past his face with I-will-kill-you eyes as the fear in his eyes causes him to take a step back and go silent.

Just when you think you are the star of the show, the showstopper on stage, entertaining the audience and having a good time, the ringmasters crack the whip to remind you who is in charge. But sometimes it feels good to remind the ringmasters you are still a fucking bear that can rip him apart with one swipe of the wrist.

The circus bullshit has gotten so bad, the only way Vega and I get through the insanity is by making a big joke out of it. Any time the MP's or Staff Sergeant Jackson has us do something that doesn't make any sense like having a tiger jump through a hoop for no fucking reason at all, we start singing,

"doot-doot-doodle-oodle-doot-doot-do-do."

It's all good though. We got back at the MPs for making us do KP. The one good thing about Vega is he is highly intelligent when it comes to reading books, especially books on regulations. He ought to be a fucking lawyer. And wouldn't you know it, it just happens to state that repairing tires is "operator level." So instead of us spending hours taking the tire apart and putting it back together with a prayer and a hope that it sealed correctly, we brought it up to Staff Sergeant Jackson who shockingly agreed with us. Let's just say after the MP's had to do a few tires themselves, they never asked us to do anything again.

So it goes, motherfuckers. So it goes.

But just when you think the maintenance tent is the biggest circus show in town, the big Army comes rolling in like The Ringling Brothers Barnum and Bailey Circus who bill themselves as the "Greatest Show on Earth."

And with it comes salute zones, uniform Nazis, and Sergeant Majors who have no real job except to make sure the sand is raked, that you don't smoke near a tent, and that you stay off the fake grass around his building.

doot-doot-doodle-oodle-doot-doot-do-do.

And with every circus there comes food, drinks and merchandise. Lots of merchandise. So of course, the military's friendly overpriced neighborhood store, AAFES (Army and Air Force Exchange Service), has moved into our base and kicked out all of our enemy prisoners of war from the Iraqi Air Force hangar we housed them in and forced them into tents surrounded by barbed wire and the unforgiving sun. The prisoners are gone now, replaced with chips, sodas, Gatorade packets, CDs, Iraqi freedom T shirts, DVDs, and price tags that seem more fitting for the Hamptons than the middle of the fucking desert.

I do find it strange that AAFES would show up. Especially since they keep telling us we will be home by the 4th of July. We are just here to capture Saddam Hussien and will turn the country over to the Iraqis when we are done with that mission. But in another turn of events that seems strange is that a finance unit showed up at the exact same time with footlockers full of cash. And they are all too willing to give us $200 a week to spend at the AAFES store and deduct it from our paychecks. Here we are fighting for our country for pennies on the dollar and they can't even give us a little hometown discount? Can't even give a free bag of chips? Nope, we are paying top shelf prices.

What the fuck, over?

doot-doot-doodle-oodle-doot-doot-do-do.

But one of the good things about the circus showing up is we got a new chow hall that was built and operated by Halliburton/KBR. They serve hotdogs and hamburgers and freedom fries, which beats eating MREs and T-rations. It blows my mind how fast the conditions on Tallil Air Base have improved from just a couple of months ago when we first took control of it. What once was a deserted Iraqi Air Force base has turned into a bustling city full of people from around the world walking around in camouflaged uniforms. It's become a giant ant bed of tiny fire ants, building up nothing into something. There are the British and Italians. There is the U.S. Army and Airforce.

The chow hall is not the only thing that has improved around here.

We've nailed up the windows to our room with plywood so we no longer wake up with a light coat of sand covering us like a late-night snow shower. We put five generators behind the building and ran wires to everyone room for lights, DVD players, air fans, and whatever else we need. We even have a phone that, unlike the phones for which the communist AT&T bastards down in Kuwait charge an absorbent price that makes you blow through your calling card faster than a prostitute during a political convention, is free. The phone, which resembles more of Alexander Graham

Bell's prototype than any modern cordless technological wonder, is a black plastic handle hooked up to a green speaker box that's connected to a long black wire. There are no buttons, just ringing that lasts for 20 minutes before an operator answers and connects me to MacDill Air Force Base. After about 15 more minutes, I finally got connected to my dad's house phone.

It felt so good to hear his voice, no matter how cracked the sound was. But just as the happiness began flowing through my chest, the line went dead, sending a telegraph of anger and sadness bursting through my vocal cords. You get what you pay for, I guess.

Fuck.

We also now have a makeshift apocalyptic looking shower made out of a rusted piece of metal with a giant square water tank on top. It's a lot nicer than using a bottle of water and a poncho liner. At least we have that going for us. The shower is split into 4 stalls that expose each person from the shoulders up and from the knees down. But the shower is a double edge sword. If we take a shower during the day, we are guaranteed a third degree burn from the water boiling under the sun. And if we go too late, we are guaranteed to get frostbite on our dicks when the cool air comes blowing in. The best times to shower are about an hour after sunrise and an hour after sunset. But it's pointless for us mechanics to shower in the morning before work. And by the time we get off at night the water is too frigid. But the absolute worst time to shower is when Sgt. DeJesus, an MP, is in one of the other stalls. He loves to talk to me just like he did back in Ft. Stewart.

In the old WW2 cinder block barracks, there were ten stall-less toilets in a row and I would always sit at the farthest one from the front door like a normal person, so we don't have to sit next to each other. And unlike a normal person, he would always sit his chubby Puerto Rican ass in the seat next to me, drop his pants to his knees, open his newspaper and look over at me, asking the same thing every time.

"How's your baby momma, Private?"

"Um, I don't have a baby momma, Sergeant," I would reply, completely horrified.

"Ah, come on, I see what you're working with there, I bet you have several baby mommas."

Now, the venue may have changed to Iraq, but he's still performing his same old act, looking over the shower stall, asking about my baby momma and commenting on my private parts and lack of manscaping.

Don't ask, don't tell.

What a circus.

But this shit show is far from being a stationary performance, though. No, my friends. This is a traveling circus as well. Now, if you think the show has been entertaining up until this point, wait until you experience the street circus…

I am laying on my cot after a long day's work.

"Hey Ruger, sit up for a minute," Staff Sergeant Jackson says, kicking my cot with his desert combat boot while hovering over me with his notepad in hand. "In the morning after chow you are going to go on a mission with the MP's. The First Sergeant personally wants you as his gunner for the mission."

"What's the mission?" I reply, taking a drink out of a plastic water bottle.

"An Air Force colonel wants to take a tour of Nasiriya," he says, shaking his head. "You guys will be escorting him around town. So be in full battle rattle down at the staging area at no later than 0700, hooah."

"Hooah," I reply.

I report to the First Sergeant's vehicle. After our usual blah, blah, blah, everything is a possible threat safety brief, I climb up into the gunner seat where there is a Squad Automatic Weapon with a 200-round belt of 5.56mm ammunition underneath it and a Mark-19 fully automatic grenade launcher attached to the turret.

As we exit the main gate, the convoy pulls off to the side of the road. I open up the feed tray and lay the belt inside and close the tray, effectively loading the fully automatic machine gun. Then I open the feed tray for the grenade launcher, load the 30-round belt of grenades, and slam the feed tray down. The First Sergeant looks up at me and asks suspiciously, "Hey, Ruger, so what's with Vega? Is he a threat to anybody in our unit?"

"No, First Sergeant," I yell back down.

"Are you sure," he yells back up. "Rumor has it that he has been saying some pretty negative things about the war. He is starting to sound like a terrorist sympathizer."

"No First Sergeant," I reply. "He's a Buddhist—not a terrorist."

"Ok," he responds, his eyes squinted as if he still doesn't believe me. "You let me know if he starts acting suspicious, hooah."

"Hooah, First Sergeant," I reply, looking back up as the convoy starts to move out.

Once the First Sergeant gets a radio check and the green light that everyone is locked and loaded, he instructs his driver, an 18-year-old MP, to take off. The convoy slithers its way through the main streets, alleyways, and back roads. I scan the city for anything that looks like a threat, zooming in like a hawk at the forest of Iraqi citizens who have come out of their gopher holes and looking at us in awe now that the shock and awe campaign is over. The slightest movement catches my eye, jerking my head in that direction. Several kids are kicking a soccer ball back and forth. Some more movement across the street catches my attention. I try to fight the urge to look but I do anyway. More kids playing about.

It's hard to focus on just one person. The streets are lined with men, women, and children going about their lives, which is good to see for the country as a whole. Shops are opening back up. Kids are playing in the streets. But from our point of view, it makes life sketchy as fuck. It's hard not knowing who is a possible threat and who isn't. It was better when it was a ghost town. At least then it was easier to tell the friendlies from the enemies.

But there is no use in bitching about it. All we can do is adapt and overcome. We treat everyone like they are a threat. We can't trust anyone that doesn't look like us. And even then, we still have to keep an eye out just in case.

As we pull up to the first statue of Saddam, the Air Force Colonel, who's sitting in the seat behind the First Sergeant, pokes his Kodak disposable camera out the window and snaps a picture, winds it to advance the film and takes another just in case the first one didn't take well. Then we blaze our way to another site, our guns pointing in every direction. I scan the bombed-out windows in all the tall buildings for snipers, but it's damn near impossible to have eyes everywhere. There are just too many windows in too many buildings. Welcome to urban warfare.

I just rotate the gun turret in hopes of making the bastards think twice about fucking with us, but deep down all I can think about is *Black Hawk Down* where motherfuckers were shooting from everywhere. And that's when I get that sinking feeling again, that goddamn worm squirming on a fishing hook sinking deeper into my gut as the convoy is led deeper into the city.

As we make it to another Saddam statue, the Colonel tells the driver to stop. He jumps out for a quick photo of himself next to the statue, his chest puffed out like a lumberjack and his weapon held up like he is a Navy Seal. The First Sergeant snaps the picture, winds the camera and takes another of him posing with a goofy smile and his arms up in the air like he is on a goddamn rollercoaster at Busch Gardens.

We go to statue after statue, then to a few other sites that are supposedly historically biblical.

Every time I hear the click from the fucking camera followed by that damn winding noise, I look down from the gunner seat at the colonel below and shake my head. Here we are risking our lives so this jackass can take some goddamn pictures like he's some tourist visiting the Grand Canyon or Yellowstone National Park.

I can hear the reporters now asking my mother back home, "Well, ma'am, how did your son die in the war?" "Well," she'll say, "he was on a mission to protect an Air Force colonel while he took a bunch of photos of himself in front of a bunch of statues. The Army stated the mission was a matter of national security, but his fellow soldiers told me it was a matter of national stupidity. But at least the Army was nice enough to pay for his tombstone that reads 'WHAT THE FUCK, OVER.'"

Luckily, the trip is short, and we make it back to base without any physical incidents. But the field trip leaves a bad taste in my mouth worse than a thousand flies coming out of that shit cave and landing on my tongue.

I storm back up toward my room when I am stopped by Specialist Boston.

"Hey Ruger come check this out," he said with an odd grin."

I walk into his room where several MPs are sitting around watching a porn movie on a mini-DVD player.

"You think this chick is hot?" Boston asks with an unusually big smile.

"Yeah, she's cute," I reply with a confused look as to why this conversation is even happening.

But before I can even ask why, the blonde porn star with big tits whips out an even bigger dick."

The room erupts in laughter.

"Ruger is a fag," Boston yells to the grins of everyone. "You thought he was cute, you said it yourself."

"Yeah, yeah, I walked into that ambush," I reply shaking my head. "But you guys are the ones sitting around rewatching it. What does that say about you? Where the fuck did you guys even get that from?"

"We got it from the Iraqis," Boston replies. "They love the cock. You know what their saying is right?"

"No," I reply shaking my head. "But I am sure you're going to tell me."

"Women are for breeding, men are for pleasure," Boston replies with an even bigger grin."

"Don't ask, don't tell," I reply as I walk out of their room and into mine.

Maintenance squad is breaking for lunch. Vega, stretched out on his cot, looks up from his philosophy book, "Hey, Ruger, how was the trip?"

I reply, "You don't want to know. But I do have a question for you. Why is the First Sergeant asking me if you're a terrorist sympathizer?"

"He asked you that?" Vega replies, sitting up in his cot. "It must be because I asked to speak to the battalion commander about why our commander hasn't pushed my objector packet up the chain. They're trying to make me out to be something I am not to cover their ass."

"Well, whatever it is, I would watch your back," I reply. "The MPs are pissed at you."

Fuck.

There is nothing I hate more than getting dragged into some shit I have nothing to do with. Especially when it involves people I am cool with. I get along with most of the MPs. They have taken a liking to me too, that's why I get to go on all these missions.

But it isn't even a few days later when the shit starts to hit the fan. Several MPs a day come out to the Maintenance tent to taunt Vega. That goes on for a couple of weeks till it finally comes to a head. A black MP with the rank of Specialist comes back to taunt Vega again. But this time it turns physical when the MP starts poking Vega with his finger. Vega finally has enough, and a wrestling match ensues. But little did the MP know, or even the mechanics for that matter, that Vega is trained in Jiu Jitsu, and it doesn't take long for him to get the MP in a choke hold and make him tap out.

However, even having the beaten soldier slither his ass back to the pit from which he came didn't stop the taunting. Which puts me in a bad spot because I am friendly with both sides. Growing up in the streets you learn not to take sides. You try to be cool with everyone because you know life is hard enough without enemies, and it's even harder with them.

That's why I perform the high wire act, walking that tightrope between the two because, well, the show must go on, right? I still have Vega's back. He's my battle buddy. I'd jump on a grenade for him. But I do enjoy going on missions no matter how retarded the missions have become, because it gets me out of slaving away my life in some circus tent. And I rather ride around on a unicycle on the streets of Iraq than be stuck in there. I'm born to be wild. I'm born to roam wherever I want to go.

I stay cool with Master Sergeant Bragg and most of the MPs.

These field trips I get to take outside the wire are the only thing that keeps me sane these days. I would much rather be out in the shit risking my life, walking along that high wire than working myself to death in some oppressive Chinese labor camp. I don't know how my dad does it. He works all day in a factory, doing the same thing day in and day out. To me, the definition of insanity is doing the same thing over and over and over and over and over again. Punching the same clock day in and day out. Pushing the same buttons day in and day out. I am of the belief that life is not truly lived by living in room temperature. You got to jack up the heat. You got to jack up the adrenaline. Get the heart pumping. Get the blood flowing. Get it flowing through all your veins. Get it flowing until you feel that burning ring of fire, that ring of fire that makes you feel fully alive, it makes you feel like you are on top of world.

That's when you know, that's when you know what is real in life. That is when you know what is truly important. That's when all that other bullshit fades away. That's what happens when you come to grips with the fact that you may die, and you decide to live that life anyways. You will die soon enough either way. Do you really want to waste this short time on Earth being a basic motherfucker who does basic shit? Who wastes away in some cubicle all day then comes home and eats frozen TV Dinners at night while watching the evening news in fear? Or do you want to experience life to the fullest? Do you want to stare death in the face and say bring it on, asshole, you're going to take me anyways?

I am coming out guns a blazing, motherfuckers.

Personally, I want to experience life. I want to see as much as I can see. I don't ever want to sit on the bench and feel so worthless again like I did playing sports as a kid, watching from the sidelines, watching life pass me by. That's why I gear up, physically and mentally, and meet up with Bragg at his Humvee for another mission. Fuck it—if I die, I die. I should have been dead a long time ago with all the drugs I did. At least if I go out now, I will go out for something that means something.

I think.

I hope.

Though these missions are starting to make me question this traveling circus I find myself in. Now, if you thought that all those roadside circus missions that I've been going on were the pinnacle of stupidity, then, boy, do I have an encore for you.

After another "blah, blah, blah safety brief, CIA reports state that the enemy is dressed like donkeys and could potentially shit on soldiers as they pass by, exposing them to the hairy black tongue disease, soldiers are instructed to steer clear of all asses, this now covers all officers in the event something happens and someone cries that they weren't informed beforehand," I get into the driver's seat and crank up the engine.

The MP in the turret turns a CD player on, blaring Metallica's "Seek and Destroy." The adrenaline starts pumping as the warming flood of fresh blood flows through my veins, the anger gripping my chest. I am ready to fuck some people up. I am ready to go out in a hail of bullets. Let's fucking roll.

We're scanning the scene in the Iraqi city tonight,

We're looking for the Republican Guard to start up a fight,

There's an evil feeling in our soldier's brains,

But it's nothing new, you know an enemy that hides, drives us insane

Running, on their way hiding, the terrorist will pay dying, one thousand deaths

SEARCHING, SEEK AND DESTROY

The convoy snakes out the front gate, the Ziggurat fading away as we slither into the city. Iraqi men in clean white dresses and brown vests line the streets, waving, smiling—business as usual. I scan the road in front of me, looking for anything that might be a bomb—dead dogs, soda cans, anything—on the side of the road.

I scan every bridge we go under for potential threats that may try to drop a grenade on us, violently swerving if someone is standing up there. I scan the cars that pass by to see if I can see fear in the driver's eyes, a telltale sign that their heart is connected to a car bomb. I give myself a little distance from the car in front of us in case it's taken out, making sure I can still maneuver around him. I scan the landscape trying to predict an ambush.

If I were to ambush us, where would I hide?

Where would I attack from?

The convoy pulls up to the curb of several Iraqi stores. Everyone dismounts except the gunners who swing their machine guns back and forth, scanning up and down the road for anyone who looks suspicious. The First Sergeant and a bunch of MPs walk into the Iraqi shop. I take up position with my back up against the wall of the brown building, the front of my Humvee directly in front of me. I never let anyone get behind me. I feel safer that way. You never want someone to come up from behind you and stab you in the neck. Bragg stands toward the rear of the Humvee, leaning up against it while staring down the street, his right hand tapping the top of his 9mm Beretta pistol as he takes a drag from his cowboy killer cigarette.

Ten or fifteen minutes go by, and the First Sergeant. is still inside. A herd of Iraqi teens comes walking up. They seem friendly. They say "Hello, American" and wave. The ringleader, a ragged looking little shit, probably 14 or 15 walks up to me.

"Mister, Mister, give me water," he says, looking like a used car salesman on meth.

"Sorry, I don't have any to give," I say, shrugging my shoulders.

"Yes mister, give me water," he says with his hand in the air gripping an invisible bottle.

"No," I reply forcefully.

"Mister, give me chocolate," he insists with his hand out.

"Sorry, I don't have any chocolate."

The little bastard and I go round and round before he finally gives up and goes back across the street with his buddies. A few minutes later, he walks over to the other side of my Humvee and tries to open the door handle. An explosion of anger bursts through my chest as I race around the vehicle and shove the end of my barrel into his jaw.

"Get back," I scream, pushing his head away from the Humvee with my M-16. "Get the fuck back."

The rush of adrenaline fills my veins like a shot of Jack Daniels at a Motorhead concert. I can hear my Drill Sergeant from basic training yelling in my ear, "Do you know what makes the green grass grow, Private Ruger? Blood, blood, blood makes the green grass grow, Drill Sergeant."

You're goddamn right it does.

It feels empowering to not have to take anyone's shit, to finally be able to fight back. All those years being bullied in school, picked on for being white, for being skinny, for having a big nose.

I grit my teeth as I shove the little bastard away. He doesn't have to respect me, but he will respect my gun. And the fear in his eyes confirms he respects it. I look over at Bragg looking at me, grinning more than usual.

"Got damn, Ruger. I think you just made that kid piss himself."

A short while later the First Sergeant and the herd of MPs come through the door carrying 20 or so trays of long block ice that look like 4-foot fence posts and load it into the back of multiple Humvees. After paying the Iraqis in cold American cash, we race off down the road to another shop. We dismount and again take up positions with our backs to the walls. This time just the First Sergeant walks into the shop. Several chickens walk down the middle of the street like they own the fucking place, completely oblivious to these armed freaks in desert camo with enough firepower to keep every goddamn Kentucky Fried Chicken in America stocked full of yardbirds for a year.

After a few minutes, Top comes out of the building holding several of his uniforms that are spotless and pressed. What the fuck, over? Did this motherfucker really drop off his uniforms to get cleaned and pressed? Not only did he put everyone on base at risk if the enemy were to use the uniforms to infiltrate us, but here we are risking our lives so this asshole can pick up his dry cleaning? Are you kidding me? Wait till Vega gets a load of this bullshit. He's going to shit himself laughing.

I lose all respect for the First Sergeant right there. Any soldier who would put the needs of themselves above the lives of their soldiers is no soldier to me. But that's the difference between career soldiers and soldiers who only care about defending their country. We don't give a fuck if our uniform is dirty or not. We don't give a fuck about looking good. We only care about making the enemy look worse than us. And there are some ugly sumbitches in this unit.

I pull a drag from my smoke, shaking my head as I shake the cherry out of the cigarette and put the dead soldier into my top pocket. We head back to base.

These missions do nothing to help cure my conformity problem. It's bullshit missions like this that are making it harder and harder for me to conform to the rules. Not to mention the 18-hour days, 8 days a week of being grinded up like sand and worked into the ground. The tire pressure in my mind is exceeding the maximum recommended amount of PSI. I've already had several sit downs with Staff Sergeant Jackson about my attitude. It all started to go downhill a couple of weeks ago when that MP made me go do KP.

It's fucking bullshit that they had me do it. The MPs are pulling 12-hour shifts sitting on their ass in a guard tower, staring off at a bunch of prisoners staring back at them. They get a day off every now and then. And the ones that go on missions get the rest of the day off when they make it back to base. The mechanics get to go back to work in the motor pool after our missions. And we get to do all the other bullshit details around here too. But no one comes to help us out. They just dog the fuck out the vehicles then bring them to us and bitch about how it's a piece of shit when it breaks down.

Like this truck I had to work on in the circus tent today for example. Some geniuses asked me to rewire their battery system a couple of weeks ago with an electric cord extension with multiple ports so they could hook up a radio and a DVD player to entertain themselves while doing 15-18-hour long convoys. When I refused by saying, "fuck you, I won't do what you tell me, not only because it distracts them from looking for the enemy, but because it could short circuit the computer system and possibly the whole damn electrical system," the clowns decided to go all kung fu ninja and do it themselves.

They damn near set the truck on fire. The battery box looked like a bomb had gone off inside. Black residue smeared the whole inside of the battery box and the wires we melted like a candle. It's an easy fix, but it's annoying as fuck that it's extra work I have to fucking do for no good reason at all.

As soon as I am done unfucking this fuckup, I have two more fuckups to unfuck. It takes me two hours to clean out the battery box and replace the computer module. And as soon as that one goes out, Robinson drives in another—a diesel-powered—Humvee that this dumb ass MP filled up with gasoline. What a clown.

And it's not long after we drain the fuel tank and get it fixed that Vega drives in another truck. I start draining the oil, replacing the oil pan gasket, peeling the old one away from the metal and scraping off the old grimy one.

Vega starts replacing the driver side windshield. It's one of the easiest tasks in our career field, but these trucks have been sitting next to the ocean in St. Petersburg, Florida since the last time they were over here in 1991 during the Gulf War. The screws are all rusted to shit. And when we snap one off, it's a 30-minute job of trying to tap and die the thing and spin it out. Nothing is ever easy. You work until it hurts, then, somehow, you just keep working.

We all find ways to keep us going in this circus called military life. For Sgt. Rodriquez, it's the thought of doing it for his wife and daughter. For Specialist Lee, it's purely driven by his ego, to show everyone that he's much bigger than his short frame. Staff Sergeant Jackson is driven by God. Who knows what college boy, Vega, is driven by? Probably some philosophical answer I couldn't understand anyways. Robinson does it for the ladies. I just take pride that I am doing my part for the war, for freedom. To make my family proud of me.

Yeah, that's what I keep telling myself.

After getting the new gasket installed, I fill it up with oil. I look over at Vega with a look of exhaustion.

"Hey, I am going to go wash this oil off my arms and then I'll be ready to get on that starter when I come back."

"Ok, Ru," he says, his eyes never leaving the screwdriver as he struggles to get the last screw out of the window.

I make my way over to the water buffalo, a green 100-gallon tank of purified drinking water. I push the spigot and wet my hands and arms. I grab a bottle of Gojo oil and grease hand cleaner out of my back pocket and stroke my arms up and down. Out of nowhere I hear, "Hey, what the fuck? Watch what you're doing. You got just oil all over me."

I turn and look to see who it is. It's the First Sergeant standing there by himself, with a look of horror, trying to wipe the grease and grime off his nicely cleaned and pressed uniform. I am too burned out to even give a fuck or say sorry. I just silently give him a blank stare, turning around and finish washing my arms. I rinse off all the Gojo and grease and grime and dry myself off with a rag. I grab the bottle of hand cleaner and make my way back to the motor pool.

"Vega, you ready to knock this shit out?" I ask.

"Yeah, let me just finish tightening the last few screws."

He finishes up and we both slide underneath the truck on cardboard boxes. The starter is a two-man job. Of all the places to put one the heaviest fucking parts of this truck, they place it up underneath and secure it with two giant screws. I get the pleasure of holding the thing while Vega takes a ratchet and begins unscrewing the screws. Getting the anvil out is the easy part. The hard part is trying to hold the goddamn thing up while the other person can line up the screws. It is a highly difficult job; especially for a couple of screw ups like us.

I bench press the starter up into place as Vega attempts to put the screws in. My arms start to shake.

"Put it in the hole asshole," I yell at him.

"I'm trying," he replies, frantically trying to put the screw in.

"I bet if that was your boyfriend's assholes you could get it in," I say, laughing.

I reach muscle failure after about five minutes of trying to hold the Empire-State-Building-looking contraption up and bring it back down to my chest.

"Come on, Ruger," Vega yells with a laugh. "I know those skinny arms aren't that damn weak."

"Hey, fuck you," I joke back. "You try it then tough guy."

Vega holds it as I attempt to put the screws in.

"Hey, come on, hold it still," I grumble.

"I am holding it still," Vega grumbles back.

A few minutes go by, but we still can't get it into the hole.

"Fuck," Vega screams. "I can't hold it up any longer."

"Not so easy is it, asshole," I say laughing.

"Fuck this shit," Vega yells. "This is fucking insanity. Let's take a break."

After a quick smoke we crawl back up the vehicle and get the fucking thing installed and the vehicle starts right up to our relief. Finally, something is going right for a change. I look at my hands and see the grease has reappeared.

"I am going to head back to the water buffalo to wash up again," I tell Vega. I'll meet you upstairs and we can go get chow."

After getting cleaned up, I make my way toward the entrance of the barracks where several MPs are sitting around a wooden bench when the First Sergeant purposely bumps into me.

"Hey, watch where the fuck you are going, Private," he yells at me. "What the fuck is your problem?"

"I don't have a problem, First Sergeant," I reply, too tired, too worn out, much too young to feel this damn old, much too everything to be scared of his antics right now, too tired to give a fuck. Too tired to give a fuck about his rank. Too tired to give a fuck about anything.

That's how he gets his jollies, showing up Privates in front of his Sergeants. Making them shake with fear as he berates them. Which is funny he didn't have the balls to do that when it was just the two of us standing by the water buffalo. But I just stand there with my body posture respecting his rank, my hands locked behind my back in parade rest, but my eyes locked onto his showing him that I am not scared of him, that I don't respect anything about him. After a quick stare down that seems like forever, he blinks and storms off. The Sergeants sitting at the wooden picnic table look at me in shock, but I am too tired to care. I just walk away.

doot-doot-doodle-oodle-doot-doot-do-do.

As I make my way up the stairs and down the lost hallway to my room, I see Vega surrounded by Specialist Boston and several other lower ranking MPs who are berating him with insults. I cut in and ask, "what's the problem?"

The problem is this terrorist sympathizer here," Boston says, pointing his finger in Vega's face.

I get in the guy's face and growl back, "Vega is not a terrorist, he's a got damn Buddhist, and he doesn't want to kill anyone, so why don't you leave him the fuck alone!"

That's when Robinson comes around the corner and says, "Yeah, son, how about you leave him alone or you got to mess with all of us."

The MPs are taken aback, their faces looking as shocked as the First Sergeants when he couldn't intimidate me in front of his friends. The MPs whimper back to their room with their tails tucked between their legs. When I turn around, I see Vega's face looking just as taken aback as the MPs at the fact that Robinson and I stood up for him.

I'll never tell him to his filthy face, but I will always have his back, because I know what it feels like to be bullied, to be picked on for going against the status quo. But I also know what it feels like to have friends that have your back, that stand up for you when you can't. That's a great goddamn feeling to have when you don't have anything at all. That's been the story of my life. And I made a promise to myself back on the bayonet assault course, that I would never back down from anyone, and certainly not these ass clowns fucking with my battle buddy.

But I know for every action, there is going to be an overreaction.

And we've gone and opened that can of worms now.

I am getting that squirming feeling again, as if I am the worm hooked to the end of a fishing pole, slowly getting lowered down into this murky lake of fire.

What a goddamn circus.

It's going to take everything we have to make it out of here with all of our sanity, if we even make it out of here alive...

ACKNOWLEDGMENTS

I would like to thank Lisa and Running Wild Press for having the balls to publish my work. While the rest of the literary world is watering down the whiskey of the written word by neutering it in order to make it consumable for those weak-minded consumers sailing the high seas in their boat shoes and fancy Catamaran yachts, RWP isn't afraid to rock that boat, even if it means spilling a bit of boxed red wine on those people's pink polo shirts. I cannot thank you enough for letting me run wild, and for running wild with me. Cheers!

And I would also like to thank my friends and family for putting up with all my madness over the years, even when I hit rock bottom deep down in that fox hole I've been trying to climb out of for years. I cannot begin to express my gratitude for everyone who always had a couch for me to sleep on and a refrigerator full of food for me to eat when I had absolutely nothing. My work is nothing without you. I am nothing without you. You all have shaped who I am. You all have shaped what my writing style has become. The crazy wild adventures. The crazy wild nights of shenanigans and debauchery.

But most importantly, the generosity of helping me out when I was trying to make sense of all these words, trying to make sense of all those horrible experiences that kept me twisting and turning in the darkness hours of the night. I cannot thank you enough for all of it. This Bud Light is for you. Cheers you crazy motherfuckers!

And last but certainly not the least, I would like to thank my editor Ben for putting up with my bullshit. I've always been of the belief that there should be a great amount of friction between a writer and an editor. That of course, is how mountains are made. The friction between two opposing tectonic plates causes the Earth to shake and the mountains to rise. And our back and forth has given rise to this book that I believe will cause the Earth to shake and the pages to rise from the ashes of everything I am and everything that tried to destroy me. This book would not be as good as it is without you brother. You helped take it to heights I never dreamed it could go. Thank you for everything. Thank you for lifting me back up after the literary world kept knocking me down with their rejections. Real people are hard to find in this world and you've always kept it real with me. And I've always appreciated that about you. Cheers my friend. Cheers…

ABOUT RUNNING WILD PRESS

Running Wild Press publishes stories that cross genres with great stories and writing. RIZE publishes great genre stories written by people of color and by authors who identify with other marginalized groups. Our team consists of:

Lisa Diane Kastner, Founder and Executive Editor
Joelle Mitchell, Licensing and Strategy Lead
Reuben Tihi Hayslett, Acquisition Editor, RIZE
Benjamin White, Acquisition Editor, Running Wild
Peter A. Wright, Acquisition Editor, Running Wild
James Aquilone, Acquisition Editor, Monstrous Books

Resa Alboher, Editor
Angela Andrews, Editor
Rebecca Dimyan, Editor
Aimee Hardy, Editor
Cecilia Kennedy, Editor

Barbara Lockwood, Editor
Kelly Ottiano, Editor

Evangeline Estropia, Product Manager
Pulp Art Studios, Cover Design
Standout Books, Interior Design
Muzammil F., Interior Design

Learn more about us and our stories at
www.runningwildpublishing.com

Loved this story and want more?
Follow us at
www.runningwildpublishing.com/rize,
www.facebook/runningwildpress,
on Twitter @lisadkastner @RunWildBooks

www.ingramcontent.com/pod-product-compliance
Lightning Source LLC
Chambersburg PA
CBHW051306300726
48976CB00002B/284